"I CAN'T BELIEVE THEY KILLED ....
I CAN'T BELIEVE THAT SHIT."

"Who killed who?" Cream lazily asked.

"Rinaldo. He killed him. The man on the news," Nina said, still in shock. "This fool is now murdering people."

"Look at me." Cream grabbed Nina by her chin. "Act like you don't know shit. I need you to keep working as usual until I get with some people."

"You done lost your mind! That cracker ain't nobody to mess with. He is obviously connected."

Cream jumped up and slapped her. Nina fell onto the bed, and he grabbed her by her throat.

"Girl, did you not hear a word I just said?" he yelled. Nina nodded her head yes, trying to blink the tears away. She had seen Cream lose it before, but this was scary. He was acting like her keeping this job was life or death.

"I need you to continue working until I figure out how I'm gonna get this cracker for a whole lotta cake. Do you understand? You owe me, bitch. You owe me..."

SIZZLING PRAISE FOR WAHIDA CLARK AND HER NOVELS

THUG LOVIN'

"Brutally honest."
—*Publishers Weekly*

"Exciting...realistic characters...Clark provides another descriptive drama that once again pulls no punches or kicks with an in-your-face-and-groin realism."
—*Midwest Book Review*

"FIVE STARS! Wahida Clark is an excellent storyteller...I was wrapped up in the read."
—TheUrbanBookSource.com

"Explosive, hot, tempting...a rambunctious ride through the streets of LA that displays street sense from both sides of the relationship...Clark, the Queen of Thug Love Fiction, delivers a multifaceted urban tale filled with big money, big dreams, and big consequences."
—Rawsistaz.com

"Fast-moving...full of the drama and tragedy of the 'hood...If you love the Thug series you will certainly enjoy this."

—TheReviewBroads.com

PAYBACK WITH YA LIFE

"Wahida Clark has done it again...well-written...with believable characters [and] unexpected plot twists...I recommend *Payback with Ya Life* to all urban fiction fans."

—ApoooBooks.com

Payback with Ya Life
Thug Lovin'
What's Really Hood!

THE GOLDEN HUSTLA

WAHIDA CLARK

GRAND CENTRAL
PUBLISHING

NEW YORK BOSTON

Grand Central Publishing
Hachette Book Group
237 Park Avenue
New York, NY 10017

www.HachetteBookGroup.com

Printed in the United States of America

First Edition: October 2010
10 9 8 7 6 5 4 3 2 1

Grand Central Publishing is a division of Hachette Book Group, Inc.
The Grand Central Publishing name and logo is a trademark of Hachette Book Group, Inc.

Library of Congress Cataloging-in-Publication Data
Clark, Wahida.
    The golden hustla / Wahida Clark.—1st ed.
        p. cm.
    Summary: "Nina Coles makes a home in Atlanta hoping to turn her life around. But she'll learn that you can't run from trouble"—Provided by publisher.
    ISBN 978-0-446-17810-5
    1. African American women—Fiction.   2. African Americans—Fiction.   I. Title.
    PS3603.L3695G65 2010
    813'.6—dc22
                        2010007883

*To all the dedicated readers of
Wahida Clark books. There would be no me
without you. Thank You.*

ACKNOWLEDGMENTS

All praise is forever due to the Creator. My family, you guys are the best. Thank you for holding it down and for all of your many sacrifices.

To my husband, Yah Yah, I can't image no me without you. To the WCP street team, you guys are the shiznit and we always shine wherever we go. I appreciate y'all. Omar, Rahman, Al-Nisa, Hasana, Lil' Wahida, Hadiyah and Nobel. To the Lil' Street Team in training, Jordan Brown and Islama, you make me proud.

To the family behind the scenes, Lindsey, Jamil, Ebony, Kisha, Hijrah, Samataha, Sabir and Darrin. Thanks!

To my right hand, Lil' Wahida, aka Marie. Love you. Hasana, you make me proud.

Karen Thomas, my editor from day one. Thank you so much for not being a "yes man." Can I take you with me? Again, I can't thank you enough. To the rest of the Hachette Team: Latoya Smith, thanks for your happy e-mails. Linda Duggins, thanks for plugging me in wherever you could. Samantha, thanks for the support.

Acknowledgments

To all the booksellers and street vendors, thanks for your hustle. I appreciate you. Keisha Caldwell, you are counting down. Love you and thanks for always being there and remaining the same.

To the WCP Authors: Cash, Mike Sanders, Missy Jackson, Tash Hawthorne, The Country Boys, Anthony Fields, Dion Jones, and Victor Martin and those to come, it's on and poppin'!

Thanks UNC and Kisha from Pennsylvania.

2010 is my year. I am Wahida Clark, the "Official Queen" of Street Literature.

CHAPTER ONE

THE AFTERMATH

Nina! Nina! Wake the fuck up!" Michelle snapped at Nina as she shook her frantically. "Your face is all twisted up and shit. You sweatin' and slobbin' all over my seats."

Nina stared at Michelle with a look of horror and confusion on her face.

"What the fuck is wrong with you? The devil ridin' your back or some shit like that?"

"Shit!" Nina ran both hands across her face and jumped out of the Rover.

Michelle jumped out and stood watching Nina pace back and forth.

"Damn, that shit was real as hell. Shit!" Nina kept repeating as she continued to pace, trying her damnedest to make sense of the dream she just had. She couldn't stop the visual from playing in her head. It was as if it were playing in 3-D.

"Look," Michelle snapped, not giving a fuck about her girl being shook up. "It's hot as fuck out here. What we gonna do now? Did you get in touch with Reese yet?" Michelle asked as she walked around the truck to where Nina was and stood in front of her.

Nina looked her best friend over and wanted to grab her and kiss her, relieved that the dream was just that, a dream, but decided against it. Then she looked over at her brother Peedie, who had just come out of his girlfriend Darlene's house and was headed up the block. *Damn, that dream was real as shit.*

"Nina! Did you get in touch with Reese yet?" Michelle saw the blank look on Nina's face and was getting agitated. "Did you talk to the nigga or what?" she snapped.

"Damn, chill, bitch. Let me get my thoughts together." At the moment Nina was having a hard time determining what was real and what wasn't. *Damn. Did I just talk to him?* She tried to shake it off. *That shit seemed so real.* Michelle now had her arms folded across her chest and was leaning up against the truck. She was beginning to piss Nina off. "Trick, why you in such a hurry? It ain't like you got somewhere to be."

Michelle sucked her teeth. "Bitch, I don't want you to leave and the closer you get to making that move, the sadder I feel. Okay? There. I said it."

"Awww. Big bad Chelle is feelin' lonely," Nina teased her.

"Nina, did you talk to him or what?"

"I talked to him. He told me that he can move the coke in as little as two days and have the money for me by Thursday."

"Thursday, huh? That nigga gonna move ten keys in two days? I don't know, Nina. Get your head outta that cloud you were just on. Do you think he can be trusted?"

Nina gave Michelle's question some thought. "I think so. That nigga's pockets already laced, Chelle, plus up until this point he hasn't given a reason not to. And with all this shit on my shoulders and a mark on my back I don't have too many choices. Hopefully he won't try to beat a bitch out of a puck-ass two hundred grand."

"Bitch, you know how them New York niggas get down. Them niggas put the capital C in 'cruddy.' Plus, two hundred grand is two hundred grand. But fuck it. Like Lil Wayne said, 'Life is like a gamble when you all about your poker chips.' If you trust that nigga, so do I. I just hope he comes through for you. Did you tell him who the keys belong to or how you got 'em?"

"Come on, Chelle, you know me better than that. I'ma hustler. I don't let my right hand know what my left hand is doing. Just handle your part, aiight. You see Peedie up there sittin' on the fire hydrant?"

Michelle glanced up the block. "Yeah, I see him. And all I'm supposed to do is go and get the keys to your car from him, right?"

Nina nodded her head.

"Do Peedie know you got ten bricks hid in your trunk?" When Nina didn't respond, Michelle had her answer. "Aiight, damn. Let me go get them car keys because I know you fucked up about Derrick and everything that's going on, but your attitude is vexing me. I'll be right back." Michelle rolled her eyes at Nina and headed for Peedie.

Nina jumped back into the truck, cranked it up and turned on the air. She lay back on the headrest and closed her eyes for a minute. Michelle was right. Her attitude was kinda shitty, but what did people expect? She was officially the target of a citywide hunt. And her younger brother Derrick "D-Rock" Coles had just been shot and killed only a few days ago by the very same people that were hunting her. *I need some dro*, Nina said to herself and exhaled. When she opened her eyes, alarm registered in her brain quickly.

A candy apple red Dodge Viper with two dudes inside with red bandanas covering their mouth and nose stopped a few feet in front of her. Nina lowered herself in her seat but noticed that the Viper occupants' attention was elsewhere. Nina tried her best to follow their gazes. Her heart stopped momentarily as her eyes settled on the only two people standing on one side of the block…Peedie and Michelle. Just as that dream registered in her brain, the Dodge Viper began to creep up the block.

"No-o-o-o-o-o!" Nina screamed as the assault rifle came out of the window. As if riveted to her seat, Nina watched in horror as fire erupted from the rifle along with the sound of rapid-fire gunshots. Eyes glued to the scene in front of her, Nina watched bullets rip into Michelle's body and twist her in grotesque angles before she dropped to the ground and lay still. Her eyes saw the movement of her

Two hours later, Nina saw a silver Lexus LX truck pull behind Michelle's Rover. She walked out of the shadows and headed towards it. She was relieved when she saw Reese jump out and she damn near ran to meet him. They embraced, and at that moment time seemed to be standing still. She settled into his masculine arms and inhaled his scent. Nina tried, but couldn't place the cologne. She felt safe in his arms. If only for a little while. Choking back sobs, Nina said, "Thank you for coming."

"I told you I got you, ma. What's good with you? Did some nigga hurt you?" He was looking her over.

Nina started to respond, but the sheer weight of everything that had transpired over the course of the past four days hit her and she broke down. Reese held her in his arms and gently stroked her hair. He let her cry herself out while patiently waiting to hear about whatever was bothering her. He had been handling some business in Brooklyn when he got her call telling him she needed him right now. Dropping everything, Reese was up for some new pussy, so when it called he came running.

"Listen, ma. It's going to be aiight."

"It's not gonna be all right," Nina screamed suddenly. "Don't say that. You don't even know the half of it."

"Okay. Okay. Listen, Nina, you gotta tell me what's wrong, ma. If you want me to help you, I gotta know what's good, feel me? So wipe your eyes and tell me what's going on. Tell me everything and don't leave nothing out."

Nina composed herself as best she possibly could, took a few steps back from Reese and started at the beginning. "Almost two weeks ago, I came home to find my house burglarized, ransacked, I mean, tore the fuck up. Before I could file a police report, my neighbors described a nigga who turned out to be my brother, described him to a T leaving my house. He stole what I called my 'Lord Have Mercy' fund. In other words, it was my rainy-day money. Derrick breaks in my shit and takes my money, not thinking that I'ma find out it was him. I went looking for his ass and confronted him about my shit. That's the day I met you. A few days later he shows up at my front door. When I wouldn't let him in he broke down, cried me a fistful of tears and promised to make everything right. My heart was broke, but hey, that's my little brother. So I let him in against my better judgement. D-Rock then got all excited and shit, telling me that he had a way to get my stash back plus give me an extra ten stacks for my troubles. He knew a chick named Canada—"

"D-Rock...Canada...where did I...?" Reese interrupted. Scratching his head, he tried to recall where he had heard those names before.

"What?" Nina asked with a suspicious look on her face.

"Nothing. It'll come to me. Go 'head with the story."

"This chick named Canada and her mom, Serita, had some checks worth about a hundred grand that they were trying to cash in. D-Rock knew that checks and shit was right up my alley, so he arranged to hook us up. After the introduction and agreement was made, I cashed the checks and then when we go to take her the money, boom. My brother and his boys would rob 'em. That was the plan. I didn't know the chick Canada or her mom, Serita, from a can of paint, so I was like, fuck it, let's do this.

"So the day after, D introduced me to the chick and then we went to handle our business. Everything went according to plan as far as cashing the checks, and then shit went bad real fast. After we handled the business, me and my girl got ghost so D-Rock and his boys could handle theirs. I then get a call from my brother to come get him. He was all shot up but he still had some money. We dropped him off at the ER. Later that night, we found out that Canada's mom and my brother had died. It was all over the local news. I was trying not to panic, and kept telling myself that there was no way anything could be traced back to us. And the twenty-five grand my brother gave me made me feel a lot better. I thought that everything would blow over, you know? A woman and a feen getting robbed and killed in Trenton…that shit ain't nothing new.

"I knew the cops would be sniffing around and we figured that they were all we had to fear. Boy, was we wrong. We all were so wrong. The next day, while coming out of a house on Tyler Street, my brother's boy Blue was gunned down. Blue was with D that night but he got away. He must have been running his mouth. The streets got to talking and then word got back. The chick Canada had told her brother about the lick. The brother was the one who gave her the checks. When Canada's mom got killed, he put two and two together and came up with Derrick and me. Out of all the chicks to kill in the hood they had to go and kill a chick whose brother is the leader of one of the Blood gangs in the city. Ilhawn Inglewood Bloods or something like that. He put out a 'red' light on us. After that I went to my best friend Michelle's house and hid out.

"The next thing I knew, somebody set my house on fire. I lost everything, Reese. My kids' shit. My shit. The money, everything. I had to go get my car from my brother Peedie today so that I could leave town. Are you able to move those bricks? I gotta raise some more cash so that I can bounce."

"You said ten, right? Why, what's up? They got burned up too?"

"There's a small problem," Nina said with hesitation.

"What's up?"

"The keys are hidden in the trunk of my car. My brother's been driving it and don't....didn't know that..."

"Who, Derrick?" Reese asked.

"No...my other brother. The oldest one. Peedie. Me and my girl Michelle went to Peedie's girlfriend Darlene's house out in Ewing to get my car so that I could get the keys for you." At that point, Nina choked up again and her tears started anew. "We pulled up on the block. Michelle was driving...that's her truck over there...the Rover. I stayed in the car while she went to get the keys to my car from Peedie. I saw the red Viper turn the corner...they killed my best friend...they shot Peedie. I don't even know if he's dead or alive right now," Nina said and wiped tears from her eyes. "I called an ambulance for him and left him there. I left him there...Peedie might be..."

Reese walked over to Nina and said, "Peedie... D-Rock...Darlene...Canada. Small world, small world."

Puzzled, Nina looked into Reese's eyes. There was something there. The expression on his face was speaking louder than words. "What is it? Why did you say it's a small world?"

"I was in Brownsville a few days ago, at a gambling spot on Prospect. The spot was full of Blood niggas— Nine Trey gangstas out of Harlem, I believe. They had a nigga with them that I had never seen. But I remember hearing the nigga say he was from Jersey. I overheard the nigga telling the other dudes about a situation they were dealing with. He mentioned a dude named B-Murder's mom and sister Canada getting robbed. The name Canada stuck in my head. He said something about a bitch and her brother D-Rock that they killed. Then he mentioned a dude named Peedie and..." Reese paused as the whole conversation that he heard slowly came back to him. "Damn, shorty. It all just came back to me. Didn't you say that Peedie's girlfriend's name is Darlene?"

Nina paused. She felt like she just gave him too much information. "Yeah, that's her name."

"I hate to be the bearer of bad news, but Darlene is connected to the Blood niggas in some kinda way. The Jersey nigga told the other nigga that Darlene's been helping the homies and that she was going to set up Peedie for them."

"Are you sure?"

"I'm positive, shorty. When you mentioned your brother Peedie getting shot, that brought all the recollection back to me. I remembered thinking that the bitch Darlene that dude spoke of was a dirty, shiesty bitch. I'm definitely sure about what I heard. I'm sorry about your brother, but I never connected any of that to you because the dude never said your name."

The world was spinning now at a different angle for Nina and she felt dizzy, light-headed. She couldn't believe what she was hearing. Darlene had a hand in all of this shit. The botched robbery and Peedie being shot. Hell, they had planned on taking D-Rock out from the jump. *Why didn't they kill me? They couldn't because I didn't stick around like we had originally planned.* As the realization set in, the picture became that much clearer. Now everything made sense. Reese's revelation explained how the Bloods knew to catch Derrick. He had to have told Peedie his whereabouts and Peedie unknowingly had to have told Darlene. Darlene knew where she lived, that's how the Bloods knew where she rested at. Thus her house being burned down. Darlene didn't know where Michelle lived. Then Darlene must have told them that Peedie was outside her house at that exact moment...wait. Nina focused all her attention back a few hours ago, when she was sitting in the Rover watching the Dodge Viper. The two dudes in the car with the red bandanas over half their faces...the driver was doing something that she hadn't noticed at first, but it came back to her now. While both men had been looking down the block, the driver was holding something to his ear...a cell phone. Right before Peedie and Michelle were shot, the driver of the Viper was on the phone talking to Darlene. A rage that was totally unknown to Nina came over her and settled. It was like a fire that was consuming her body and soul. She knew exactly what she had to do.

"I need a favor."

"I told you I'ma help you move the keys. I figure you need the money to bounce with. I got you."

"I know that already. That's not what I'm talking about. I need another favor."

"What's that?"

"I need a gun," Nina told him.

Reese was about to protest, but then stopped and nodded in understanding. There was no need for discussion; he knew what the business was. "Are you sure that's what you want? You sure that's what you want to do?"

Without hesitation, Nina replied, "I'm sure. Here." Handing Reese the keys to her car, she said, "My car is a red 2010 Volkswagen Jetta with chrome 22s on it. It's parked on the 2000 block on Lanning State Street out in Ewing.

You won't miss it. Get somebody you can trust to drive it, but be careful because the Bloods have to know it's mine and they may be looking for somebody driving it.

"The ten bricks are in my trunk. Go in the trunk and lift the whole paneling out to where the spare tire is located. Remove the spare tire cover and the keys are right there. But in the meantime, I have something to do. When it's finished, I'ma call you and meet you somewhere. I need to ditch both of the cars. I gotta make a call, and if it's all good, I'ma drop them both off at a friend of mine's chop shop. Then I have to bounce to somewhere safe until you ready to hit me off with that loot."

Reese nodded. "I got you on all that, shorty." He reached under his shirt and pulled out a chrome handgun. "This is a Sig Sauer 9mm...It's light, small and just right for you. The clip holds ten bullets. There's one in the chamber, so that gives you eleven shots." Reese gave the handgun to Nina. "Be careful, ma. Be careful. Holla at me as soon as you can."

Taking the gun and putting it in her purse, Nina nodded her head and without another word she walked into the night.

Darlene Rojas was a bad bitch and she knew it. She prided herself on being a thorough street chick. Growing up on the mean streets of Newark's Dayton Street Projects had nurtured her and shaped her into the person she was today. When her mother lost her job and they moved to

Trenton, Darlene thought it was the end of the world. But she was exposed to a whole new world. Brian "B-Murder" Mitchell was the be-all and end-all on the streets and he loved her. Or at least that's what she thought until her world came crashing down one day. Darlene found out that B-Murder had a woman stashed in every part of the city. When she confronted him with what she had found out, he never denied anything and he never said a word. He simply stopped calling her and stopped coming around. Heartbroken and distraught, Darlene tried everything in her power to win back B-Murder's affections. But nothing seemed to work. Then she met Peedie Coles and decided to let him fill in for the love of her life, until she was able to find a way to get him back. B-Murder just needed a little time, and time seemed to be something she had a lot of lately.

When she found out about Nina and Derrick getting ready to jack B-Murder's sister Canada and his mom it was as if heaven opened its gates and rained down manna upon her.

Darlene took her direct connection to the situation to be a sign that she was meant to be with B-Murder. All it took from her was a lot of deep throating and dick riding to get all the info she needed out of Peedie. Then, like a loyal bitch, she made contact with Murder and confirmed what he said he already knew. But what he didn't have was the specifics, addresses, etc., . . . and she did.

Turning onto her street, Darlene eyed the yellow tape

that still lined the area where the girl she barely knew had been killed. *Luck was one twisted sister*, Darlene thought to herself. Death had eluded the person that it was meant for that day and had found another soul to take. Parking her car, she thought about all the questions the police had asked her as she played the role of the distraught girl-friend to the fullest. She hadn't answered not one. Darlene walked up her front stairs and saw all the blood that had dried up on her porch and promised herself that she'd remember to put the high-power water hose on the porch tomorrow to wash the blood away. But it would have to wait until after she left B-Murder. Excitement washed over Darlene as she walked into her house. She had forty-five minutes to shower and dress and then the moment she had been waiting almost three years for would come. She was about to meet and spend the night with B-Murder. And she couldn't wait.

Hitting the light on the wall, Darlene walked into her living room and almost jumped out of her skin. "What the...? Nina?"

"Hey, Darlene."

"Nina, what the fuck? How did you get in here? Why are you here?"

"I let myself in. I hope you don't mind. I had to see you before I left. Why you lookin' all shocked?"

"No, I thought you was gone," Darlene said as she tried to play it cool.

"I'm on my way out but I gotta right one wrong before

I leave town. All my life, Darlene, I have been a hustla. Going from one hustle to the next. But I never thought that one day I'd become a killer."

Darlene's eyes dropped to Nina's hand and saw the gun. Fear ripped her heart and squeezed it. "Killer? You? Who did you kill, Nina?"

"You, Darlene. For betraying my brother Peedie, my brother Derrick and me." With that, Nina raised the gun and shot Darlene repeatedly in the face.

Exiting the house the way she came, through the back door, Nina ran quickly down the alley. She came out onto the street and walked calmly back to the Rover. What Nina didn't see was the cream-colored Infiniti M35 that was parked three cars behind her. As she pulled off, the Infiniti waited awhile and then pulled behind her.

After getting rid of both cars, Reese and Nina drove to a hotel in a town called King of Prussia, located on the outskirts of Philadelphia. Reese made sure she was safe and situated, then he left. But not before he asked for the gun back. Without a word exchanged between them, he ejected the clip and saw it was only half full. His eyes met hers and that was it.

Stretching out on the bed, Nina allowed herself a moment's rest. She was dog tired. She was also relieved, angry and stricken with grief. The first thing she did was take a long, hot shower and wash her hair. Standing under the steaming spray of water, she decided to talk to God.

"I know I'm probably the last person you thought would be reaching out to you, but it's me. I know I do a lot of sinful stuff but I just wanna ask you to look out for my big brother Peedie and my brother Derrick. Please forgive him and my girl Michelle for the lives they lived. It wasn't easy growing up in Jersey. And please, please, take care of Peedie. Help him heal from all his wounds mentally and physically. But most of all, forgive me for the life I took and pray that I never, ever, have to take another. Do this for me and I promise you I'ma get my life together. Amen. Oh! And take care of my kids while I'm gone. I know you are going to do that."

When she was done, Nina turned the water off and wrapped herself in a towel. She brushed her teeth and then sat on the bed. Nina lay back and stared up at the ceiling. Her mind was cluttered and kept flashing with everything that happened over the past week or so. Ending with the phone call to her mother, who told her that Peedie was in critical condition, but he was expected to live. That news in itself was like an invisible weight lifted off her chest. But still she cried for Michelle and for Derrick. Grabbing the pillow from the other side of the bed, Nina covered her face and screamed into it as if she were being tortured.

Her stomach knotted up when she thought about her three children that she would have to leave behind. The longest she had ever been away from them was a couple of weeks. The thought of her babies, along with the rest of her drama, had her bawling like a baby. But what hurt the most was the fact that she wouldn't even be able to attend the funerals of the two people closest to her. And their deaths were all her fault. Nina rationalized that Derrick's death was her fault because had she not gone after him about the money he took from her house, the caper with Canada and her mom would probably have never happened. The death of D-Rock and Michelle was a rude awakening, and she swore that after the ten keys were sold she was walking the straight and narrow.

Thinking about the kilos of coke made her remember where she'd got them. After D's death, Nina finalized her plan to leave Jersey for a while. And since everything she had had burned down in her house, she had to hit a lick to come up with the going-away money she would need to live outside of Jersey. That's when she remembered her ex-boyfriend's stash. Cream kept no less than fifty to one hundred keys stored in a public storage space, and she was the only one who knew where it was. Getting into the storage space without a key had been easy. She had been there enough for the dude who worked the desk to be familiar with her. After a little flirting and a promise to hook up behind her man's back, she was in. Nina had planned on taking only one or two kilos, but when she thought about the reasons that she and Cream were no longer together, she decided to get back a little and hurt his pockets at the same time. She grabbed ten keys and left. Later that night she hooked up with the dude who worked at the storage spot, sucked his dick until he begged her to stop and gave him a promise of more to come that would fortify his silence about her trip to the storage space.

Nina then contacted Reese to put him to the test. He had told her that if she ever needed anything to call him. She needed him now more than ever.

After two days, Nina was well rested and getting restless. Yesterday she walked across the highway to the movie theater and she started to do it again today but Reese called and said he would be coming through.

Reese. She barely knew him, and everything she learned about him was from their few but lengthy phone conversations. He had been relentlessly trying to get with her but she was focused on getting everything together for this move. She kept giving him rain check after rain check and still he never stopped trying. But when it came down to it Nina trusted him and just as she anticipated he came to her rescue and he wanted nothing in return.

It was almost eight and she was bored shitless. Nina had taken another shower, threw on some sweatpants and a wife-beater. She ordered a pizza from Pizza Hut and was getting ready to call them and cuss them out. She placed the order at seven and here it was eight and they were just knocking on the door to deliver. She decided to make them wait. Finally, she went to the door and snatched it open. Nina looked up and Reese was standing there wearing a sexy grin, a pair of jeans, a gray Versace sweater, a black leather vest and a pair of black Mauri gators. He caught her completely by surprise.

"Hey." She eased over to where he was and kissed him on the check, surprising herself. *Did I really do that?* He took both hands, pulled her to him and kissed her on the mouth. That surprised her as well. His tongue and mouth tasted like peppermint. Nina, in a panic, was the first to break the kiss. She just stood there in the doorway looking at him.

"What? I can't come in?" Reese teased, looking down at Nina. Beneath all of that toughness, she was incredibly sexy and childlike to him.

She looked at him and stepped back. "Of course you can come in."

His bald head glistened and his smile let her know that things were going as planned. "I was beginning to think that you forgot all about me," she said seductively.

"Never that, shorty. I told you I got you." He closed the door and put the chain on. "You all right?"

There was another knock at the door and Nina saw Reese's hand slide behind his back.

"Stand down, baby boy. I ordered pizza. It's only the pizza guy," she told him as she went and opened the door. He still kept his hand behind his back until he was positive it was *just* the pizza delivery.

"Well damn, I thought y'all had to go to Italy to bake the pizza," she snapped. "How much do I owe you?"

"Sorry about that, ma'am," the young white girl said.

"They told me to deliver to the hotel next door. That's where I went first, but that'll be sixteen dollars and forty cents."

Nina gave the girl a twenty-dollar bill and snatched her pizza and soda. She then slammed the door and slid the chain back on.

Reese watched her set the pizza down and then go sit on the edge of the bed.

"Is everything all right with you?" she asked him.

"Oh, we good, shorty." Reese took off his jacket and hung it up. He moved towards the bed, unzipping the compartments on the vest and allowing the stacks of money to fall onto the bed. "That's the whole two hundred stacks. Count it if you want, but it's all there. Now you can bounce whenever you want to. That shit went so fast it scared me. When all this shit blows over, you gonna have to introduce me to your connect. If he keep that fish scale like that, he is definitely somebody I need to know. Feel me?"

"I feel you and you got that," Nina lied. "You don't know how much I appreciate this." Breathing a sigh of relief, she grabbed one bag at a time and emptied it. The bag contained ten stacks of big-face hundreds. Emptying the second bag, she saw it contained ten stacks of money.

"That's twenty stacks altogether, shorty. Ten grand a stack. Go 'head and count it. TRUST NO MAN, NINA. NOT EVEN ME."

Reese and Nina sat on the bed and began counting the money. Nina stopped counting periodically to look at him. After a while, he caught her stealing glances. He smiled mischievously and kept counting.

"Yo, what's up? Why you just smile at me like that?" Nina asked.

Reese ignored her and kept counting stacks. After he finished counting all the money, he took off the vest and went to hang it up. He looked over at Nina and said, "You look like you need a hug. Come here."

"I'm okay," she said. He looked at her again, thinking about how vulnerable she was.

"Come here." When she didn't move, he went over to the bed and grabbed her hand. He pulled her up, wrapping his arms around her. "What?"

She stood there limp, arms hanging loosely by her sides. "I'm okay," she mumbled.

"No you're not. You damn near ripped the poor delivery girl's head off. You order pizza and leave it sitting there untouched. You were sitting over there on the bed with a blank look staring out into space somewhere. Plus, you've been cooped up in this room for damn near four days."

"I went to the movies yesterday," she protested.

Reese started laughing. "Wow! The movies," he replied, teasing her.

"What's so funny about that?" She was now smiling. That was the first time she actually saw him laugh.

"You need a hug." The way he said it gave her goose bumps and made her shiver. "It's all good. I got you." He pulled her close and began rubbing up and down her back as he held her tight. She closed her eyes and surrendered to his embrace. It was feeling so welcoming she couldn't help but wrap her arms around his back, releasing a soft moan.

"See, I told you, you needed this," he said in that same seductive tone as he slid one of his strong hands down and began massaging her ass. Her heart fluttered, she opened her eyes and looked up at him. She wanted to ask him what he was doing. But he leaned in and kissed her. The kiss was commanding so she couldn't help but to kiss him back. His kiss was wet, sweet and silky smooth.

She pulled back and said, "So I *needed* my ass felt on along with a kiss?" She turned around to walk back to the bed but he grabbed her from behind and held her close so she could feel his dick harden as one hand circled her nipple and the other hand slid down the inside of her sweats. His fingertips rubbed across her pussy back and forth.

Later for the kiss.

"Feeling how wet you are I can also tell that you *need* some of this dick."

"Reese, you don't want to go there," she teased.

"Yes I do. And why wouldn't I?" He was massaging her tits and playing inside her pussy while her ass was subtly rocking side to side, grinding against his hard-on and on his fingers.

Her surrender gave him the green light to move forward.

"Shorty, you know you ready for this so why you frontin'?" His fingers slid out of her warm pussy and went to her clit. She spread her legs wider and a moan escaped her throat.

"See, I told you," he whispered in her ear. He played and mashed on her swollen clit, causing her knees to buckle and cum to squirt in his hand as her trembling body fell back into his. He pulled her wife-beater up over her head and turned her around. She unzipped his jeans, slid them and his boxers down off of his ass and got on her knees. His dick sprung out, tapping against her cheek. "He's glad to finally meet you."

She grabbed on to it and licked the head. Reese watched as his joint disappeared into her mouth and then reappeared again. She went back and forth, teasing the head and said, "I don't think you're ready for this." She swallowed him up.

"I damn sure ain't." He grabbed her head, ready to fuck her mouth but she seductively and slowly slid her lips away. The veins on his dick looked as if they were about to pop. His dick was standing straight out. "Oh, so you got jokes."

Nina stood up and slid her sweats down over her hips and to the floor. "Ladies before gentlemen. I gots to get mine first."

Reese got out of his clothes and shoes as if he was on a mission. Nina went over to the bed and climbed on all fours. "Uh-uh, that's too easy. You said you want to get yours, right? Come over here." He motioned to the recliner. "Do you, lil' mama."

Nina climbed up on it, placing one knee on each armrest,

leaned forward and wrapped her arms around the back of the chair. Reese came up behind her and allowed his dick to slide across her pussy. He went back and forth, teasing and stimulating her clit with the head of his dick. "Reese, stop playing." Nina groaned, unable to move in the position that she was in. *Shit.* She wasn't in control. She needed to be in command of the dick. He kept sliding back and forth, getting her wetter and wetter. Her teeth bit down into the chair before he plunged up into her. "Ohhhh," she moaned, her juices were sliding down her thighs. "Oh shit," she gritted. "This feels so good," she panted.

Reese pounded away, loving all of the control he was having. He was able to get in deep as he wanted and when it felt like he was ready to bust he pulled out.

"Nooooo, no, wait," she begged. "Finish fucking me," she pleaded.

"Don't move," he commanded as he began to plant soft kisses on her neck, shoulders, all down her back. When he got to her ass he spread her cheeks and began licking her crack.

Nina's body, from the lips, to her toes, all the way up her back and tits caught fire.

"What...are...you doing to me?" She shivered.

Reese kept licking until he was about to cum, then he stood up and got back up into her pussy, while playing with her clit until she could hold out no more. She began cumming and shaking, trembling and screaming. He let loose at the same time, their bodies connecting as one.

And that's how Reese came into the picture.

After he moved those ten keys and laid the pipe he was in. He got someone to drive her U-Haul to Georgia and the two of them rode in his truck. He stayed with her until she found an apartment and transportation. He was her knight in shining armor and the most important thing was he wanted nothing in return. Nina was finally off to starting her new life.

As soon as she stepped foot onto Georgia soil, Nina took off running. She quickly discovered that as long as you had good credit, getting an apartment in Georgia was a cinch. It only took her two weeks. She and Reese went to a car auction and she walked away with a silver Volvo that looked nice, ran good and most of all it was paid for. She found a chic one-bedroom apartment in Decatur and was quite pleased.

After Reese went back to New York she buckled down and began job hunting. She didn't have a degree and the only skill she had was hustling. *Fuck working at some fast-food joint*, she constantly thought to herself. Telemarketing jobs were plentiful and didn't require a résumé so that's what her focus was on. She started calling around and setting up interviews. She learned that just about everything was sold over the phone. Magazines, vacation packages, security systems, furniture and even coupons...you name it they sold it. And it was all bullshit. Getting the consumer to buy stuff they didn't need.

She ended up accepting a gig selling magazines. It was a new company, the facility was new, she liked the atmosphere and she didn't have to travel too far and battle that Georgia gridlock. After she got the job she felt accomplished and on her way to stability. She got settled in less than two months. All during those two months she called home and checked on her children every day. It was excrutiating to talk to them over the phone and not be able to see them. And her baby, she tried not to think about her because Jatana would always bring her to tears. She imagined her wondering why her mother, sister and uncle and auntie Michelle all of a sudden disappeared.

She had a new cell number and told her mother and Jatana's grandmother to give it to Jatana's daddy, Supreme. He stayed into something so he would probably never get out of prison. He was bent on making her life on the outside a living hell. And on top of it all he still hadn't bothered to call her yet. She knew he was pissed at her for moving out of state and he did keep true to his word. He promised her that she would not take his daughter so far away. He was determined to make her suffer. She couldn't believe she used to be in love with such a vindictive nigga. Finally, after three months he sent her a message, to not worry about their baby, she was fine.

Her brother Peedie was finally out of the hospital and doing well, despite being paralyzed from the waist down. He was convalescing and laying low with a woman he knew in Englishtown. The detectives assigned to his shooting kept asking about Darlene's murder, but he told them nothing. And that was because Nina had told him nothing. Even if she did, Peedie would not violate the code. Nina vowed to herself that one day she would be honest with Peedie and tell him about Darlene's betrayal and her death. But now was not the time, she decided. Not while Peedie was dealing with his paralysis and maintaining his sanity because of it. The last thing he had said to her was, "Live the life of a square while you're down there and be safe. I love you, Sis." That piece of advice Nina took with a tablespoon of salt and two grams of sugar. All she did was go to work and come home. Her plan was to add a lot more money to the stash she already had and buy a big house so that she could send for her children in a year. That was the plan. But so far, the plan was not coming together fast enough, and discouragement was quickly creeping in. After buying everything she would need for starting anew in Georgia and pinching to send money home to her mom for the kids, her stash was lowering somewhere around a little over a hundred grand. And she wasn't going below the hundred for nothing in the world. Her job was paying the rent, car insurance, gas and providing food, but that's it. Nina wasn't saving anything or adding to her stash. Her dead-end job constantly reminded her of when she started hustling, why she never stopped.

Hustle money was fast and it was huge. She knew that if she did a little something every now and again, she'd be able to stack in a week what it took her months to stack on a job. The hustle that flowed in her veins was starting to call out to her, so discreetly, Nina began to look for a come up.

Reese started out visiting her two to three times a month and he had her wide open. She was in love with him but was noticing that lately he was only coming once a month. Today was her six-month anniversary living in Georgia and she was celebrating all by herself. She was in her living room getting comfortable preparing to watch a movie before she turned in for the night when she was startled by the sound of someone ringing her bell. *Who in the hell is at my door? And at this hour of the night?* Nina wondered as she headed to check it out. When she looked out she saw her knight in shining armor, Reese. She quickly opened the door while smiling from ear to ear and jumping into his arms.

"Aren't you a sight for sore eyes!" she said excitedly. "And you made it for our six-month anniversary." She was busy raining kisses all over his face and lips. When she slid off him, Reese flashed his sexy smile. As soon as he stepped inside her apartment, Nina was all over him again. It had been a month since she had seen him and she was jonesing...bad.

Reese came up for air. "I need to talk to you, Nina."

"Well, whatever it is, it is going to have to wait until morning. Maybe I'll be done with you by then." She grabbed him gently by the back of his head and began to kiss him passionately while at the same time rubbing her hand up and down his dick. Reese had not planned to sleep with Nina tonight. He made this trip because he was on a mission. He had something important to tell her but she was making it hard for him to stay focused on the task at hand. He could tell that she was glad to see him and had been anticipating his visit. And it was obvious that she was not taking no for an answer.

"Nina." He interrupted her. His head was foggy and his dick was ready to put in work.

"You don't miss me, big daddy? It's been a whole month."

"Of course I do. But that's what I need to talk to you about." He tried once again to do what he came there to do but she was making it hard.

"Like I said, it's going to have to wait because I'm gettin' me some of this dick. Now act like you miss me and haven't seen me in four weeks. As you see, I have been counting."

Damn, he said to himself. Then decided to go with the flow. "We do miss you, girl." He was kissing all over her neck and had his hand up her pajama top feeling her breasts.

"I miss you more." She was breathing heavy and ready to fuck. "Wait a minute. Who is we?" Nina teased.

"You know who *we* is." He took Nina's hand and slid it down the front of his jeans. "Me and him. And he said he is *extremely* glad to see you."

Nina giggled and ran her hand along the length of his dick. It was stiff and long, just the way she liked it. She slid her thumb back and forth across the head, playing in the pre-cum. "Mmm. I got a few words I need to say to this guy right now," she purred. She got on her knees and gave him some head.

They then ended up fucking right there in the hall-way but Nina was not done with him. She noticed that he started fixing his clothes. "Uh-uh, I know you don't think you finished." She was now pulling him towards her bed-room. They were walking backwards. Nina was tugging at Reese's shirt and trying to unzip his pants all at once.

"Wait. Hold up, Nina, we have to talk."

"Daddy, all I want to hear come out of your mouth are moans," she whispered as she continued to get ready to get some more dick. "That was just round one."

They made it to the bedroom. She undressed him and Reese was now lying on his back, one hand behind his head the other rubbing his dick. Nina was standing over him holding on to the rail attached to the canopy bed. She was playing with her clit and on the verge of cumming.

"Hold up, baby, not so fast. Let me finish you off."

Nina moved her hand to her breast and spread her legs. Reese climbed over to where she was and started lick-ing her pussy. Nina grabbed on to his head to stabilize her trembling body. Reese kept licking until she pushed his head away. He then lay back down on his back, dick standing straight up. Nina squatted over him backwards, and eased all the way down on his pole, her hands around her ankles. Reese wrapped his hands around hers so she couldn't move and began pumping up in her slowly. Each time he would slide all the way out of her and would go back in deeper. This drove Nina crazy.

"Reese," she moaned. "My spot. Keep hittin' my spot." He came out and went in deeper. When he felt her spot he hit it until he felt her pussy muscles strangling his dick, she started cumming, let go of her ankles and fell forward.

Reese smiled as he hurriedly climbed on top of her limp body and started hitting it from the back until he went limp and fell beside her. She dozed off while Reese rose up and sat on the side of the bed. He lit a blunt and looked around the room. He got up and started packing all of his stuff. After he was done and fully dressed, he rubbed Nina's back. "Baby, I came to talk to you about something."

Nina's eyes popped open, and when she looked around at his stuff packed her face frowned up and she jumped out of the bed and threw on her robe. "Baby, what's the matter? Where are you taking your stuff?"

"Look, Nina. I care about you and I have been trying my damndest to make sure that I don't cause you any unnecessary heartache."

He now had her undivided attention. This didn't sound good. Nina backed up a little to brace herself for what was about to come out of Reese's mouth. "Nina, I know it's been a while since I have been down here. But it's not just because I'm real busy." An unsettling pause came over the room and with hesitation in his voice he took a deep breath and said, "I have a family."

Nina looked at Reese as if she did not know him.

"What did you just say?"

"I have a family, Nina." He stood up and came towards her.

She looked at him as if he had lost his mind.

"You came all this fucking way to tell me you have a family? You could have called me and told me that shit over the phone," Nina said, unable to mask her disappointment. She turned to walk away from him but he grabbed her arm and she quickly snatched away from him.

"Nina. I respect you too much to call you on some damn phone and tell you something as sensitive as this. I owe you and respect you more than that."

"At least it would have been a littler easier and less embarrassing for me." She felt as if she was just stabbed in the heart, and was hoping for him to tell her he was only joking. When he didn't say anything she said, "Look, you don't owe me anything, Reese. You helped me when I really needed you and I guess I paid all my debts in pussy. But hey, it was good while it lasted." And she meant that. She was so caught up that she failed to see the signs. He didn't move in with her, his visits started getting too far in between, shit, he was just too good to be true.

Reese stood there feeling like shit. "Nina, you know that ain't right. You know I got mad love for you, and it's because of those feelings I knew I had to be honest with you. My conscience wouldn't have it any other way." He could have kept enjoying the best of both worlds. But from past experience he knew that eventually somebody would have found out.

Shit, the way I'm feeling you, fuck your conscience. You could have kept that honesty shit to yourself. Nina looked at him with disgust and hurt in her eyes as the tears began to trickle down her cheeks. "Well if you are done being honest, I guess you have a plane to catch." She proceeded to walk to the door.

Reese was right behind her. He grabbed her by the arm and pulled her close to him. Nina wanted to resist but his strong arms felt too good wrapped around her. She took a minute to enjoy what she knew would be their last embrace. She thought about all of the contentment and joy he had brought to her. How he was there when she needed someone the most. Then she finally got the strength to break away. "Go, Reese. Don't make this harder than it already is." She put her head down and turned to open the door, refusing to look at him. "Go." Her voice trembled.

"Nina, don't be like that." Reese tried to plead with her.

"Please, Reese. If you meant any of what you said about how you feel about me, you would just leave." With that, he walked out of her house and out of her life. She closed the door, slid down on the floor and cried.

CHAPTER TWO

GBI

A year and a half later...

Congratulations, Bob! You did it! Are you sitting down?" Alexis Greenspan shouted in excitement. She could feel Bob's adrenaline rush through the phone.

"Oh God, Alexis. Did I really do it?" Bob could barely contain his breathing.

"You did it, Bob Tokowski! You have just won your fair share of one million dollars of American Eagle gold coins! One million!" Alexis screamed out. "I told you to hang in there, Bob! The road was rocky, but you did it! Your perseverance paid off. Again, congratulations to ya, Bob! You deserve it! You finally hit the big time."

Bob was now crying tears of joy. "Thank...you. Alexis. Oh my God. Thank you."

"Now, Bob, I need you to grab your pencil and paper. You must write down this claim number. Go ahead, Bob, grab a pen and a pad." Alexis could hear Bob piddling around in the background. She heard glass crash, a moan and then a thud. Then there was an eerie silence.

"Bob! Bob?" Nina heard her own voice call out.

Click. Agent Houser turned off the recorder. Houser had been lead investigator for the Georgia Bureau of Investigations for the past seventeen years. He had two more years until retirement. Houser reminded you of an older version of the white detective Crockett on *Miami Vice.* The cool swagger, loose linen trousers, flowery Florida short-sleeved button-up with a few of the top buttons left open. Everyone was beginning to think that in his mind maybe he thought he *was* the actor. However, at this point in his career he was very ready to retire. His impetigo was spreading and pus was oozing out of the skin infection on his legs. But he told himself it would all be over soon. *Retirement, here I come!*

The bright side of his gloomy lining was that he lucked up and got an interview with Nina Coles, aka Alexis Greenspan, aka Kelly Kennedy. She was one of the top salespeople at WMM advertising, aka We Make Millionaires. All of law enforcement knew that this was one of the biggest and hardest-to-penetrate fraudulent telemarketing firms in the state of Georgia. The firm knew all too well how to operate in that gray area.

Houser had screamed at his team, "Screw the FBI! We can do just as good a job as they can." He pulled one of the oldest tricks in the book. He sent Nina Coles what appeared to be an official certified-looking letter explaining that she had inherited some money, to the lovely tune of $250,000. The letter stated that she would have to come and get processed to see if she was eligible to claim it. That is how he got her to come down.

Hell, in her mind she was 99 percent sure that it was a fake document. But she wanted an excuse to go in late to work. Plus, what if it wasn't a fake? When she pulled up to the bureau's fictitious office they had set up down the street, Houser flashed his badge, introduced himself and told her to follow him. She did. To the bureau's main office.

"Why are we at the GBI?" Nina's curiosity was piqued.

"We have to make sure that you are claiming what's rightfully yours," Houser simply stated.

As they walked past the front desk and down the long, bright, white corridor, Nina got suspicious. "Are you sure I'm here to claim some kind of inheritance?"

Houser smiled. "Depends on how you look at it."

"How I look at it? What does that mean? Don't have me down here on no bullshit! I got better things to do with my time," she spat.

Houser pulled out his keys and unlocked his office door. He moved to the side and motioned for Nina to step inside. "Please have a seat, Ms. Coles. Would you like a cup of coffee? Tea? Bottled water?"

"No. I just want you to tell me what this is really all

about." Nina was growing agitated. There was obviously no inheritance.

Houser sat his six-foot-one, two-hundred-pound frame behind his desk. He lifted his spectacles off his nose and rubbed its bridge. He then leaned back into the chair, resting his hands behind his head. Nina cringed at the patches of impetigo on his chin and elbows. He obviously picked up on her discomfort because he hastily sat up, resting his arms on the chair's armrests. He hit the intercom button on his phone. "Doris, tell Parker and Radcliff to bring the WMM file."

"WMM? Is this what this is about? You fucker! You tricked me to come to your office under false pretenses! I should sue your ass!" Nina stood up and grabbed her purse. "My name is Nina Coles not WMM." She turned to leave the office.

That's when Houser hit the play button on his recorder. Booming through its speakers was the conversation between her and Bob Tokowsky. Nina abruptly turned around at the sound of her sales voice and stood frozen in place.

Agents Parker and Radcliff entered the office. They both slid several folders in front of Houser and took their seats. Agent Parker looked as if he had a blond toupee sitting on top of his head. His wrinkled plaid suit drooped over his scrawny frame. He reminded Nina of an anorexic Homer Simpson. Radcliff was grossly overweight and sloppy looking. His oily black hair was slicked back into a ponytail. He looked like a goldfish.

After they listened to Nina yell, "Bob! Bob!" Houser turned off the tape.

The room grew silent. Except for Radcliff's wheezing.

"Please, have a seat, Ms. Coles."

Nina clutched tighter onto her Gucci bag under her arm.

"Fuck you! I am going to sue your ass for purgery and for wasting my time. Kiss my ass!" And she stormed out of the office.

Houser jumped from his chair, stood in the hallway in front of his office and said, "Murder, Ms. Coles. If you don't get your ass back in here, you're going down for murder."

Nina spun around and practically ran to get in Houser's face. "Murder? You wannabe FBI agent! I ain't got nothing to do with no murder. You people have really lost your minds! Find someone else to fuck with," she said through clenched teeth.

"Ms. Coles, your client Bob Tokowsky died. Dropped dead of a heart attack while you were trying to scam him with your 'millions' in gold coins." Houser motioned with two fingers from each hand to emphasize quote-unquote "millions." "That's right, we know all about the scamming and scheming of WMM. We know your boss, Rinaldo Haywood, aka Brian Stout, aka Tommy Green, aka John Bennett. We know about his office in the Florida Keys run by his cohorts Brandon Ingram and Charlie Adams.

We know your phone name Alexis Greenspan. Very catchy. We—"

"Hold up, you asshole. I don't give a fuck what you know. I'm a sales associate. A damned good one at that. I sell to business owners. If the client decides to patronize our firm and at the same time gamble at a chance of getting a bunch of gold coins, so the fuck what? That's not illegal! This is America, you muthafucka!" Nina ranted as she turned to walk out.

"Nina, Alexis or Kelly, whatever character you're in right now"—Radcliff chuckled as Houser began his negotiations—"this is your only chance to help yourself. You know what's going on over there is against the law. All I have to do is say the word and the feds will be all over that place. Not only will you go down for money laundering, conspiracy and wire fraud, you also have a murder hanging over your head."

Parker finally decided to put his two cents in. "Look, Ms. Coles. He's right, the company is going down whether you help yourself or not. If I was—"

"Look." Nina sighed as she stepped back into the office and shut the door to emphasize her point. "If y'all really had something, then you wouldn't need me." She snatched open the door and then slammed it shut behind her. "Fucking pigs!" she yelled out. Then mumbled, "Ain't nothing snitch about Nina muthafuckin' Coles."

CHAPTER THREE

HOW IT ALL GOT STARTED

After leaving the GBI headquarters, Nina drove straight home and was now parked in front of her condo in the Cherry Ridge subdivision in Decatur, Georgia. Sitting in her brand-new Mercedes E430, she sucked hard on a swisher sweet filled with purple haze and allowed her thoughts to drift. Going back to work was no longer on her agenda for the day. Nina glanced at the facade of her condo. The four-bedroom, three-bathroom condo was her dream home, but in reality, she hated it. It was lonely. There was no laughter to come home to, no kids running around, no live parties or friends to share it with. It was a place to live, but deep inside Nina didn't feel that this house was really a home. WMM and her co-workers had sadly become her whole life.

"Shit!" Nina slapped her steering wheel after putting out the blunt in the ashtray. *I didn't come all the way to Atlanta to catch a murder case. I was lucky enough to commit a murder and get away with it, then barely escape New Jersey with my life intact.*

After everything that had happened back in Trenton, New Jersey, relocating to Atlanta had been the best answer to her problems. Then shortly after that, she learned that her youngest daughter's father, Supreme, who was incarcerated, had successfully orchestrated the kidnapping of their child.

"That bitch beefing with the Blood niggas, done got one of her brothers killed, one paralyzed and her best friend got smoked, too. Now she's on the run and hiding out in Atlanta somewhere. She's an unfit mother and I don't want my seed around all that negative shit."

Nina could hear Supreme's words coming from his mouth as her mother relayed them to her. To compound her grief, she hadn't been able to attend the funerals for her brother or her best friend. The only solace she had been able to find was in the small gesture of secretly paying for both funerals. With one child gone, that left her with two children to worry about. They wanted their mommy and couldn't seem to understand at first why they couldn't be with her. Their tears had hit her hard and permeated her heart to its core. Even as she struggled to withstand her mother's scathing tirades. Her middle-aged mother, who wasn't supposed to be raising two small children, was the same mother who had kicked her out into the streets when Nina became pregnant while still in high school.

All of that had been over a year and a half ago, and since then she had not stepped one foot on New Jersey soil and had no plans to do so anytime soon. Even though she missed her kids something awful and they begged her to come and get them, she felt as if she wasn't ready and that she let them down. She felt like she had to learn to be a mother all over again. The private investigator she hired to find her daughter still had no leads. The only peace she had was in knowing that her missing daughter's father wouldn't let a hair on her head be harmed, but still he wouldn't let her know where she was. WMM had certainly turned her into someone that she didn't even know. Yes, she had come a long way. She came from being a Section 8 mother to masterminding prosperous check-cashing schemes to now having a corner office and making over $100,000 a year. She thought that her Jersey hustling and scamming days were something to brag about. Shit, those hustles were a joke compared to that of WMM's. They took shit to a whole 'nother level. Undoubtedly she was proud of her accomplishments...up until recently. Now there was the possibility of being under investigation by the GBI and brought up on murder? Nina had to laugh at that one, in order to keep from crying.

Now, instead of leaving her children behind in Jersey, she wished she had left something else. The toxic relationship that she was back involved in. The one with Akil, aka Cream, her ex. Cream was the person responsible for her plush job at WMM.

"Once you take out the trash, you never go outside and bring it back in."

Nina leaned her seat back and let the purple haze's seductive embrace will her into a peaceful place as she thought about what her mother had always told her about men and trash. But contrary to what her mother had told her, bringing the trash back into the house was exactly what Nina had done. After robbing him for those ten keys in Jersey, she had run into him in Georgia, of all places, and allowed herself to be persuaded into picking up right where they left off. It was too late to curse the afternoon that she ran into him, but it was definitely a day that she wished had never happened. Closing her eyes, Nina allowed that day to replay in her head as if it were being projected in HD…

"Can I help the next person in line?" the cashier asked.

"Yeah, gimme two grande hazelnut lattes. Put a shot of vanilla in one of them. But make both light and sweet. Throw in an orange juice as well."

The hairs on Nina's neck stood up. That voice. Oh, hell no. It couldn't be! *She turned around and looked at the dude next to her. He had his cell phone glued to his ear while going through his wallet. She turned away and started easing off before he could recoginze her.* Damn. *He still looked good. Light, curly fine hair, medium build like the singer Christopher Williams. He had put on a few pounds but he still looked the same.* The coke. *That was his coke in the trunk of her Jetta. The last time she actually saw Cream was the night she busted him driving some hood rat around in her car. That was the same night she vowed to leave him alone.* Forever. *That night ended with the police taking him away in handcuffs.*

"Nina?" Cream's *voice boomed, causing her body to tremble.*

Shit. *She realized she didn't walk away quick enough.*

"Nina. What the fuck? Look at you. It's really you. This is un-fuckin'-believable. Yo, Mo, this my lucky muthafuckin' day. You not gonna believe who I'm standing here looking at. Nina, man. Let me hit you right back. Make sure them niggas is layin' down those tracks. Time is money, nigga."

"Cream," Nina said dryly.

"Cream? That's all you can manage to say to the nigga who used to fuck yo brains out? Have you creamin' all in yo' jeans?"

Nina sucked her teeth. *"Don't flatter yourself, Cream."*

"Give me some love, girl. You still fine as shit." He grabbed her, feeling her ass, and pulled her close. Then he kissed her on the cheek. *"So this is where you ran off to?"*

"Tell everybody my business, why don't you?" She made an attempt to break away from him.

"Girl, these people don't know you like I know you." The tone of his voice went from warm to ice. He grabbed her by the back of her neck, snatched her out of the line and took her outside.

"Nigga, what the fuck is the matter with you?" She tried to break away from his grip.

"Bitch, don't get cute. I'll snap yo fuckin' neck."

"What do you want, Cream?"

"Nina, where you rest at?" He squeezed her neck harder and it was making her dizzy. "Answer me, girl!" He slammed her against a truck. She was seeing different colors.

"I'm in Decatur," she said, damn near out of breath, almost pissing on herself.

"Decatur, huh? You better not be lying. Let me see your license." He snatched her bag that was already hanging off of her shoulder and dumped its contents out onto the hood of the truck. She scrambled trying to gather everything together but he snatched up her wallet.

"Give me my shit, Cream."

He pushed her hard enough to cause her to go tumbling backwards. She almost fell. She charged at him, lunging for her wallet. He quickly turned his back to her and was able to take out her license and social security card.

"Give me my shit, Cream." She was grabbing for her ID. "What the fuck is the matter with you?" She punched him in the back.

"Bitch, yo' dumb ass stole ten kilos that wasn't even mines. I took the rap for that shit and had to pay them muthafuckas off and leave from up East. That's what the fuck is the matter with me. Girl, you owe me. I know your slick ass figured that you would just take the coke and dance happily off into the sunset."

Damn. Those keys. She swallowed hard. Those ten kilos had come back to haunt her.

"Cat got your tongue?"

"Your keys? Muthafucka, you forgot how y'all got

away and that bastard held me hostage for almost two weeks? That shit is just as much mines as it is yours," she snapped.

"I been paid you for that, Nina."

"The fuck you did! You crazy! You could never repay me for that shit."

"Get your bag, let's go back inside. We need to talk for a few minutes."

Nina was trying to buy time by gathering up the stuff that had been inside her purse. She was considering jumping into her car and pulling off but since he had her license that wouldn't do any good. She had to get her license back. Cream was standing over her watching her every move. "You should be putting my shit back into my purse. You dumped it out," Nina snapped.

"C'mon. Let's go. I'm right behind you." He grabbed on to her elbow.

Nina sighed but led the way back into Starbucks. She went to the counter and paid for their drinks.

"How's the children?" he had the nerve to ask her as if he didn't just finish tossing her around.

"They're fine." Nina grabbed her Frappuccino off the counter.

"Who you down here with?"

"What do you mean who I'm down here with? I'm down here by myself. You should already know that since you seem to know about every other goddamn thing," she snapped as she headed for the exit.

He grabbed her hand. "Naw. I ain't finished with you yet. Let's grab a seat. We gotta talk. We gotta play catch-up."

"I gotta go, Cream. You're making me late for work. What do you want?"

"You work?" He asked skeptically. "Where you work?" He wouldn't let her hand go.

Nina caught the sarcasm in his voice. "In Chamblee. A company called APS."

"What do you do?"

"It's a telemarketing job. I sell magazines," she stated dryly.

"Magazines?" Cream started laughing. "The check queen selling magazines! Well I'll be damned. What has the world come to?"

"Nigga, fuck you!" Nina snatched her hand away.

"Naw, wait. Magazines? I can't have my girl going out like that."

"I'm not your girl, Cream."

"Sheeit. You'll always be my girl. And like I said, you owe me but I'ma help you out. I can get you a much better job than selling some damn magazines. Plus, you'll be doing me a favor."

"Cream, excuse me. But I make nice money at this job. It pays my rent, car expenses, food and I have a savings account. And most importantly I'm legal. I actually like sales and I'm good at it."

"Sales, that's what's up. Today is really my lucky day. So how much you make?" Cream challenged.

"That's none of your business, Cream."

"What? You make four hundred a week? Five hundred?"

"I told you it's none of your business." Nina was still easing her way towards the exit. But this time he grabbed her by both of her shoulders, led her to a table and sat her down. He sat down in the chair across from her.

"I can hook you up with a job paying triple that. How does six hundred times three a week sound?"

"Cream, I don't have no time for your get-rich-quick schemes and I'm definitely not trying to go to prison."

"Prison?" A sly and mischievous grin spread across Cream's face.

"It's funny that you mentioned that, Nina. Remember outside when I told you that you owe me? Well, you happen to owe me for a lot more than those keys you stole."

"What the fuck are you talkin' about, Cream?" Nina asked indignantly.

"Remember that movie called I Know What You Did Last Summer? The one that had Brandy—"

"Cut the shit, Cream, and spit it out. What else do I owe you for?"

"My silence, then and now."

She didn't know why, but all of a sudden, there was a creepy, eerie feeling in the base of her stomach. The self-assured look on Cream's face gave her the chills. "Your silence?"

"That's right, baby. Let's just say I know what you did a year and a half ago."

"Cream, if you don't tell me what the fuck you're talkin' about, I'm getting up and I'm gonna leave. You can keep my license ..."

"You ain't going nowhere, Nina. Not till I say so. After I discovered that my spot had been tampered with, I know you were the culprit. But I couldn't prove it. So I copped me a cream-colored Infiniti M35...one that you had never seen before, and followed you around for a while. I know all about the robbery that went bad back home, Nina. I know that your punk-ass brother D-Rock was involved and eventually killed behind it. I know that the Bloods back at home want to kill your ass.

"I also know that you gave Peedie your car while you rode around with Michelle. I know that the Bloods killed Michelle and shot Peedie up. And here's the best part of all, I know that you went back to a house out in Ewing, but you went through the alley to get there. I know that Peedie's girl Darlene lived on that block, and for some reason after Peedie was shot, Darlene ended up dead the next morning. I was parked on the block when you came out of the alley that night, Nina. I know that you killed Darlene. That's why I say it's funny that you say you don't wanna go to prison. I never told a soul about that night, Nina, and I also let you go. At that point, I didn't care if you had the keys or not, you were knee-deep in a pile of shit that stunk to the heavens. You didn't duck me, baby. I could've killed you that night, but like I said, I let you go ... and I kept my mouth shut then, and I'ma still keep my mouth shut now.

I can call up top and talk to a few niggas and them Blood cats would be on your ass down here in a New York minute. And you know what I'm sayin' is true. So you help me and I'll help you. And I'll continue to keep quiet. How does that sound?"

When Nina had failed to respond, Cream went on.

"You said you can sell, right? I told you I know people, and the job I need you to take is in sales. You'll be selling high-priced promo shit to businesses. Fuck, a five-dollar magazine! What's your cut? Fifty cents? Who you think you foolin'? You know that ain't even your steelo. Hustling is in your blood, Nina."

"Cream, you know people? What kind of people?"

"The kind of people that will kill you and your family for stealing their dope." He glared at her.

Damn. *She was stupid to think that she would never cross paths with Cream again. Not in this lifetime.*

But now here he was. Cream had Nina's attention, but in her stubborness and pride she didn't want him to know it. Plus, she knew it would be major strings attatched. But...six hundred times three a week? That's eighteen hundred dollars. Shit, that was hustle money for her. He damn sure knew what to use to get her open.

"Nina, you still the same girl. You better grow up and let bygones be bygones and get this money. You know you want to," he said, as if he were reading her mind.

"Give me the info, Cream."

He knew he had her.

"Not so fast. We gotta do this my way. Give me your phone." He held out his hand for her phone.

"Just give me the info, Cream." Nina was getting impatient.

So was Cream. He snatched her phone out of her hand. "Here. I'm putting my number into your phone. When I call you, you better answer. I'll meet you back here on your lunch break."

"I get off at seven, Cream. Let's just meet then. I'm not going to have time to come here, talk to you and be back in an hour."

He thought briefly about it and then said, "Aiight then, bet."

Nina did not like the excitement in his voice and attitude. Something was definitely up but for now she could play his game. "Can I have my license back now?"

"When we meet back here at seven, we'll talk about that."

She stood up, looked down at him and started to go off but decided it could wait. "Bitch ass nigga," she mumbled under her breath as she stormed away from him.

As soon as she disappeared, he dialed his girlfriend Diamond. "Yo, baby, you don't have to worry about taking that job. I got somebody to fill that spot."

"I wasn't worried. Who did you get?"

"What the fuck you mean you wasn't worried? I should make your ass take it just on g.p."

"Cream, don't start. I'm going on seven months and you

talking about taking some damn job," Diamond said in disbelief.

"This shit is important. I see you ain't the ride-or-die chick you professed to be. I needed you to do one simple fuckin' thing for us and you couldn't even do that."

"I'm going on seven months, Cream!" Diamond yelled in an attempt to force him to understand.

"You wasn't going on seven months when I first asked you this shit."

"Cream, you got yourself into this mess. Why do I have to be responsible for bailing you out?"

"Bitch, you know what? Nah, fuck it." He hung up on her.

He dialed his partner in crime, Mo. "Yo, Mo, you ain't going to believe this. I just ran into Nina. I'm good now!" Mo knew Nina from Jersey. He knew she was ride or die and could understand Cream's excitement.

Back at APS, Nina could hardly focus. Triple than what I'm making now? I could send for my kids and move to a bigger apartment. Better yet, a house! And running into Cream? He was one of them thug niggas that was a cheat, loser and asshole all wrapped into one. But he could fuck you into a coma. And that had always been Nina's weakness. A long, hard and some superior dick. Running into him was already taking her off her square. She watched the clock on the wall hoping for more time. Something she never did. She was always on point on the job.

"Nina, are you all right?" Maggie, the floor supervisor

stopped by her desk and asked her. Maggie glanced up at the clock. "It's five thirty. You usually are more focused and have your quota by this time. Is everything cool?"

"Maggie, I just ran into my ex and I'm spooked. This nigga is supposed to be in Jersey somewhere. How did he end up in the same place with me?" Nina spoke in hushed tones.

"Didn't I tell you Georgia was small as hell? You believe me now, don't you? And guess what? This seems to be the place where everyone migrates. It's crazy," Maggie told her as she squeezed Nina's shoulder. She then went to the front of the room, stopped and turned around. She pulled out a twenty-dollar bill and pinned it to the corkboard. "This is for the next person to make a sale. C'mon, people, time to hustle! Shift's almost over!" She clapped her hands together for emphasis.

"You might as well bring that twenty right over here, Maggie," Nina announced.

"Uh-oh. Do I hear a challenge?" She turned to Nina's competition. "Sammie, you don't have anything to say about that?" Maggie wanted to get the salespeople on the floor hyped up.

"I'm already at the top of the board. That twenty is actually mines," Sammie teased.

"You won't be there for long. You know that's my spot and I only allowed you to be there because I felt sorry for you," Nina teased right back.

That comment got oohs, aahs and snickers from the entire room.

"Okay, simmer down, people. And work those phones,"
Maggie interrupted. "But who thinks Nina can take her
spot back, raise their hand." Everybody raised their hands,
including Sammie's girlfriend. When he smacked her
hand down everyone burst into laughter.

"See there, Sammie. I rest my case." Nina stood up and
curtsied.

By the end of the shift, Nina and Sammie were tied.

Nina sat in the back of the Starbucks drumming her fin-
gertips on the table. Cream was almost a half hour late,
but she sat glued to that seat for several reasons. For one,
she didn't know what he was up to and her curiosity was
piqued. She didn't know if he'd make good on his threat
to sell her out to the Bloods back in Jersey. Nina knew
enough about the Blood Organization to know that they
had become the largest street gang in America and sim-
ply didn't give a fuck about anything or anybody. Just the
thought of niggas dressed in all red gunning at her on the
streets of Atlanta terrified her to no end. But most of all,
she didn't doubt for one second that Cream was vindic-
tive enough to violate the "no snitching street code" and
rat her out to the cops about the murder she committed
back in Jersey. Secondly, she needed her license and social
security card back. Last but not least the possibility of her
making hustle money, legally? That had piqued her inter-
est the most. After all she was discreetly on the lookout for a
come-up. And of course Cream knew what buttons to push.

Hell, after two years together, she knew what buttons to push of his as well. With a good fuck and a blow job she used to be able to get whatever she wanted from him. Even down to the location and keys to his stash spot. She never stole from him, all she ever did was upgrade his ass. Hell, she put him on the map.

They both were muling for this dread named Wicked who was head over heels for Nina. He kept saying she was the real Janet Jackson and he was infatuated with her. Every time he saw her he would stare at her like she was a piece of prime rib. He always made her very uncomfortable. He would tell Cream, "You betta not slip, boy, not even a likkal bit me a be right here to snatch up that punnany."

Nina held Wicked's attention while Cream and his boy Mo stole a shit load of his weed. In their haste they had taken the wrong package. They had left the dope behind. However, the weed was still the beginning of Cream's come-up and he and Nina were Bonnie and Clyde from that point forward.

Months later, Cream wanted to strike again but this time for the dope. Nina was down but once again things didn't go as planned. Cream and his boys got away, leaving her caught red-handed. Wicked held her captive for almost two weeks, torturing her sexually. The only reason he didn't kill her was because he really had a thing for her. But that didn't stop him from making her fuck and suck him to pay off the debt. If Nina didn't know why they

called him Wicked, by the end of her captivity she found
out. The entire time he held her captive, she wore a metal
dog chain around her neck and when he would fuck her,
just as she started cumming he would tighten the chain,
cutting off her oxygen supply to heighten her orgasm. During the day she crawled around the house on all fours and
he kept his dick in her mouth, even when he was conducting business. If she acted like she was tired, he would say,
"Wa ya not se cum and mash up me rod." And then he
would yank at her leash.

One night Nina didn't know whether to laugh or scream
when he came into the bedroom wearing latex and
chains. He would tie her up and continuously pour hot
wax all over her nipples and clit. And each time before a
sexcapade, he would chant the words of Shabba Ranks,
"Me a bad, bad and a wicked in the bed, wicked bad and
bad in the bed now all the girls tell all the guys that I'ma
wicked."

For hours he would beat her with whips that had fine
pins on them. Nina's ass was raw, she couldn't bear to
sit on it. He would make her straddle him sore and then
demand, "Let push back your blood clot ting."

If she wouldn't ride him hard, he would slide out of her
pussy and force himself into her ass until she could no longer scream. When she was done he would make her suck
him off until her tongue was numb. If she thought about
stopping, he would say, "Don't make me haf to jook pon
ya face." She didn't know what that meant but the way he

would growl it she didn't want to find out. So she would suck him off as if her life depended on it.

Another night he told her, "Let me get pon yor bumpa." He swallowed some stay-hard and fucked her doggy-style, until she bled. He did that for about two hours real rough while her hands and legs were tied down and mouth gagged. The last night he used an anal probe with beads on it and jacked off while he watched Nina's pain and ejaculated all over her face and hair. When she got back home it took weeks to heal and rid her skin of his body odor. And as for her pain, to this day it never went away because every time she thinks of him, she gets sick to her stomach. The whole time she was recovering, she couldn't find Cream. It was always in the corner of her mind, Did he make a deal with the devil? When she got out and about she went looking for him and he was riding some ho around in her car. That was the first time she caught him doing that. The second time she caught him was when she cut him off. So as far as she was concerned the dope was more hers than it was his.

She took a sip of her latte and cringed. Why did I waste my money on this high-priced caffeine? It never tastes good and I'm nauseous after a couple of swallows. *Nina got up, dropped the latte into the trash and ordered her favorite.*

"Yo, Nina, get me an orange juice and two slices of cake," Cream yelled out as if he just entered into the local bar.

"I'll order it, but this time you pay for your own shit," Nina told him.

"Girl, please. I'm about to put you up on something big and you trippin' over five dollars? I'm insulted."

"Seven dollars, nigga. Now pay for your shit and come and sit down. Let's get this over with."

"Well damn. What's with the attitude? If you weren't finer than the day I met you, and hadn't stolen my coke, I'd tell you to kick rocks," he teased.

Nina rolled her eyes at him and went to her table. Cream told the cashier to add another slice of cake to his order, paid for everything, grabbed a straw and some napkins before joining Nina. As soon as he sat down, he immediately began to wolf down his cake. She could smell the weed on him, and the way he housed the slices of cake, there was no doubt that he had the munchies. She leaned back into her chair, took a sip of her Frappucino and studied Cream. I actually used to be head over heels over this cheatin', slimy-ass nigga? How did I end up, way in Atlanta, Georgia, sitting across from him? Why am I even entertaining the thought of considering any proposition he comes up with?

"Okay, listen." Cream interrupted her disgusting thoughts of him. *"Since you comfortable with selling shit, then this should be a piece of cake. No pun intended,"* he said, wiping the crumbs off his mouth. *"And Nina, do this shit, take it serious and you can get paid. I mean major paid."* He flailed his arms around for emphasis.

"What am I selling?"

"Yo, Montblanc pens, golden brass calculators, golden brass key chains, all engraved with the business owner's slogan or business name."

"Pens?" Nina interrupted in disbelief.

"Yo, you know how much a Montblanc pen cost? Them shits cost damn near two or three hundred dollars." Cream didn't give her time to answer his question. "Now hear me out. They buy the product and then that automatically enrolls them into some kind of million-dollar promotion for gold coins. Them greedy crackers be spendin' guap. Fifteen, twenty-five, fifty g's in a clip!" Cake crumbs were Flying off of Cream's lips.

"So what do you get out of this deal?"

"What?"

"I know you, Cream. What do you get out of hooking me up? You got me fucked up if you think yo gonna be pimpin' me."

That sneaky-ass familiar smirk appeared on his lips. "I told you. You owe me. You put me in a fucked-up situation when you took my coke. I almost got killed. That's how I ended up down here. After I paid the shit back, it was either my life or get the fuck outta Jersey. I left my clientele and everything. You cost me big-time, Nina. You set me back big-time. Them ten keys was just the beginning of the snowball effect. They wanted me to tell them where you was, but I didn't know. So they made me eat the loss, with hella interest."

"*Are you finished, nigga?*" Nina snapped. "*Do you have any idea what I went through for damn near two weeks?*" Nina screamed out, causing everyone to look over in their direction. "*I think that makes us even. As far as I'm concerned your ass owes me! So now what?*" Nina folded her arms across her chest, daring him to say the wrong thing, but knowing Cream the way she did, he would.

"*Don't even try that bullshit. You stayed with that nigga because ya wanted to.*"

"*You slimy muthafucka!*" She hauled off and slapped the shit out of him. Catching him completely by surprise.

"*Bitch, you done lost your mind.*" He liked the fact that he was now under her skin. He had her right where he wanted her. He touched the cheek that she smacked and burst into laughter.

"*Cream, y'all probably flipped the shit you talking about ten fuckin' times, minimum, so get your math together. You can add. So we are back to square one, where I don't owe you shit, you owe me.*"

"*I ain't sweatin' that. And yeah, you right,*" he confessed. "*I just need you to get this job and we will be even. You will earn my silence. Plus, you'll be livin' large in less than a month. You ain't seen no hustle until you checked out the Golden Hustle. And Nina, you hit me again and I'ma fuck you up. But get this job and I'll let you know after you get in there and get situated what's next.*"

"*Cream, what does that supposed to mean?*"

Cream grinned. "*Nina, you ain't even got the job yet.*

How about they don't like you? Or what if you can't sell the shit? Don't you want to triple or quadruple what you're making?"

"Yeah, but at what cost?"

"At what cost? You know you don't give a fuck. That's why you here. You about that paper. But all you got to do is get in there and do good and I'll inform you of the next step."

"So that's it?" Nina asked.

"That's it for now. Like I said, you got to get in there."

"Get in there and do what, Cream?"

"Get in there and work, stack you up some paper." He slid her license and social security card over to her. "I made a copy, so if you try any funny shit I know where to find you."

"And what if I don't get the job?"

"You don't want to know the answer to that. So I suggest you get the job." He started laughing. "I'm messin' with you, girl. You'll get the job." He saw from the expression on her face that she was getting ready to go off. Cream stood up and looked at his watch. "I'm glad I ran into you. I swear, I would have never thought this would of happened. I got to go, but I'll be in touch."

They ended up in the parking lot.

"So what happened with dude from New York that you left me for? Where he at?"

"Left you for? Me and you had been over way before I met him. Give me the info so I can set up an interview."

"What's his name? Tyrese right? But the streets call him Reese."

Nina's jaw dropped. How in the hell did Cream know so much of her business? Laughing, Cream said, "Close your mouth before a bug fly in it. You thought I didn't know about your little boyfriend, huh? I told you that I followed you all over the city after my keys came up missing. I saw you all up in his arms after you left the scene of your brother's shooting. That was the same night you went back out to Ewing and mercked that bitch. I never knew you to carry a gun, Nina. He the one that gave you the gun, right? And you gave him my ten keys, didn't you?"

"Just give me the name and number of the person I'm supposed to be seeing."

"Oh, it's like that?"

"Cream, ask me about my business again and I'ma leave your ass standing here in this parking lot all by yourself," Nina snapped.

Before she left Jersey, she and Reese were only talking. They hadn't even fucked until right before she left for good. So how did asshole here know all of her business, including his name? Why did he have to bring up that nigga's name? *Every time she thought about him her spirits sank into the bottom of nothingness.* Why can't I have someone to love? Why do I attract either the losers or somebody else's man? *Nina asked herself. For the next couple of months after Reese left her high and dry she was bummed out about Reese's* "I got a family" revelation. *That shit had her down in the* dumps and she felt like she would never, ever shake his ass. Then to make matters worse she had to run into this nigga. Could shit get any worse? *She looked at him only to get reminded of how much he disgusted her.*

"Aiight, chill out." *Cream pulled out one of his business cards and wrote a name and number on the back.*

Nina snatched it out of his hands and headed for her car. Cream followed behind her.

"Yo, I'ma do right by you this time. Believe what I'm telling you. And you need to leave those married niggas alone. Dude got a wife and kids." *Cream thought he was snitching Reese out.*

"I already know that. Thank you very much. Goodbye, Cream." *Nina jumped into her Volvo and pulled off not believing that Cream had resurfaced back into her life.*

After about two weeks Nina finally got an interview with WMM. She arrived at her interview a half hour early. She had on a simple Jones New York pantsuit and a pair of Nine West flats. She was buzzed in by the receptionist, who introduced herself as Deanna, and led to a small waiting room. Deanna handed her a clipboard with an application and several employment forms. She instructed Nina to fill them out and then told her someone would be with her shortly.

As soon as Nina finished, out came a thin, short white guy with bags under his eyes and thick brown hair. She dug the Brioni suit he was wearing and he introduced himself as Simeon. He took her clipboard and she followed him to his office where he motioned for her to sit down and then tell him about herself, including where she currently worked and what she did.

At the end of the interview he held out his hand and told her he liked her attitude and it would be a pleasure to have her on board.

That was easy, *Nina said to herself. She was ready to get started. He gave her a tour of the beginning salesroom and it was triple the size of APS.*

Later that evening when she called Maggie and told her about her new job, Maggie got quiet. "Awwww, Maggie. You miss me already? Girl, I'll be making three to four hundred dollars a sale!"

"But what are you selling, Nina?" Maggie challenged. "Pussy?"

"Girl, please. We call qualifying business owners and sell them engraved products with their business names."

"What are the products?"

"Nice golden brass calculators, key chains and Montblanc pens. The smallest order is two grand. It beats a five-dollar magazine," Nina told her.

"Nina, I hear that they are crazy over there. The dude that runs the joint is crazy and plus they are under investigation. I suggest that you check them out thoroughly before you start counting the dollar signs."

"You heard that from who?"

"People talk, Nina. All of you guys bounce around from

one telemarketing room to the next. But listen, don't take my word for it. Ask Jake. He worked there before."

"Jake?" Maggie could hear the frown on Nina's face over the phone. She sounded as if she had just tasted a lemon. "That loser. I can outsell him. Plus, he don't even come to work every day. I can imagine why he no longer works there."

Maggie let out a chuckle. She knew Nina was telling the truth. "Girl, I'ma miss you. You about the only sane person in the whole damn office. So whenever you want to come back, you know I'll have you a desk."

"Awww, how sweet. Thanks, Maggie. I'ma miss you too. Plus, you know I'll keep in touch." Nina hung up.

Today she had vowed to start anew. Take control. She was determined to make her life work. New job and new attitude. Fuck Reese, it's his loss. She couldn't believe she was mourning over him for so damn long. She ain't never did no shit like that, especially not over some nigga.

She was in the kitchen broiling a porterhouse steak and making a couple of baked potatoes along with a salad. She had a Carvel ice cream cake in the freezer, a bottle of wine and was only missing some of that sticky icky. She was serious about starting anew. She had the music blasting and was dancing around the kitchen. Her spirits were finally starting to pick up and she had cleared her mind and was actually starting to feel back to her confident and gangsta self.

There was a knock and she figured it was the sister across the hall wanting to borrow something as she danced *and sang her way to the door. She peeked out the curtain. Speak of the devil. It was Cream. She wasn't unhappy to see him because she had been thinking about him and had already decided to use him, the way he was hoping to use her. And it didn't hurt that he was looking good, standing there in a State Property sweat suit with some red roses. She opened the door.*

"My. My. My. What a pleasant surprise. I'll let you in only if those roses are for me, you got some weed and you gonna give up some dick." She shifted her weight to one side, twisted her lips and then looked at him, daring him to say the wrong thing.

As she waited for an answer, he handed her the roses, felt in his inside pocket for the weed and then ran his other hand across his dick, giving her a naughty smile, and said, "Oh, I got you."

"Then come on in," Nina said as she danced her way back to the kitchen to check on her meal and to get a vase for her roses.

"Uuuummm. It smells good up in here. I'm a nigga with impeccable timing," Cream said real loud and in anticipation of getting him a plate.

"Yeah, I just threw a little something together. What brings you on this side of town and with some roses? It's not Valentine's Day, so what's up?"

"I come in love and peace." He threw his hands up as in surrender, then licked his lips as he admired her in her coochie-cutting shorts and sports bra.

"Oh, really? So why the roses?"

"The roses are just to say congratulations for your new job. What? It's been two weeks? Read the card."

"Okay and you came to see me about what? To start some shit?"

"Nina, for real, I'm just wishing you well, and I didn't mean to manhandle you when I first saw you and we a team now, so why should I start some shit? I'm just mad that I fucked up and let you get away." Without waiting for her to respond he moved close to her and put his hand between her thighs and began rubbing her pussy.

He lifted her up and sat her on the counter. She liked that about him. He was not one to wait when it came to fuck. Forget all of the games, foreplay and the rest of the shit.

"So we gonna fuck now or after we eat?" he asked as he was already trying to pull down her shorts that seemed to be painted on.

Nina pushed him back. *"My steak is in the broiler."* Cream was standing between her legs with his hard dick right on her pussy. She slid off the counter, but not before getting a little grind off. When she went over to the oven and bent over to open the broiler, Cream was right behind her grinding on her ass.

"Cut if off. I'm ready to fuck. Right now."

She did. When Nina stood up Cream took her by the waist and started to walk out of the kitchen. They made it as far as the couch before he had stripped off the little bit of clothes she had on and was hittin' it from the back. Every feeling that Nina ever had for Cream began to surface, causing her to enjoy him even more. Cream must have been feeling the same way because he was stroking Nina nice and slow, causing very sexy moans to escape her mouth.

"Ooooohhh . . . Cream."

"You forgive me, Nina?" he whispered as he continued to search for that special spot.

"Yeeeessss . . ." Nina managed to moan out. Shit, the way he was giving her that dick she would have sold the family jewels.

Right after that Cream went in deep and fast and she began to cum and yell out his name. He pulled out slow and turned her around, looked her in the eyes and whispered, "Let's go to the bedroom so I can handle this pussy like it needs to be handled." She looked down at his hard ten inches and led the way.

Nina went from beginner to intermediate sales rep in three and a half weeks. She had set a goal for herself to make two sales a day. Those sales would gross her five thousand a week. She hadn't reached that goal but was close to the halfway point and was sure as hell trying her best. She was ecstatic about her accomplishments and was shocked when she was called into Rinaldo, the big boss's, office along with Shawn, Milt and Pete.

Rinaldo reeked of cash. New money. Money that she

wanted. Nina checked out his calfskin shoes and tailor-made Brioni just like Simeon's and he had a big-ass diamond in his left ear. She didn't even want to think about what was on his fingers. She studied him. He stood about five-foot-nine, a muscular one-hundred-ninety-pound frame and had dirty-blond hair that he kept pulled back into a short ponytail. His beady blue eyes reminded you of a hawk. And he didn't miss anything. His tailor-made suit and shoes made him look like a model off GQ magazine. And for a white boy, which wasn't Nina's taste, he was very easy on the eyes. It didn't hurt that he had lips like a brother's.

He stood up and paced back and forth a few times before beginning his spiel. Nina had no clue as to why she was called into his office.

"All of you are here because you were handpicked. Several factors were taken into consideration. Such as your attendance, your work ethic, how hungry you are and no drug habits. Well, at least for the most part." His attention went to the brother sitting in the corner. "Pete here is my only Platinum Member and he needs some competition. Once you get comfortable in this business, my business, I have a problem with that. You have to stay hungry to keep me happy. Comfort is not good. My wife is pissed at me because my mattress is a wooden plank. Fuck being comfortable. Y'all get the picture?"

Everyone nodded except for Shawn, who chuckled.

"I'm offering you all the opportunity to be a part of my

Platinum Sales Team. I promise, you'll make a minimum of ten g's a week."

"Yeah, right," just about everybody mumbled.

Rinaldo started laughing. "I know that y'all don't believe me."

"I don't believe you." Nina spoke up first.

"I want to know how," Shawn barked.

"I'm listening," Milt added.

"You don't have to ask me. But ask Pete over there."

Pete only nodded.

"I designed the program, so I know it works. But the key is to do like I tell you. And don't get comfortable," Rinaldo went on to explain his Platinum program. And when he finished there was no doubt in anyone's mind that ten g's was just the starting point. "Now, if you are in, be in my office tomorrow morning at seven sharp."

Her cell phone vibrated in her lap, waking her outta her purple-hazed fog of what happened almost two years ago. The screen lit up and the words FUCK YOU BOSSMAN flashed across the screen, causing her to frown. She pressed the speakerphone button.

"What's up, Rinaldo?" she asked with absolutely no enthusiasm.

"What's up? What the fuck you mean what's up? Your clients are blowing up your phone, that's what's up. How come it's going on noon and you ain't at work? That's what's up. The fact that—"

"Rinaldo, please spare me the theatrics this morning," she cut him off. "I'm in front of my house on my way now." She regretted those words as soon as they escaped her mouth. "Give me twenty minutes."

"Home? Alexis, I mean Nina or Kelly, whoever the fuck you are, you need to get your ass here to this office!" he screamed before slamming down the phone.

Nina tossed the phone over to the passenger seat and sighed. "This muthafucka!" She cranked up the engine and headed for the offices of WMM.

CHAPTER FOUR

WE MAKE MILLIONAIRES

Nina pressed on the buzzer to the offices of WMM Advertising. From the outside, the office was set up like Fort Knox. At the parking lot entrance, you gained access by using a plastic card, and then you had to key in your password. Nina had one of the four elite parking spaces right in front of the building, and she would keep that spot as long as she was top sales associate. She turned the engine off and hurriedly jumped out of her Porsche SUV.

"What's up, Alexis?" A short and stocky sales associate greeted her by her phone name as he held the door open for her. Around the office, everyone was often called by their sales name, except Rinaldo, the boss.

"How are you?" she asked dryly.

"I'm good," he chirped as he headed for the parking lot.

Nina tried to recall the young guy's name but shrugged it off when she drew a blank. She pressed the buzzer to the main entrance again, which was the only way you would be able to get into the staff offices. She waved at the security camera above her, in hopes of getting the secretary's attention. After a few minutes, she leaned on the buzzer again, steam hissed out of her ears at the thought of her encounter with Houser and his hounds from the Georgia Bureau of Investigation. She focused her gaze out into the parking lot, which told her who all was at work. Rinaldo, "bossman" as she sometimes called him, had his $300,000 Bentley Arnage Drophead Coupe, which was always taking up two parking spaces. He was so scared somebody was going to scratch up his precious Bentley. Nina told him how ghetto he was being that if he could afford a $300,000 car then he surely could get a scratch repaired. *He is such an ass*, Nina said to herself. There was Shawn's $120,000 Mercedes S500, Milt's $65,000 custom-made Cadillac Escalade, Pete's $60,000 Porsche Cyanne, Angelia's SAAB, Vera's Mercedes 430, Tony's $70,000 Range Rover Sport and Rocky's Lexus, to name a few. The parking lot on any given day could pass for a fed's confiscation car auction or a luxury car show. Rinaldo had some kind of hookup with a car broker that kept him laced with anything his Platinum Team wanted.

"Yes, may I help you?" Deanna the receptionist chirped.

"It's me. Alexis."

Bzzzt. The steel door popped open and Nina went to see Deanna. "What's up, girl?" Deanna asked her. "You-know-who is on the warpath as usual, and you being three hours late only added fuel to his already raging fire."

"Fuck him! Because I'm on the warpath too," snapped Nina.

"And here are your messages. *Please call Garvin Meese*," she emphasized. "He has been calling every hour on the hour. The Lampkins called twice."

Nina snatched the messages from Deanna's hand. Then did a double take. Deanna was the only black girl she ever met from Wyoming. She was weird. Ditzy. She dressed like she was a homemaker who lived on a farm. On top of that she was also tall, almost six feet, and shaped like a box. And God, her hair! Nina was sick of the Afro. She wanted to snatch a whole fistful and drag her to the nearest beauty salon. Maybe then she would look more like Macy Gray instead of Don King in drag.

"Why are you looking at me like that?" Deanna snapped. "Just because guys around here tell you that you favor Janet Jackson, doesn't mean you gotta look at me all crazy!" Nina was glad that she said what she was truly thinking.

By no means was she trying to disguise the disgusted look she had on her face but now Nina was shocked. *No, this rural bitch did not just go ghetto on me.* She never heard Deanna talk like that before. Neck roll and all. "You can call yourself a psychic today, but bitch, don't hate because I'm fine. You need to let me give you some beauty lessons," Nina said as she headed down the hallway to Rinaldo's office, trying not to laugh.

The entire office was just redone with dark burgundy carpet and light gray walls. She could hear the intense chatter of the sales workers through the closed doors.

When she barged into Rinaldo's office, the other secretary, Vera, was between Rinaldo's legs. She got up off her knees and adjusted her miniskirt.

"Hey, Vera." Nina eyed her with disgust.

"Hey back, Alexis. I like that pantsuit. Donna Karan, right?" Vera smiled as she grabbed a stack of folders off of Rinaldo's desk, acting as if she was not just caught in an uncompromising position.

"Well, well, well. Look what the cat drug in. Close my door, Vera, on your way out."

She walked past Nina with her head held high.

Nina waited for Vera to close the door before she turned to her boss. "Rinaldo, I could have been your wife barging in here. I heard that you make chicks who want an advance suck your dick. I *wish* I was your wife so I could have kicked your ass. If I didn't see if for myself I wouldn't have believed it. You are so nasty. Getting head *at your place of business*, as you always say. What a fucking loser."

Rinaldo laughed. "Yeah, you said it right. You *wish* you was my wife."

"Man, go 'head with that. I don't do the white meat. So don't flatter yourself."

"And so what if I bust a few nuts at work. You should try it sometime. You need to mind your business and concern yourself with bringing my money up in here. Besides, she was sucking my dick for a reason. Want to know why?" he asked with a smug look on his face.

"Hell to the no. And you're right. It's none of my business."

"Too late, I'ma tell you anyway. She wants to have this weekend off."

"You are disgusting."

"Enough about me, I gotta hear what excuse my top salesperson is going to give me for why she lost two of her best clients and missed out on thousands of dollars." He waved two sales sheets in the air.

"What do you mean lost two clients?" She tried to grab the pages from his hands, but he kept fanning them in different directions. They went at it like a pair of kids with Nina being the victor as she grabbed hold of the sales sheets.

Rinaldo chuckled while leaning back in his chair. He picked up one of his favorite cigars for the week, a Davidoff. He ran it under his nose before lighting it.

Nina scanned both of the sales sheets that Jeff signed. All that did was add more fuel to her already raging fire.

"This is a joke right? I know you didn't give my clients to Jeff!" She was standing in front of his desk with a hand on her hip.

Rinaldo took a deep drag of his cigar with the designer's name, held it, and then blew smoke up towards Nina's face. "I sure did!" He was trying not to laugh.

"Rinaldo, you know damned well the Prestons and Don Friedman are two of my favorite clients. I've been selling to them for years now!" she screamed as she threw both sales sheets at him and began pacing the floor.

"You weren't here, Alexis. And they called for you. They were ready to be sold," Rinaldo stated with a smug nonchalance. "You know the rules. If the sales rep is not here and the client is ready to be sold it goes to the next man."

"That's bullshit, Rinaldo, and you know it! You could have told them I'd get back to them and I was out of the office. You are so full of shit!"

"Get back to them when? How could I tell them that when you didn't even call in? I didn't know if you quit or not." Rinaldo smirked.

"You are so evil," Nina growled as someone knocked on the door.

"Come in," Rinaldo yelled. It was Jeff.

"I'm talking to you, Rinaldo. Get out, Jeff," she gritted at him. "This is my time. Rinaldo, you are so fucking evil and rude."

"How fast can we ship to the Prestons and old man Friedman?" Jeff asked, ignoring and avoiding eye contact with Nina.

Nina stormed to the door, pushing Jeff out into the hallway and pulling the door shut behind her at the same time, holding on to the doorknob. "Jeff, how you gonna sell my clients? You know how grimy Rinaldo can be and we agreed that we wouldn't do that."

"Let go of my doorknob, Nina!" Rinaldo was yelling from the other side of the door, while trying to pull it open.

"Look, Nina, you know how Rinaldo is. If the shoe was on the other foot you wouldn't have turned down twenty thousand dollars' worth of commission," Jeff said, trying to justify his actions.

"You faggot!" Nina pounced onto Jeff and began slapping and punching him. She was whipping on him as if he was her bitch.

"Nina!" Rinaldo stepped out of his office. "What is the matter with you?" Rinaldo snatched her off of Jeff, and shoved her back into his office. Half of the workers in the company were now playing spectator or heading towards the direction of the commotion.

"Jeff, I'll get with you later. Everyone else, if you want to keep working here I suggest you get back on them fucking phones! Whoever doesn't make a sale today might as well clean out their desks and don't show up tomorrow," Rinaldo warned. A warning the entire office knew was serious as cancer. No one comes before Rinaldo's money. Not even his wife. He turned to go back in his office, slamming the door.

"Okay, little Muhammad Ali. Don't let that bullshit happen again."

"Fuck that shit! Whoever sells any of my clients I'ma whip their ass. And Jeff better make sure he spreads the word."

"Stop acting so ghetto. This is a place of business not a goddamn boxing ring. Just like you lost that twenty grand you could just as easily make it again."

"Can I? Are you sure about that?" She glanced down checking out her freshly manicured fingernails. "I was told that they are trying to close us down. Why didn't you tell your Platinum Team that we were under investigation? You always question our loyalty, where is yours?"

"Investigation? Who told you that?" Rinaldo feigned ignorant. His blue eyes stared at her, remaining focused on her like a hawk.

"Don't play dumb, Rinaldo. And on top of that you're lying. How can you keep lying like this? I got scammed into going to the GBI this morning. Your ass knew damn well Bob Tokowski died. And I asked you!" She was getting madder and madder. "Your response was, 'Nooooooooo he is no longer a client.' Of course he couldn't be a client. The muthafucka is dead. Then you said some bullshit about his son finding out he was sending us all of his inheritance money and that he had his father's number changed. All of it bullshit and lies, Rinaldo. Well guess what, *boss man*?" she emphasized. "I ain't going down for nobody's murder." Nina was steaming mad.

Rinaldo started clapping. "And the award for leading actress in a drama goes to..." He stood there shaking his head in disbelief. "I hope you are finished because I need to know how the fuck you wound up at the GBI."

"I told you, they are investigating us. They know your name, all of your phone names, my phone names. They know Brandon and Charlie," Nina stated in exasperation.

"So what? But what were *you* doing down there? How long and how often have you been talking to them?"

"Those slick bastards sent me a certified letter to come down and claim some inherited funds."

"And you fell for that? That is the oldest trick in the book. Why would you go to the GBI to claim some money, Nina? I thought you were smarter than that." He shook his head as if to say, I don't believe this.

"It didn't have GBI on it. It had some law firm listed, and when I got there, they were there flashing badges and asked me to follow them. So I was curious. That's why I went. I wanted to know what the fuck was going on," Nina spat, lying about the badges.

"I need you to get me a copy of the certified letter they sent you. I need to get that to Mack, our attorney. This is going to be embarrassing. I can't believe that you fell for that shit."

"This is fucked up, Rinaldo. The GBI is itching to come up in here. Have you heard anything I just said? We are under investigation."

"What else is new, Nina? Every telemarketing firm in Georgia and everywhere else in the country is being investigated. We're talking the fuckin' GBI not the FBI. Fuck them plastic-shoe, cheap-suit-wearing dicks. I'm not worried about them!"

"What about Bob's death? Why didn't you tell me? They said I could be charged with murder."

"Murder? Nina, don't be stupid. They are the GBI! There's no way they can charge you with Bob's murder. He died of natural causes and I didn't inform you of it because there was no need to. He's not your relative. You sold him over a month ago. If you were going to be charged with murder, don't you think the FBI would have arrested you and brought you in for questioning by now? Come on, Nina, use some common—no I'll do you one better. Use some goddamned street sense!"

"Whatever. But, still, why didn't you tell me?"

"Because you didn't need to know. We are about making money not mourning over the fuckin' dead."

"This is crazy, Rinaldo. I'm not going to prison for nobody."

"Look, Nina, nobody's going to prison. Let Mack and the other attorneys worry about the punk-ass GBI. You have a lifestyle to maintain. I have a lifestyle to maintain. And just how you are adamant about not going to prison, I'm even more adamant about allowing nothing or nobody to ruin my company or send me back to some fuckin' trailer park. Not even you. Now I suggest you get yourself together mentally. Stay away from any officials or wannabe FBI agents. You need this job and you need me. Don't cross that line again, Nina. Trust me. I ain't the one to be fucked with. Don't ever think about fucking with my paper. If this shit is too hot for you, go flip some burgers or some shit like that. Remember our slogan, We Make Millionaires. Now get on that phone and bring us in some money!"

"You punk-ass muthafucka," she spat, before slamming his door. She could hear his laughter as she walked down the hall. "I should take my ass home now. I need some dick."

CHAPTER FIVE

STAFF

"Peedie, what's up?" Nina asked her big brother. He gave her a call to check up on her. "How is everybody? You been to Mommy's? What are my babies up to?"

"I just came back. Jermichael was on his computer and Daysha went to church with the deacon. What's up with you, big-timer? Moved down to Atl, making all that cheddar." Ever since he was paralyzed he had been taking it easy. As she was talking to her brother, Cream was standing behind her, butterball naked, kissing on her neck. "So what's really good? How was your day at the j-o-b?"

"Same ole shit."

She definitely couldn't tell him about her morning at the GBI and then her bout with Rinaldo in his office earlier. When she left WMM she couldn't get out of the parking lot without lighting a blunt and calling Cream. She had a big-ass problem and he had all of the answers. Ten inches of dick. After that first time when he brought over the roses and they fucked, they never stopped. As soon as the money started coming in, then the Benz, the

Porsche, after that the condo, he sealed the deal on her pussy. They had a mutual understanding. She didn't sweat him about his baby mama and he didn't sweat her. Even though she wasn't seeing anybody. Hell, she didn't need to. Whenever she needed some dick, he was just a phone call away. Everybody was happy.

"Nina, what you doing, exercising? Yo ass breathing all hard," Peedie cracked.

"I'm cleaning up, boy."

"Yeah right. You better not be fuckin' with that rat bastard, Cream."

"Boy, is that all you called me for? To tell me who I better not be fuckin'?"

"You damn right."

"Well in that case, I gots to go." Nina hung up on him.

Cream turned her around and pointed to his dick. He had a clit tickler strapped around it. He backed Nina up against the wall and lifted her up. She put him inside her and wrapped her legs around his back.

"Who fucks you better?" he asked as he plunged into her pussy.

Nina moaned and grabbed both of his ass cheeks. "You do, baby." She closed her eyes and began riding the clit tickler. She liked being in control, that is, up to the first orgasm. After the first one she would lose control. Cream and the clit tickler would take over and have her climbing the walls having orgasm after orgasm until she sometimes fainted.

*   *   *

WMM offices were divided into two sections. The back
of the building held the bathrooms, break rooms and two
huge rooms for the beginning and intermediate salespeople. It also held the office of Vera, the other secretary,
and the floor manager, Simeon. His job was to oversee
the thirtysomething sales team. Simeon's voice was louder
than he was tall. Rinaldo's older fraternal twin by four
minutes was a crack fiend, who you never saw wearing
anything other than a tailor-made suit and a tie. He had
impeccable work habits except when his paycheck hit the
five-thousand mark. Like clockwork he would go off on
a crack binge and disappear for four or five days. And
like clockwork Rinaldo would be screaming mad, pulling
his hair out because even though he tried not to show it
he worried about his twin. But, even worse, he left all of
the work to Rinaldo, and the task he hated the most was
babysitting the little salespeople.

The front of the building had the receptionist, Deanna,
Rinaldo's office and the offices of the Platinum salespeo-
ple, which were Nina, Jeff, Greg, Shawn, Milt and Pete.
The copier and fax machines were in a room next to
Deanna's office. On the left wall hung a huge whiteboard,
detailing the quota for the week and all the sales activity.

It was the job of the beginning and intermediate salespeople to lure the client in. Their potential clients were
mostly senior citizens who loved to gamble and were constantly filling out sweepstakes forms. WMM would buy the

sweepstakes forms, which were called leads. Those leads were then distributed among the beginning and intermediate salespeople. They would call the client and inform them that after they purchased supplies for their business they were then eligible to pick a prize of their choice: a new car, a trip to Hawaii or an undisclosed amount of pure gold American Eagle coins. The salesperson's goal was to hype the prizes up so much that the clients would be salivating at the mouth. The goal was to excite them to the point where they got going as fast as possible for their checkbook to write out the three-thousand-dollar sum to purchase engraved office supplies with hopes of winning that new car, an all-expense paid trip or thousands of dollars worth of gold. The salesperson would then give the client a claim number that was to be treated as if it was the key to a bank vault.

That's how it all began.

Two weeks later, after the engraved office supplies were delivered with about six hundred to a thousand dollars worth of gold coins, the Platinum salespeople would call the disappointed client. The Platinum Pro would tell the client not to look at it as a loss. Now that their foot is in the door, they have the golden opportunity to play with the high rollers. They now have a chance to win their fair share of one and a half million in gold American Eagle coins. But this time the client would have to shell out fifteen thousand big ones. When the client would gasp, the Platinum Pro would remind them that they are now in the big leagues and then would proceed to make them understand that to play you gotta pay or you gotta be in it to win it. The customer was constantly reminded that $15,000 is nothing but a drop in the bucket to claim their fair share of one and a half million dollars in gold American Eagle coins. Again, the sales pitch consisted mainly of painting a picture of the client running his or her hands through and tossing up in the air hundreds and thousands of gold American Eagle coins.

Of course, you could go to a bank or coin dealer and purchase the gold American Eagle. But where was the fun in that? These were rich, greedy, living-on-the-edge, gambling individuals who wanted something for nothing. And WMM wasn't the only vice they played with. There were companies in Vegas, Canada, New York and Hawaii with high-stake offers and oily tongued salespeople. Now mind you, the first phase with WMM or first $15,000 was just a teaser. The client already had in their possession several denominations of pure gold coins individually cased, thus whetting the appetite.

Then again, after several weeks, additional engraved products would be delivered and their fair share of gold American Eagle coins, which would be ten to twenty percent of the $15,000. Then the sales pitch would start again. Each time the cost to play would go higher and higher. Some clients were paying $50,000 to $100,000, determined to beat the odds. This game was indeed a gambler's vice. WMM was bringing the Las Vegas tables right into their homes.

The day after Nina's GBI experience and Rinaldo's not so subtle threat, Nina was seated in Milt's office. Out of all the people at WMM she favored Milt the most. He was true to his era. A tall, distinguised, older brother who rocked a salt-and-pepper 'fro, black-rimmed glasses and polyester suits. His conversations were always centered on the advancement of his people and how far they came and how far they had to go. When Rinaldo said they had to work on Martin Luther King's birthday, Milt damn near formed a mutiny. But not before giving a speech on Dr. King's accomplishments, how far we've come as black people and the importance of this holiday. Milt worked his ass off to support his wife, two kids both in college, a nephew and a niece who was a single parent with two kids. Family was always first with him.

Shortly after, Shawn stuck his head in Milt's office. The three of them along with Pete were close because they were the top salespeople, worked at WMM the longest and had formed an alliance against Rinaldo. Jeff wasn't included in their circle. He came aboard well after the bond was already formed.

"Yo, Nina, what the fuck is going on?" Shawn wanted to know as he invited himself in and shut the door behind him. "Why you spaz on Jeff like that?" Shawn was black as midnight with bright white shiny teeth and thick wavy hair. He had the voice of a smoker. It was deep and gruff. He considered himself a Casanova. He had a baby on the way, three different baby mamas and three children who he referred to as the terrible three. He was only twenty-seven and was determined to open his latest baby mama a beauty salon and launch his hip-hop magazine called *#1 Stunna*. He balanced out his co-workers with his hair-trigger temper. Milt was laid-back and smooth like a shot of Jack Daniel's. Nina was the feisty, gangsta-chick and they both treated her like a little sister.

"Rinaldo gave that nigga two of my best clients. Y'all know I've been selling the Prestons and Don Friedman for almost a year now. I remember when Rinaldo tried to give me one of Jeff's clients, I acted like I was calling and couldn't get through. And he was able to get him back."

"Don't sweat it," Milt tried to console her.

"Don't sweat it? Shit, Milt, that's almost twenty grand in commission. What the fuck you mean don't sweat it?" Nina snapped.

"Listen to me now and calm down," he said soothingly. "We all know Rinaldo is always on some bullshit and try-ing to sow dissension amongst us. He thinks that if we are at each other's throats, more money for him. Let it go. Just like you got those clients, you'll get more," Milt tried to assure her.

"Fuck that, Nina! I would have took it to his ass too! Money is money and this cracker done sucked us into liv-ing all lavishly, talking about 'you only live once, and we work too hard to not treat ourselves' and all that bullshit," Shawn spat. "I could name a number of things I could have done with twenty stacks."

As soon as those words left Shawn's mouth, Rinaldo burst into Milt's office. "So this is where everybody is? What are y'all talking about?"

"Damn, Rinaldo. We ain't talking about you!" Shawn snapped.

"We're just talking about how to handle these clients," Milt said, making an attempt to throw Rinaldo off.

"Why you want to know what we talking about?" Shawn challenged. He and Rinaldo were constantly trying to prove who the bigger man was.

"Because this is *my* company. Y'all on *my* time," Rinaldo snapped. "Y'all work for me."

"Man, go 'head with that. You act as if we can't break to socialize. You just want us to stay on those phones non-stop. You don't even want us to breathe," Shawn snapped right back.

Rinaldo loved to throw his weight around. Everyone else would let him have that and go on about their business, but Shawn never missed an opportunity to argue with him.

"Motherfucker, you *need* to stay on the phones non-stop! Look at that board." Rinaldo stepped back out of Milt's office and motioned to the huge white sales board up on the wall. "Look at that. Thirty-seven thousand dollars in sales and it's already Wednesday. I should erase your name, Shawn, and write 'Lazy'! Yeah, that's your new name from now on."

"Man, please. Go 'head with that bullshit. It's something

up there! You act like thirty-seven thousand dollars ain't nothing."

"Anyway, as we were saying…" Shawn wanted Rinaldo to know that he could not get under his skin. This angered Rinaldo more because now he had stepped all the way into Milt's office, closed the door behind him and stood in Shawn's face.

"Back up, man. You ain't gotta stand all in my face," Shawn warned.

"Thirty-seven thousand dollars ain't shit! Maybe you belong back there with the beginning salespeople. Pulling in three to ten thousand dollars a week in sales. Leave the big money to the Pros."

"Man, whatever. Do what you gotta do. Like I said, we are allowed a break and as long as I make my quota, you can take that lazy bullshit elsewhere."

"You are lazy. Y'all back here lounging around when you should be focused on that board out there. Milt, or should I say Martin Luther, you ain't no better. You got less than him," Rinaldo cracked.

"I'm getting ready to close this client right here. He's worth fifteen thousand dollars," Milt countered.

"Yeah, well, the check ain't in here yet. So that means nothing to me. The only person who can afford to lounge around is Alexis. And I gave away two of her sales. I can't understand how y'all let a girl outperform y'all. Where is your pride?" Rinaldo asked in disgust.

Alexis rolled her eyes, got up and stormed past Rinaldo. Her cell phone vibrated and she answered it. "What's up, mama?" It was Supreme, her baby's daddy.

"How's my daughter?" Nina asked, trying her damndest to be friendly to someone whom she now considered to be her enemy.

"She's fine, I just spoke to her. She misses you."

"Can I talk to her?"

"Yeah, hold on." He had to click over and call her on a three-way.

Supreme was doing a bid down in Trenton State Prison for murder. He had been locked up going on his fifth year. Now here he was calling her on a cell phone from prison. He wanted Nina back into his life and to move back to Jersey. The longer she kept refusing, the longer he would keep her from Jatana.

"Jatana, I got Mommy on the line," Supreme told her.

"Mommy!" Jatana yelled with glee.

"Hey, baby. Mommy loves you. You know that, right?"

"Uh-huh. I got a Wii."

"You got a Wii? Who bought that for you?"

"My grandma."

"That's so nice. I miss you. You talked to Daysha and Jermichael?"

"Uh-huh. They got a Wii too."

"I know."

"Mommy, when you coming to get me?"

"Okay, Mommy gotta go now," Supreme interrupted.

"Wait, Supreme. I love you, Jatana." She didn't want to end the conversation so quickly.

"Love you too, Mommy."

Nina waited until she was sure that Jatana was no longer on the line. "Supreme, how long do you think I'ma let you get away with this?" Nina asked through clenched teeth. Her rage and hatred for him building by the second.

"Come see me and we can talk about it," he replied as if everything was everything.

Nina hung up the phone on him. She went into Milt's office, sat down and started crying.

The only thing to make her sob in this day and time was her children. And Milt was the only person who saw her shed a tear.

"Nina, let everything play out. Jatana is fine. You'll get her back. Make this money while we got the chance. Trust me. Everything will work itself out." Milt became quiet to allow Nina the chance to pull herself together. This wasn't the first time she came into his office and simply collapsed in defeat.

When Nina managed to get herself together she got up and went back into her office.

It was closing time at WMM. It was Friday and Rinaldo was already gone. Deanna and Simeon were left to close the office for the weekend. Simeon had about seven grand and he was ready to go get high and Deanna had a plane to catch. She was going to see her parents in Wyoming. It was their twenty-fifth anniversary.

She had just copied the sales sheets for the day and counted the twenty-six hundred dollars she collected from the beginning sales team. They were always asking for draws against their upcoming paychecks. Rinaldo would give it to them…at ten percent interest. She was preparing to seal up the envelope to be given to Rinaldo when she remembered that she didn't get the two grand from Shawn.

She paged him on the intercom. "Shawn, can you come to the front office? Shawn, I need you to come to the front office," she repeated.

After five minutes, Deanna stormed towards his office and barged in. He was sitting there smoking a cigarette, thumbing through a *F.E.D.S.* magazine. On the cover was the New World Nation of Islam. The phone was resting on his shoulder. He ignored her so she started flicking his lights on and off.

"Hold on, Marge, dear. The front office is paging me for something. In the meantime, you mull over what I've just proposed. And remember, you've come too far to back out now. Do you understand me, honey? Fine. I'll be right back." He put her on hold. "What the fuck is the matter with you? Can't you see I'm working?" he snapped at her.

"Shawn, you are the last one here. We are trying to lock up. I have a plane to catch and I need Rinaldo's two grand that you owe."

"Girl, I got a customer trying to send in fifty grand and you sweatin' me about two? Somebody needs to stay here and keep this muthafucka open until I make it happen with this client."

"Shawn, it's Friday. I have a plane to catch and I gotta get this money over to Rochelle. I'm locking the door in five minutes," she stated with conviction.

"Come on, girl, stop playin'. Where's Simeon?"

"He just left. You got five minutes," she warned him.

"I can't close this customer in five minutes," Shawn barked.

"Okay, I'll give you fifteen minutes, but you will have to drop this money over to Rochelle's for Rinaldo. That would help me out a lot. Can you do that for me? Pleeassse, Shawn. Pretty pleeeease?"

Shawn waved her off and got back on the phone with Marge.

"Thank you!" She threw a kiss at him.

Shawn pulled his S500 in Rinaldo's driveway and deaded the engine. He got out and walked to the front door. The screen door was closed but the front door was open. He rang the bell. Rochelle came dressed in a Prada crystal-embroidered tank top, Prada jeans and a pair of Chanel calfskin clogs. Her hair was bone straight and hanging loosely. She had Shawn drooling at the mouth.

She opened the door and told him to come in and have a seat. When she turned around and he saw that ass in those jeans he asked her, "Why the fuck is you with him?" It just came out and he knew you couldn't take back spoken words.

It shocked her. "What did you say?"

"You heard me. Why the fuck are you with him?"

"Would I be better off with you?"

"Yeah, you would."

"Why the fuck do you work for him?" she snapped back.

"That's different. I ain't got to fuck him."

"Who says I'm fucking him?" She looked Shawn up and down, liking what she saw. In fact, she always liked what she saw.

"Come on, playgirl. Ain't no way in hell you staying in the man's house, spending his money and you ain't giving up no pussy. That's bullshit."

"You *wish* you knew the intricacies of our relationship." Rochelle smirked.

"Well, I'm sure you set for life. If you ain't I suggest that you get with the program. This shit ain't promised forever."

"Can I get you something to drink?" she asked him. She wanted to hear more of what he had to say.

"Only if you got something to smoke with it." Shawn sat down on the huge soft leather sectional and made himself comfortable.

"No, I don't have anything to smoke, but if you do, light it up. I'm down. My baby is at his grandmother's."

She didn't have to tell Shawn twice. He took the envelope

that Deanna gave him and set it on the coffee table. He put his two thousand in there and sealed it up. He pulled out a plastic bag of dro, his Phillies and went to work.

She reappeared with a bottle of Patrón and two champagne glasses. She turned on the CD player and Sade's *Soldier of Love* began oozing out of the system.

She sat down next to him and watched as he skillfully rolled the blunts. Rinaldo or their son wouldn't be back until Sunday. It was the weekend, and she did not want to spend it alone. But now she believed that it was no coincidence that Shawn showed up at her door. She had been looking for someone to play her game and she planned on taking full advantage of his visit.

Shawn lit the first blunt as she poured the drinks. "Would you fuck me?" she asked him while watching him closely to gauge his reaction to her very direct question.

He took another pull of his blunt and his eyes roamed across her body, in an attempt to memorize her curves. She lifted her champagne glass and took a sip of the Patrón.

"What's in it for me?" he finally asked her.

"What do you mean what's in it for you?"

"Cut the bullshit, Rochelle. I mean, you obviously ain't stupid. Shit, you latched on to that muthafucka. I mean, I can't stand his ass but the muthafucka is brilliant. I'll give him that. Now I'm sure you got some shit up your sleeve. So again, what's in it for me?"

"Let's talk about it over dinner." She stood up and took the Patrón and two glasses of champagne and disappeared.

Shawn stood up and mumbled, "This is going to be interesting."

"Now that everyone is back from lunch, I want all the Platinum Pros in my office in the next ten minutes. I want all of the Platinum Pros in my office," Rinaldo announced, yelling over the intercom. And, inevitably, right after Rinaldo would make an announcement, he would come flying around the corner to tell them the same thing in person. It was as if he thought that they didn't hear him.

"I need to go over some things." He stuck his head in Nina's office. He closed her door. "Including you, lazy!" Rinaldo then barked, "And get on those phones in the meantime. Standing here shooting the breeze. You can sell somebody in ten minutes. Stop being so fuckin' lazy!" He stuck his head in Milt's office.

"Can you believe this guy?" Shawn looked at Milt in disbelief. He was standing in Milt's office talking.

"Hey, man. He's the boss." Milt decided to kiss some ass.

"Whatever, man." Shawn waved them both off and headed back to his desk.

Fifteen minutes later, the entire Platinum crew was seated in Rinaldo's office. Everyone staring straight ahead. Rinaldo stood up, slowly rattled the lid off his cigar box and set his gaze on Shawn.

"Why you lookin' at me? All of these other people in here and you looking at me."

Rinaldo ignored Shawn as he ran his fingers across the

remaining cigars in the box. The room was silent as they watched Rinaldo grab his lighter in anticipation of what bullshit he was going to pull next.

"C'mon, Rinaldo. I hate that cigarette smoke," Nina whined.

"It's cigar smoke, Alexis, and this is *my* office." He lit the cigar anyway.

Nina grabbed her chair and moved it as far away from his desk as she could. "I never seen somebody so damn rude and inconsiderate," she spat.

Rinaldo sat down, propped his feet up on the desk and puffed away.

"This is going to be short and to the point. Everyone in here is on my Platinum Team. Whatever is said in this office remains in this office. If you get any strange phone calls or visits, don't say shit, and notify me immediately. Even if you have to call me on my cell or home phone. Does everyone understand me?"

"What do you mean strange visits or phone calls?" Jeff wanted to know. Jeff was thin as a rail. He wore wire-rimmed glasses that rested on the tip of his nose and he looked like a rat. His shirtsleeves were always rolled up and he always had ink pens in his shirt pocket. He was often in and out of jail for DUI.

"What the fuck you think? Phone calls asking about our organization. About what we do and how we do it. Questions about Florida. As long as you do like I'm telling you, you'll be fine. Otherwise, you are headed for big trouble.

Trouble that I won't be able to get you out of. Again, does everyone understand where I'm coming from?" Rinaldo rested his gaze on everyone in the room. "Good. Moving right along. I'm raising the late fees."

He got outbursts from the entire room.

"I knew it was some sheisty bullshit getting ready to come out of his mouth," Nina barked.

"This doesn't make any sense. C'mon, man," Milt pleaded. "Is this the way you treat your employees? I mean, we putting money in your pockets!"

"Man, you crazy!" Shawn yelled. "Raising them to what?"

"I don't believe this." Pete rocked back and forth in his chair. The afternoon sunlight glared off his bald head. Rinaldo was once again finding a way to cut into his get-high money.

"Rinaldo, man, you said we supposed to be family, man. Is this the way you treat family?" Jeff asked.

"It is when y'all start getting slack and lazy. Obviously, what I'm already charging ain't enough."

He opened his desk drawer and threw a stack of time cards in the air. "Look at these time cards. Eight-oh-five, eight twenty-two, eight forty. Y'all muthafuckers gettin' later and later. And Alexis came in damn near three hours late last week and she didn't even bother to punch in. She conveniently said fuck Rinaldo."

"You know why I was late, Rinaldo," Nina snapped.

"Yeah, but you didn't call, and like I said, this is a place of business. I provide a very comfortable and professional environment for y'all to come in and to make money. The least y'all could do is be on time. So instead of five hundred dollars a day, now it's a thousand dollars a day."

"Man, fuck this!" Pete shouted, finally coming to a figure of how much Rinaldo was cutting into his get-high stash. Pete was a heroin addict with excellent sales skills who was late almost every day except for Friday...payday. His clients loved him. As long as he made enough to easily feed his habit for a week and money to keep Jill happy, he never complained. But this...he wasn't going for. "A thousand dollars a day? You need money that bad? What? You tryna buy another car? You got me fucked up, man!" Pete ranted.

"Yeah, well tell Jill to go half with you. Since y'all like to be late together and get high together. A heroin addict and a cokehead. What a fuckin' combination," Rinaldo teased. "But I don't need y'all fuckin' late fines to buy me a car. I gots money. A shitload of it."

Jill was Pete's fiancée, who introduced him to snorting heroin. Coke was her vice. She liked to dress fly, throw parties and snort coke as if she lived in Hollywood. She kept very close tabs on Pete, which is why she took a job at WMM. She was an intermediate salesperson who was just that...intermediate. No matter how hard she tried she couldn't graduate to a Platinum Pro. Nina and everyone else was convinced that Rinaldo would make sure that never happened. She was a tooter and Rinaldo simply did not like her. He felt that Pete was only getting high because of her. The two had been planning this huge wedding since forever. The date kept getting pushed back, it seemed every other week she was announcing a new date or passing out new invitations.

"Well, you got me *and* Jill fucked up," Pete ranted again.

"You got me fucked up!" Rinaldo mocked Pete's high-pitched voice. "Have yo' lady come suck my dick and I might cut your fine in half."

"What the fuck did you just say?" Pete jumped up and charged at Rinaldo. Rinaldo snatched his burner from under the desk, cocked it and pointed it at Pete.

"C'mon, money. Put that away," Milt said in an attempt to defuse the situation.

"What's it gonna be?" Rinaldo ignored Milt and was testing Pete, who was frozen in place. After staring Rinaldo down, he stormed out of his office. "And whoever else don't like it can leave now. You're either a professional or a bum. All bums leave." He slid the burner back under the desk.

Shawn got up and headed for the door. Rinaldo started laughing. "I knew you were going to be the first one to go."

"Rinaldo, come to the front," Deanna was yelling frantically over the intercom, interrupting the late-fines debate. "Mr. Branson's son is out here. He will not stop kicking the door. He says he wants to talk to the owner. And he keeps pushing on this friggin' buzzer. Should I call the police?"

"Naw, I got it." Rinaldo felt under his desk and this time he pulled out a .45 automatic. He stuck it in his waistband. "This meeting is adjourned. All of y'all get the fuck out!"

"Drama queen," Nina hissed.

CHAPTER SIX

WE DON'T GIVE REFUNDS

"Sir, can you stop laying on the buzzer? Someone will be with you shortly," Deanna pleaded with exasperation.

"Why can't you open the goddamned door? I want to see the owner, now!" the persistent man yelled into the intercom as he kept pressing the buzzer.

Rinaldo made his way into the receptionist's office. "What the fuck?" he mumbled as he adjusted the security camera to get a close-up on what he was dealing with. "Whose son is he?" Rinaldo was eyeing the huge white man with a Texas hat and cowboy boots with silver spurs. His tight blue jeans were tattered on both knees. He carried an expensive briefcase. His face was fire-engine red, as if he had just downed one too many drinks. His pudgy nose was even redder. The buzzer was still ringing.

"Ted Branson." Deana was thumbing through the file cabinet in search of the Branson file.

"Ted Branson doesn't have a son. Ask him his name," Rinaldo barked, priding himself with knowing every detail regarding everything about each and every one of his customers.

"Excuse me, sir. I didn't get your name," Deanna stated into the intercom.

"What?" he yelled.

"I didn't get your name."

"That's because you didn't bother to ask. I'm Darwin Branson and I'm here on behalf of my uncle, Ted Branson."

"Okay, sir. Someone will be right with you." Deanna sighed.

Rinaldo was looking at previous sales sheets. Ted Branson was a client who loved Alexis. He had been buying from her for almost eight months now and had spent almost $150,000. Rinaldo looked at Darwin again. Branson's file said nothing about a nephew. "Alexis, come up front," Rinaldo paged her as he continued going through the file.

"Is the owner gonna come talk to me, or do I have to call the law?" Darwin Branson threatened.

Deanna looked at Rinaldo.

"Tell him the owner is in a meeting but will be with him shortly."

"Mr. Branson, the owner is in a meeting but will be with you shortly. Just be a little more patient."

"What's up, Rinaldo?" Alexis asked as soon as she stepped into Deanna's office.

"What's the story with Ted Branson? Is he a satisfied or a disgruntled customer?" Rinaldo asked.

"He is very satisfied. He even wants me to come visit him. I keep telling him I have a sick grandmother who I cannot leave, not even overnight. If he was disgruntled, you know I would have told you."

"Yeah, well, what I'm trying to figure out is, if Ted Branson lives all the way in Fort Worth, Texas, why is his nephew down here in Georgia, and how did he know this address? Our satellite office and everything else is in the Florida Keys!"

"I don't know." Alexis shrugged.

Rinaldo snatched the phone up and dialed Armand. "Hey. How soon can you get over here? We may have a situation."

"Fifteen, twenty minutes," Armand assured Rinaldo.

"Make it ten." *Click.*

"You want me to call Charlie?" Deanna offered.

"No, no. Not yet. Let me see what's up first," Rinaldo told her. This was a small matter to Rinaldo. Nothing that he and his enforcer Armand couldn't handle. No need to bother his business partner with this trivial bullshit.

"Okay. Anything else?" Nina questioned.

"No. I'll take it from here."

Nina headed back to her office.

"When Armand gets here, send him to my private lounge. Mr. Branson and I will be back there."

"I got it," Deanna said, relieved that she did not have to do any more of Rinaldo's dirty work.

"Buzz him in." Rinaldo stepped out into the hallway,

awaiting Darwin's presence. Rinaldo pasted a grin on his face and held out his hand when Darwin stepped in the hallway. "Mr. Branson? I'm Tommy Green." Rinaldo was trying to size him up right quick as they shook hands. "That's quite a grip you got there. Are you a Texan like your uncle?" Rinaldo joked and then slapped him on the back. He could smell the alcohol oozing out of his pores.

"I'd like to think so. Are you the owner, Mr. Green?"

"Tommy. Call me Tommy. I'm one of them. Let's go back to the lounge area, where we can talk in private. You don't look like you're from around these parts. When did you get into town?" Rinaldo prodded.

"I work for a Texas telecommunications company and we had a couple of seminars and a convention to attend to right here in Atlanta. I've been in your town since Monday."

Rinaldo keyed in the access code on the keypad to gain entry into the private lounge area. It was very plush and decorated in mauve and black. There was a small refrigerator, microwave, coffeemaker, a fully stocked wet bar and a huge black and mauve conference table surrounded by black leather swivel chairs. Rinaldo could see the approval on Darwin's face and his demeanor calmed drastically.

"What are you drinking, Mr. Branson?"

The Texan smiled. "My kind of man. Darwin. Call me Darwin, Tommy. How about some black coffee with a shot of vodka?"

"Coming right up." Rinaldo poured the steaming black coffee into a mug and then put several shots of vodka in it. He poured himself a tall glass of carrot juice, placed the beverages on a tray and headed for the conference table. Darwin was approving the motivational plaques on the wall. "Here you go. Have a seat."

"I thank you kindly," Darwin drawled as he placed his briefcase on the table. He reached for his coffee and remained standing.

"Make yourself comfortable," Rinaldo encouraged.

"Can you make this a tad bit stronger?" Darwin frowned as he sniffed his drink.

"Sure can." Rinaldo went and brought the bottle to the table and placed it in front of him.

"Don't be shy. Drink up. It's just us fellas here." Rinaldo watched as Darwin filled the rest of the mug up with the vodka. Then he sat down.

"I sho' do appreciate this. Nothing like some strong joe with a shot of vodka!"

"So, Darwin, what can we do for you? You didn't go through all this trouble to find us just to get a cup of joe with a shot of vodka. You can get that anywhere. Speak your mind."

"Hell, I sure didn't. But it definitely makes my efforts worthwhile. 'Cause it wasn't easy trackin' you buzzards down. So I guess you would want me to cut to the chase?"

"Cut to the chase," Rinaldo again encouraged.

Darwin poured more vodka into his coffe mug. "Well I'm sorta watching over my uncle Teddy. You know he's pushing up on eighty years old soon and his mind ain't at all like it used to be." He popped open the briefcase and took out a red Pendaflex folder. "Okay, Tommy, I'm going to level with you. My uncle has been retired for almost sixteen years now. He retired from Enron." He placed several Montblanc pens, golden brass calculators and golden brass key chains on the table. They were exquisitely engraved with the name TDB Enterprises. "Are these your products?"

"They sure are," Rinaldo stated proudly.

"They're very nice, but like I said, my uncle has been retired for almost sixteen years. And he is not a business owner. He barely gets around." He pulled out some WMM sales sheets. "Now, what I'm trying to figure out is why would he spend fifteen thousand, fifteen thousand, thirty thousand, thirty thousand, and this one here fires me up, fifty thousand on these here trinkets?" He slid the sales sheets across the table to Rinaldo. "Exactly what kind of scheme do you people have going on here? He's a senior citizen for Christ sakes!"

"I understand your concern, Darwin. But does Mr. Branson know that you are here on his behalf? Because from what I understand he may be up in age, but he is very competent. We are a very reputable company and I believe that Mr. Branson buys our products just so he can get the gold American Eagle coins. And more than anything he is very fond of his sales rep. I think what he's actually buying is happiness, entertainment and attention. Who are you to stop him?"

"Geesh!" Darwin slammed the coffee mug down onto the table. "One hundred seventy thousand dollars?"

"Darwin. It's his money. Let him have some fun. He's earned it. Wait. Wait a minute. Is he cutting into your inheritance?"

"You damned right he is! I'm the last of Uncle Teddy's family that's worth leaving anything to," Darwin unashamedly belted out. "This is fucking ridiculous and you know it!"

"So, what do you want us to do about it? Stop selling him happiness because he's now dipping into your pockets? What are we going to tell him? Uh, Ted, your nephew Darwin said you can no longer do business with our company anymore, because he feels that what you are shelling out could be better used by him?"

"Look, Tommy. We can do this the easy way or the hard way. Just give my uncle a refund of his money and we could end this amicably. Give me the refund and you have my word, I'll go quietly."

"Refund? What are we supposed to do with all of these products? We can't resell them. They have his name all over them, and what about the gold coins? He has thousands of dollars in gold coins, which I *know* he's not going to return. So you see, Darwin, we don't give refunds."

"Okay. You wanna play hardball? The Georgia Bureau of Investigation and the FBI would just love to get a complaint from a concerned citizen whose eighty-year-old uncle is being bilked and extorted out of hundreds of thousands of dollars. Now wouldn't they? I have my resources and they are patiently collecting ammunition, and like I said, I would quietly walk away and not give them any help. You wouldn't even remember that I was here. Just write me a check for a hundred and seventy thousand dollars and don't contact my uncle anymore. Can we deal or not?"

Rinaldo started laughing. "Darwin, you Texans got more balls than I imagined. I mean, to come into my place of business and threaten me? Blackmail me? Are you serious?"

"I'm very serious. I didn't spend all of this time and energy tracking you bastards down for nothing. At the rate my uncle is going, by the end of the year he would have given you bastards damn near a half million dollars. And that's my damn money!" He reached for the vodka bottle and filled the coffee mug halfway once again. Can you pour me a little more of that black, would ya, Tommy?"

"You're the boss, Darwin."

"Okay, so we got a deal or what?"

Rinaldo sighed as if he was seriously contemplating his offer, running his hands over his face and then scratching the back of his head. "Let me talk it over with my partners and get back to you."

"Tommy, Tommy, Tommy. Are you listening? When I leave this office I'm going back to Texas with two hundred seventy thousand dollars or I'm going down to the FBI."

"Two hundred seventy thousand dollars?" Rinaldo yelled. "Texan boy, you must be drunk already. 'Cause you just said a check for one-seventy and now you want another hundred thousand!"

"Two seven zero. I must get back my investment. It took many resources to track you people down. Surprising what a few dollars, combing through phone records or trash cans find ya. I know about your office in the Florida Keys. You see, my uncle thinks your operation is in Florida. But I know it's in Georgia. Real cute setup you got here. Real cute. So that's why I'm upping the ante to two-seventy!"

"Okay." Rinaldo feigned an act of surrender. "I've heard enough. But there's something still eating away at me. Who's to say that once I give you what you want, you don't leave me alone?"

"Tommy. I'm from the old school. And in case you didn't know, with us old-schoolers a handshake, a smile and our word is all that's needed."

"Okay. Okay." Rinaldo placed the pot of coffee in front of Darwin.

"Good. Good move, Tommy boy. I'll just help myself to another drink while you go and get that check."

Rinaldo stood up and asked, "So, who knows you're here? Does your uncle know?"

"Not a soul, Tommy boy," he said as he loosened his tie. "Not a soul. Go ahead. Run along. I'll be right here waiting on that check." Rinaldo could see the gleam in Darwin's eyes. He headed for his office, where Armand was patiently waiting.

"What's the deal, boss?" Armand stood up to greet

Rinaldo. His tight suit looked as if it was about to burst. His hands were big as baseball mitts. He was a Rinaldo wannabe. His dirty blond hair was slicked back into a greasy ponytail.

"You wouldn't believe it if I told you. I have a Texan guest in my office. I want him to follow you to the other office. He wants to pick up a check." Rinaldo eyed Armand. "Take care of him." Those were the only words needed.

Darwin Branson was seated patiently in the law offices of Bells and Gray. The relaxing music was teasing him and luring him into a nod. Almost thirty minutes ago, he shook hands with Rinaldo, thanked him and followed Armand to the lawyer's office. Oblivious to the figure easing from behind the sliding door, Darwin was fantasizing on what he would do with the two hundred seventy thousand big ones. He couldn't believe how easy it was to muscle Tommy Green. His first order of business would be to handle the $150,000 gambling debt. Everything else would fall into place. Just as he stretched his arms and yawned, a thin wire was wrapped around his neck. Armand pulled tighter and tighter. Darwin kicked wildly while trying to grab Armand and loosen his grip. No longer receiving oxygen, Darwin's eyes damn near bulged out of their sockets as he pissed and released his bowels on himself, all while concentrating on catching a breath. There was no more.

Darwin was dead.

CHAPTER SEVEN

SHOW ME THE MONEY

We Make Millionaires was the name of the company, and the company's slogan. It didn't apply to the clients, but to the salespeople. And Rinaldo was relentless when it came to making that money.

Rinaldo was born and raised in Centralia, Illinois, in a trailer park community called Central City. It was on the north side of town, where most whites were considered poor, white trailer trash. Times were not too bad while their father, Simeon Sr., was there. But when Rinaldo turned seven, Simeon Sr. was gone. His mother, Hazel, did the best she could during that first year. She applied for welfare and took a job at a local tavern. She was uneducated but made sure the boys went to school. The next year, Hazel picked up a drinking habit and shortly after that, the family of three was living from shelter to shelter and eventually on the streets. Rinaldo swore that once he was able, he would make as much money as he could. Making money became an obsession.

In the office, he hounded the salespeople the entire

shift. There was only one of him but he made you think he had a bunch of clones. He was all over the office. Two nights out of the week, Tuesdays and Thursdays, were late nights. The salespeople had to focus on potential clients on the West Coast. He also made them work on Saturdays whenever the sales numbers for the week were below his quota. Below quota was when sales were less than $500,000. Alexis would bring in over $100,000 a week by herself. She remained hungry and was determined to be the best at whatever she did.

All the Platinum salespeople barged out of the morning sales meeting wanting to draw blood. Besides already hitting his Platinum Sales Team up for $1,000 every time they were late, he was also assessing $1,000 per day that they did not make a sale. He told them that there was no reason not to make a sale in an eight-hour period. He claimed that he did not need the measly $1,000. It was the principle of the matter. He prided himself with training and handpicking his Platinum sales force. He had to admit that they were damned good. Five Platinum salespeople at $100,000 a week, that was almost a guaranteed half million dollars in sales every seven days. What the beginning and intermediate reps brought in was gravy.

So what that they were pissed off! They would eventually get over it. There was no other telemarketing firm in the world where they could go and enjoy the type of moneymaking opportunity that he created for his Platinum Team. Just like a drug, they were all addicted, and Rinaldo made sure he fed that addiction. Every one of those luxury vehicles in the parking lot were leased to his Platinum staff by WMM. And you better believe he was getting his cut off of that. His friend owned one of the biggest corporate leasing companies in the area. And whatever Rinaldo wanted to drive, it would be delivered personally. Whatever his sales force thought or mentioned that they wanted to drive he made sure he would have it brought right over and put in their face. And all of them had a minimum of two rides. Lease payments were ranging from $800 to $2,000 a month.

All staff was required to wear suits into work. And just like Rinaldo, they all had good taste. Taste ranging from Armani, Brioni and Joseph Abboud to La Perla and Ermenegildo Zegna, to name a few. Rinaldo had a jeweler who would bring to the office various selections of Rolexes, Cartiers, Corum, Chopard, Hublot and several other custom-made watches to wear. He had diamond cuff links, earrings, necklaces—you name it—to sell to the Platinum Team. His line of thinking was the more you had, the more you would want.

Everyone lived in a condo or townhouse with pools or access to a pool, which they were either leasing or had a hefty mortgage attached to it. They all were living beyond their means. If WMM shut down tomorrow, and they did not have a nest egg, they would lose it all.

Then there were drugs. His manager and twin brother, Simeon, was a crack fiend. Of his Platinum members: Jeff an alcoholic, Pete a heroin addict, Shawn a weedhead with three baby mamas and four kids, including the one on the way. Milt was also a weedhead and had a daughter attending Howard University, a son at Columbia, nieces and nephews, all of whom he was supporting. Nina had her mother, three kids back in Jersey that she took care of, and they all knew about her boyfriend Akil, who had the so-called record label that drained a lot of her cash. Then there was Supreme, the control freak in prison who kidnapped her daughter. Therefore, yes, he had them and he made it his business to make sure they had bills up the ass. He had everyone where he wanted them…dependant on him.

Rinaldo was definitely king. He lit a cigar, threw his feet on top of his desk and blew smoke rings at the ceiling.

"Hey, mama. How are ya doing?"

"Oh, I'm all right. How are you?" With everything going on, Nina needed to talk to her babies. They gave her a sense of sanity.

"I'm okay. How's the babies?"

"Nina, I don't know why I gotta keep telling you, you ain't got no more babies. Them children are grown. Daysha is eight, Jermichael is seven and Jatana is six."

"Mom, I know how old they are. But they are still my babies. I just called to hear their voices. Let me speak to my little man."

She heard her mother suck her teeth before going to get Jermichael.

"Mommy!" He sounded so excited as he got on the phone.

"Hey, baby. Are you okay? I miss you and I love you."

"Miss you too. I want to come to the South."

"I'll be up to get you. What have you been up to?"

"Nothing." He was on his computer and half of his attention was on the phone while the rest was on the computer.

"School is fine," he sang.

"Go get your sister because I see you are not trying to talk to me."

Jermichael giggled. "I'm on my computer."

"Give the phone to Daysha." She was standing over him looking at the computer screen.

"Hey, Mommy."

"Hey, beautiful. I love you and miss you. I called you last night. You are always hanging out. You must like church, huh?"

"No. I don't like going with the deacon. When can you come get me?"

"Soon, baby."

"I don't want to go to Bible study."

"Girl, give me that phone." Ms. Coles snatched the phone from her. "Nina, I need a favor."

Oh shit. Here it comes. I wonder how much this time?

"I need seven thousand dollars."

"Seven thousand?" Nina shrieked. "Mom, what the hell do you need seven thousand dollars for? I just sent you five thousand, and forty-five hundred right before that. What do you need all of this money for?"

"I know how much you just sent me. But it is all for the Lord."

"The Lord? What Lord?"

"Nina, don't be yelling at me. It ain't but one Lord."

"Yeah, but who's collecting all of this money for *the Lord*?"

"Nina, can you send me the money or not?"

"Tell me who you are sending the money to," Nina pushed.

"Pastor Will Wilkins."

"Oh God, Mom. I saw him on TV. That guy is as fake as they come."

"Nina, watch your mouth."

"How long have you been sending this guy *my* money, Mom? I don't believe this," Nina said as she paced back and forth.

"Pastor Wilkins is a good man. A real servant for the Lord. I will not listen while you cast your negative judgment upon him."

Click.

The phone line went dead. Nina could not believe her mother had the gall to hang up on her.

Nina eased back into her chair and decided to rest her eyes and brain for a minute. *God I'm starting to really hate this job!* she screamed to herself. *Sometimes I just want to pack up, run, and run far, far away.* Each day it was getting harder and harder to come into work. *Does money buy happiness? FUCK NO! Sometimes I would rather be broke than deal with all of this stress and pressure.* She squeezed her eyelids tighter and tried to relax. *And now some televangelist is milking my own damn mother for the money that I'm milking my clients for. This shit is crazy.* Her cell phone vibrated and she answered it without checking to see who it was.

"Baby girl, what's good?"

Nina sucked her teeth. It was Supreme.

"Well, damn. It's good to hear from you too."

"Can I speak to my daughter?"

"I just called over there and no one is picking up. They must be out."

"Then why are you calling me?"

"To see how you're doing."

"Supreme, why are you doing this to me? You're in prison, she needs to be with me."

"Nina, you are way across the fucking country some-where on the run and don't even have your other two kids, so how could she be with you? I begged you to stay so I would be able to see my daughter. But no, you had to go chasing behind some lame-ass nigga. So fuck that. I can be a father to our daughter."

"Supreme, I was not chasing behind some nigga. Shit was hot for me and you know that."

"You left with some lame, Nina. That nigga from New York. You left your kids."

"Supreme, you know I was on the run and he was only helping me out."

"Nina, I was helping you out. And he damn sure wasn't helping you more than I was. Whenever you said you needed something I made it happen. You didn't want for nothing while you was up here. I—"

"Supreme, I was tired of Jersey. It was getting too hot for me. You know what? I'm hanging up now." Nina cut him off and turned off her phone. She rested her head back and closed her eyes. Just about every time they spoke to each other, they argued. She knew Supreme still had feelings for her, but she told him from the door that she was not doing time with him. So she wasn't going to fake it. She wasn't going to do him like that. Instead of him respecting that and accepting it, he tried to manipulate her by helping her out, but with all types of strings attached.

She needed to get away from Jersey and him too. But he pulled that real fucked-up and ultimate move by taking their daughter and stashing her away with his relatives. Relatives that she did not know nor had any idea where they lived. Even his mother was in on the shit. Nina hired a private investigator but as of yet nothing turned up.

BOOM! Her body twitched and tensed up, but she kept her position and eyes closed. Rinaldo had barged into her office like he usually does, yelling, farting and bringing lots of drama with him.

"Alexis, why aren't you on the phone?" He picked up

the phone and held it out to her. She kept her eyes closed and sighed.

"I will get on the phone in a couple of minutes. Can I at least enjoy my coffee?"

"Coffee? You're in here sleeping!"

"Rinaldo, I'm not asleep. How could I be asleep when I just left your depressing sales meeting?"

"Depressing? What was so depressing about it? My meeting wasn't depressing."

"You're always trying to find ways to take money from us. You always on some bullshit." Her eyes remained closed.

"Taking money from y'all? No, I'm not. I'm not trying to take y'all's cash. If you are on time, no cash gets taken. If you make at least one sale a day, no cash gets taken. Y'all lucky I didn't say two a day! Y'all seem like y'all ain't hungry no more. Maybe it's time for me to get some new blood in here. What do you think?" He yelled out into the hallway, "Milt, Shawn, Pete and Jeff come here!"

"Oh God." Nina groaned. "Rinaldo, you are so full of yourself and when can I resell on Ted Branson? What happened in the meeting with his nephew?"

"I'll discuss Ted with you later."

"Rinaldo, Rochelle just pulled up," Deanna announced over the intercom.

"Shit," Rinaldo said, his whole demeanor changing. He looked at his watch.

"What's up, big boss?" Milt was playing the kiss-ass. Everyone was standing around Nina's office.

Shawn just stood there with Pete and Jeff. "I was just telling Alexis that y'all ain't hungry no more. Maybe I should bring in some fresh blood."

"Man go 'head with that. You need to be keeping an eye on the ones you got. Letting hot muthafuckas up in here. I ain't going to do time for no other muthafucka. If I go down it's gonna be all because of me," Shawn belted out.

"Man, what you been smoking? What the fuck you talking about, Shawn? You need to stay outta them goddamn rap magazines. Coming up with all of these conspiracy theories. Who's hot?"

"Fuckin' Jeff, man." He said it as if Rinaldo should already know it.

"Me!" Jeff yelled in disbelief. Nina, who was half-asleep, opened her eyes and was just as shocked as everyone else.

"Yeah, nigga. I don't trust you. My gut is telling me that you ain't right." Shawn snapped and of course was not backing down. "Rinaldo, you so busy trying to get paid, you not recognizing these hot muthafuckas you got up in here! You're gonna fuck around and it's going to be too late."

"Fuck you, man." Jeff charged at Shawn, trying to shut him up. Milt and Pete grabbed Shawn as Rinaldo slammed Jeff's skinny ass up against the wall.

"Hold the fuck up!" Rinaldo screamed. Once again, the entire office was heading towards all the commotion. "This is a place of fuckin' business." Rinaldo was now stomping. "Everybody back to their desks and get on the fuckin' phones! Right now! Shawn and Jeff, y'all get in my office!"

Rinaldo's face was beet red as he pointed to his office as if he was directing traffic.

"Damn!" Nina said to Milt. "What the fuck is really going on? Two battles in one week."

"Get on the phones!" Rinaldo yelled as he headed back to his office.

"All right! All right!" Nina stepped into her office and slammed the door.

"Sit y'all's asses down," Rinaldo ordered as he kicked the office door shut behind him. Jeff was the first to ease into a chair. Shawn defiantly remained standing as he leaned up against the wall behind Rochelle. Whatever she had brought Rinaldo for lunch smelled good and it was smelling up the office.

"Rinaldo, I have the travel package on hold for this weekend's trip to Saint-Tropez. Do you want me to put it on your American Express card and swing by and pick up the tickets?" Rochelle asked as if she and him were the only two people in the office.

Silence. Rinaldo had forgotten that she said she was dropping off his lunch this afternoon.

"Rinaldo, you forgot, didn't you?"

Hell yeah I forgot. I gotta make this money this weekend, not lay up with you on some damn island. We can do that anytime. "No. I didn't forget, baby. I told Charlie I would be up to meet him this weekend."

"I knew you were going to do this. That's why I went and cancelled the damn reservations. I just wanted you to show me once again that your fuckin' job comes before your wife and son," she ranted.

Jeff was pretending to be thumbing through a Robb Report and Shawn had a smirk on his face. They were both all ears, Shawn never taking his eyes off Rochelle. She was dark like Shawn and reminded him of a young and beautiful Lauryn Hill. What some bitches would do to live the lifestyle.

"Baby, look, you know if I could get away, I would. Shawn and Jeff, wait outside."

"Bullshit, Rinaldo! It's your fuckin' company. You're the damn boss." She stood up to leave. Jeff and Shawn didn't move.

"I know it is but—"

"But what?" she cut him off. "Don't give me that same old spiel about us living good because of your work, blah, blah, blah. Fuck you, Rinaldo! I see your crackhead brother more than I see you!" She stormed out of his office, slamming the door.

He ran behind her and snatched it open. "What the fuck is that supposed to mean?" He slammed the door back.

"Damn, Rinaldo," Shawn picked at him.

He waved her off as if it was nothing. "That spoiled bitch! I mean, what the fuck? I work too much. She doesn't complain when she goes on them fifty-thousand-dollar shopping sprees. Or when she's zooming around the city in a fuckin' Porsche. Or—"

"White boy, let me school yo' ass. Your arrogant ass forgot that you married a sista. They usually see right through the bullshit. They know what they want and they want it. And you do. You work too much. You are greedy, man. It's never enough for you. You act like your life is over if you don't make a half a mil a week."

"Jeff, check this out. Lazy-ass Shawn muthafuckin' Dr. Phil is trying to give me some marital advice? Dude, you got how many baby mamas?" Rinaldo snapped.

"Aiight, man. Later for your personal problems, back to what I was saying about Jeff. You're so greedy you can't see a hot muthafucka when he's staring you in the face."

Jeff jumped out of his seat and charged at Shawn. Rinaldo came from behind his desk and broke them apart.

"Jeff, step out. Go to your office. Let me talk to Shawn." He was pushing Jeff's tall lanky frame towards the door, and knocked off his glasses.

"If you don't like me, man, just say it. Don't be talking about I'm hot," Jeff spat. Shawn was coming towards him and stepped on his eyeglasses.

"You hot, nigga, and it's not that I don't like you. I just don't trust you," Shawn spat as Rinaldo shoved Jeff one hard time, shut and locked his door.

"My glasses! My glasses!" Jeff banged on the door.

"Man, what's up with you? You know what? I think you're jealous because he's starting to make more money than you. That's what this is really all about. I've noticed that you haven't been working as hard as you used to. Stop being lazy and trying to shift the heat off yourself."

"Whatever, man." Shawn smirked. "But don't say I didn't tell you. Hiring a fuckin' hot-ass crackhead." He unlocked the door, opened it and stepped out. Jeff went in and picked up his glasses.

Rinaldo was following him laughing and taunting him. "Shawn is jealous, y'all. You are jealous and you lazy."

Shawn slammed his office door in Rinaldo's face and locked it.

"Rinaldo, Charlie is on line four," Deanna announced over the loudspeaker. Rinaldo went into his office and shut the door.

Nina came out of her office to go to the break room. As she turned the corner, she saw Rochelle, Rinaldo's wife, most likely having a bullshit conversation with Deanna. Nina immediately noticed the cream Chloé pantsuit she was wearing. *Damn that would have looked fierce on me.* She had just seen the same one at Saks but didn't get it.

Deanna yelled out, "Hey, Alexis," as if they were the best of friends.

This bitch, Nina thought to herself, then threw out a phony greeting, "Hey, ladies."

Rochelle turned around and smiled at Nina. "What's up, girl? Damn, you look like you need a vacation. Is Mr. Asshole working you to death? I told you to check that fool. Don't let him play you out," Rochelle advised. "Us sista-girls gotta look out for one another."

"Well, sistagirl, some of us do have to *work*," Nina teased. She figured Rochelle must be bored to come hang out at the office. She didn't know that she had just left fussing Rinaldo out because he forgot about their pre-planned trip to Saint-Tropez this weekend.

"I *work*. Don't get it twisted." Rochelle made a little chuckle. "But enough about all that. What I really want to know is if you wanted to hang out with me tomorrow night. Friday night is ladies' night. Let us get out and get our groove on. I refuse to stay in the house *alone* for yet another weekend."

"Yeah, let's go," Deanna chimed in, all hyped up.

Both Rochelle and Nina looked at her as if to say, "*Bitch, please*. You must be *crazy*." Neither one of them would be caught dead in a club with her.

"You mean tomorrow Friday?" Nina asked Rochelle in surprise.

"Yes, tomorrow Friday." Rochelle wasn't going to take no for an answer. "It's ladies' night out, my treat." By Thursday of every week Rochelle was pissed as usual, adding up the countless weekends Rinaldo had been away from home. For the last four weekends Rinaldo had been running back and forth to Florida and not spending any time with her. Shit, their sheets were going from cold to icy. And she felt like if she did not get out she was going to explode.

Deanna interupted her train of thought by saying, "Oooohh…hell yeah, let's get out and have some fun."

Because Rochelle's back was to Deanna she gave Nina the eye and as if on cue Nina said, "Maybe next time. I already have plans." And she headed for the break room.

"All right, Nina, maybe next time. Let me make my rounds, Deanna, and I'll check in with you on my way out."

"All right, girl. When y'all do go, don't forget a sister," Deanna said as if she had a friend.

Rochelle gave her a phony smile and walked off.

Rochelle popped up a minute later in the break room and closed the door. They both started giggling like two high school teenagers.

"Her homely ass is always trying to hang out," Rochelle whispered.

"That's what you get for revealing your business to her nosy ass. You know she's Rinaldo's watchdog," Nina reminded her.

"Why do you think I said it? Anyways, later for her. You down or what? You know I don't have anyone else to go with."

"Just name the place and time." Nina gave in to Rochelle's request.

"I'll pick you up around nine." Rochelle glanced at her Cartier. "Shit. I'ma be late for my massage."

"You got entirely too much time on your hands," Nina teased her.

Rochelle winked at her and hurried out of the break room. She and Nina were not tight or anything. However, since neither one of them had a close girlfriend, every now and then they would have lunch or shop together. Never clubbing. But Nina had a feeling she was getting ready to see a whole other side of Rochelle. And she was looking forward to it because she hadn't been out in quite a while.

TGIF...

Sitting at her desk Nina began thumbing through her phone messages. "I need money," she mumbled. "Show me the money. Aha. Rita Cornwell of New Mexico. Nah." She began shuffling through her sales orders. "Ahh. The Bartzes. Carol and Ed. The real estate tycoon and land developers. They love to play. These two will definitely play all day if I coach them right."

Nina smiled as she dialed their number. She placed her headset on her head and stood up. She was now in closing mode as she dialed the Bartzes and waited for someone to pick up.

"Hello," the female voice chirped.

"Hello, Carol? This is Alexis from WMM. How are you this beautiful morning? Is it beautiful there in Poughkeepsie, New York?"

"Oh, Alexis," Carol squealed in delight. "I haven't been out yet but it looks beautiful. Ed, honey, it's Alexis from WMM," she said to her husband. "Alexis, do you have some good news for us?"

"Don't I always? Tell Ed to pick up the other line." Nina paced back and forth in her office with her hands behind her back.

"Ed, honey, Alexis wants you to get on the line. She has some good news for us."

Ed was still in his plaid, silk, Burberry pajamas reading the *Wall Street Journal* and sipping on a glass of orange juice.

"All right, hon," Ed said as he headed for the phone in the living room. Carol was on the phone in the kitchen.

"He's coming, Alexis," Carol eagerly announced.

"Great. Just great."

Nina still couldn't figure out who the biggest gambler of the two was.

"I'm here, Alexis. Top of the morning to ya!"

"Top of the morning to you too, Ed."

"Carol said you had some good news for us. I hope it's better than the last time. We didn't make out so well. We got back only a handful of gold coins. Tell me something good, Alexis," he firmly stated.

"I have some very good news, but it's going to take another fifty thousand dollars." Nina cut to the chase, allowing $50,000 to roll off her tongue as if she had said fifty cents.

"Aww, come on, Alexis," Carol belted out.

"Not another fifty thousand," Ed chimed in. "We've already given you guys two hundred and thirty thousand dollars, Alexis."

"Let's get this straight, Ed and Carol. Are you listening to me?"

"Yeah," Ed and Carol said simultaneously.

"Good. You haven't *given* us anything. You guys purchased products for your business. You made an investment for your business. Am I correct?"

"Yeah b—"

"But nothing," Nina cut Ed off. "There are no buts. You purchased products for your business. You invested in your business."

"But we wanted more gold," Carol whined.

"It's gonna take another fifty thousand dollars." Nina dangled the carrot.

"Alexis, this has to stop. We've already given, uh, invested two hundred and thirty thousand dollars." Ed tried to exude finality.

"You're exactly right!" Nina continued to pace back and forth.

"So do you see this thing from my side of the fence?" Ed asked.

"Of course I do," Nina assured him.

"Then you see why we can't give—er, uh, invest another fifty thou?" Ed felt like he was winning this battle.

"Carol, are you still with us?" Nina wanted to know.

"I'm here, Alexis," she replied, her voice beginning to fill with defeat.

"Well talk some sense into that head of your husband's."

Nina was beginning to yell, in an attempt to get her point across. "You guys"—she paused to let her point hang out there—"I honestly don't understand where all the skepticism is coming from. I just don't." Nina tried to sound as if she was insulted.

"Alexis," Ed said. She didn't respond.

"Alexis, are you there?" Carol checked, but Nina said nothing. "Where did she go, Ed? Alexis? You don't think she hung up, do you?" Carol was getting nervous.

"How the hell should I know?" Ed was whispering into the phone to his wife. "I don't hear a dial tone. Alexis, are you still there?"

"Do you think she's angry with us?" Carol too was now whispering.

"Angry? I didn't do anything," Ed countered. Nina was listening to both of them go at it.

"You insulted her. She's only trying to help us. Maybe we should give her the fifty thousand."

"Maybe nothing. We already gave her two hundred and thirty thousand dollars."

"Invested," Carol interrupted. "Not gave." They were both still whispering.

"Invested. Gave. It doesn't matter, it still has been two hundred and thirty thousand and we only got about twenty-five thousand in gold."

Nina decided that she had heard enough. Enough to know how to close this deal. "Sorry, guys, are you still there?" Nina's voice boomed through the line.

"Yes, we're still here, Alexis," Carol assured her, sounding relieved.

"Where did you go?" Ed wanted to know. "We thought you hung up."

"I apologize. This is one hell of a phase WMM is now in. And I'm going to give you a tip." They both were on the edge of their seats. "If you guys back out now, you'll be the laughing stock of the company as well as with the other participants. This is *really* big, guys."

"Alexis. We understand, but you don't understand where we are coming from. We've already invested two hundred and thirty thousand dollars," Ed said.

"You're absolutely correct. I don't understand how you could invest two hundred and thirty thousand dollars and now quit. Where's the logic behind that? Stop at two-thirty or invest fifty? Lose the two-thirty or invest another fifty? You guys are scaring me. Have you been drinking this morning or out partying all night? I'm worried about you two. Maybe I should call back tomorrow. Let me put you on hold while I consult with one of the owners. Both of whom happen to be in the office today for this special promotion. Let me figure out how to explain that one of the top contenders are ready to bail out over a measly fifty thousand dollars and that they already invested two hundred and thirty thousand. When I explain that to them I hope they won't disqualify you."

"Oh, noooo!" Carol shrieked.

"Wait, Alexis," Ed chimed in.

"Wait for what, guys? I need to put you on hold. I need a consultation. You guys are obviously not in your right frame of mind."

"Alexis, we're just concerned, that's all. You realize that $50,000 is nothing to sneeze at. We're retired," Ed pleaded.

"That's it. I've had enough. I'm hanging up."

"No. No, wait!" Carol begged. "We're not drunk. We're in our right frame of minds."

"Of course we are not drunk," Ed stated indignantly. "Just give us some time to decide."

"Time? We've been on this phone now for twenty-five minutes. You realize how many other contenders wish they were in your position?" Nina chastised them. "And you need time to decide? They are *hoping* that you back out. More for them."

"Oh my!" Carol gasped.

"How many others are there?" Ed's greed was getting the best of him. Nina was just about convinced that Ed was the biggest gambler of the two.

"On your level? Not many. But it doesn't matter, does it?"

"Yes. Oh yeees. It does," Carol chimed in, sounding as if she was on the brink of an orgasm.

"This is what I'm going to do. I'm going to see if I can find out how many others are on your level. I'm going to put you on hold, and when I come back, you need to tell me whether you guys are in or out. Now you aren't drunk, are you?"

"No. We are not," Ed assured her.

"Good. I could get in trouble if your judgment is impaired while we are trying to handle this serious matter. You need to make up your minds. I have to go down the hall. I should be back in ten minutes."

"Okay, Alexis. We'll be here." That was Carol and she sounded as if she was exasperated.

Nina took the headphones off and pressed the hold button, activating the smooth sounds of the day. Stepping out into the hallway, she saw that Milt's door was cracked so she peeked in. He was just sitting there looking over sales sheets.

"You got a sale?" she asked him while easing into the chair facing his desk.

"Not yet. Crazy Emma said she's going to the bank, but you know I can't count that." He started mocking her in an old lady's voice. "'Mr. Bank Manager, I need a cashier's check for ten thousand dollars.' And I can hear Mr. Bank Manager saying, 'Wait right here while I call your daughter!'"

"Damn, Milt. You better get your ass on that phone and call somebody else." Nina couldn't help but laugh.

"You got a sale?" he asked.

"I got the Bartzes on hold. They were bitching at first, but I believe I broke them down."

"I hear you! How much?"

"Fifty thou."

"I heard that." Milt held his fist out to give her a fist bump.

"Yeah, it's Friday and I'm glad to get away from the offices of WMM."

"What you and your ole man gonna do this weekend?" He wanted to know.

"He wants me to go to some party."

"Oh, yeah? You're going? You don't sound too enthused."

"Hell no. I'm hanging out with the ladies tonight. Plus, I haven't seen him in a while. He hasn't been coming around like he used to. I just call him when I need some maintenance."

"Girl, you need to find you a husband."

"Milt, don't start with that. Is Shawn outta Rinaldo's office yet? I can't wait to get the four-one-one." Shortly after those words left her mouth, Rinaldo barged into Milt's office.

"Alexis and Martin Luther! Lunchtime was hours ago. Why aren't y'all on the phones?"

Nina stood up. "I was just leaving. I got the Bartzes on hold."

He stood over Milt's desk. "Get on the phone, *last place*." He used last place as a nickname for Milt. "You got a sale yet?" he asked him.

"I'm working on it," Milt assured him, as he shuffled his papers around.

"Well work harder." He backed out of his office, slamming the door.

"Alexis, are they going or what?" Rinaldo asked, referring to the Bartzes sending the check.

"How come you call me by my phone name and nobody else?"

"Them lazy bums don't deserve to be called by their phone names. Are the Bartzes going or what?"

"Yeah." Nina sat down and placed the headphones on her head.

"How much?"

"Fifty."

"All righty!" He raised his hand up to high-five her. "At least somebody's working."

"Can you close my door?" She left his hand hanging as she hinted for him to get out of her office.

Ladies Night . . .

Rochelle pulled up to Nina's at ten p.m. in Rinaldo's Hummer. Nina sashayed down the steps and jumped in the front seat. "Why did he have to get gold? No, wait. I don't even know why I asked that dumb question. Gold coins."

"Girl, you know he likes to floss and make sure everyone knows he's the shit. Later for him. But girl, you look fierce. You gonna be stoppin' niggas in their tracks tonight," Rochelle complimented Nina, who had on a simple Derek Lam hookup. A black blouse with a hot red wraparound miniskirt. On her feet were a pair of red Jimmy Choo stilettos.

"Girl, look at you." When Nina gave Rochelle the once-over she didn't know what to say. She was so used to seeing her in suits, but tonight she had on Balenciaga from top to bottom. She knew she saw that shit in a *Vogue* magazine. "I don't even know what to say."

"Say, 'Velvet Room, here we come'. And I hope you ready to party because a bitch is about to let her hair all the way down," Rochelle said with a devious smile on her face.

"Oh shit. That's where we going?" Nina asked in excitement.

"Yes, ma'am."

"Aiight then. Velvet Room, here we come!"

They pulled off, heading for the infamous and upscale Velvet Room. She knew that it was supposed to be one of Atlanta's hottest spots. Nina knew that the athletes and hip-hop stars frequently partied there and hosted special events like birthday celebrations and album release parties. So it was on tonight. When they pulled up as anticipated, the scene was jumping. There was a line but it wasn't too long. But there were many cars pulling into the parking lot. Rochelle was trying to make her way to a parking spot but people were walking all in the street, making it almost impossible to get from one end of the street to the next. Finally Rochelle got the Hummer parked and they headed towards the entrance. The minute they stepped out of the truck, they noticed that bitches were looking them up and down. Nina guessed they would really have an attitude when they realized that they would not be waiting on line with them. Rochelle had pull with the owner so they walked right past the haters and straight up to security. She whispered in the guard's ear and, just like that, proceeded through the velvet ropes.

This was Nina's first time inside the club. She was surprised to see that it was one humongous red velvet room decorated with stunning glass chandeliers. As her stilettos took her across the dance floor, she looked down. She had heard that it was the only liquid nitrogen dance floor in the dirty South. Whatever that meant. It must have meant something because she noticed guys in black and white on point, ready to wipe up any spill or mishap. *Impressive.*

"Mr. Michael Vick to your left, Rochelle." Nina nudged her partner for the evening.

"Petey Pablo to your right," Rochelle teased and nudged Nina right back.

"Who?"

"Don't even try it. Petey muthafuckin' Pablo." They both started laughing.

The sound system and lighting were crazy. Nina was definitely ready to get her party on. There were huge plasma screens all over the place.

"Can I get you ladies a drink?" a good-looking, brown-skinned young brother asked. He was standing at one of the bars with his partner and introduced himself as Vince. His partner said his name was Dante.

Nina and Rochelle looked at each other and simultaneously said, "Sure." They introduced themselves and, while they all stood there, Nina and Rochelle noticed that there were several bars with plenty of arm space for standing there and people watching or catching an eye, and there were also multiple VIP tables with nice off-the-floor or over-the-floor views where they could see or be seen. "We gotta get over there in VIP before the night is over," Rochelle whispered.

"I'm down," Nina said back.

After the drinks started to kick in, the four of them couldn't help but submit to the music. Vince paired up with Nina, Dante with Rochelle, and they danced nonstop for almost an hour. Nina had not danced like this since she had hung out with Reese.

She and Rochelle were dancing back to back. "Gurll, let's take a bathroom break," Rochelle leaned into Nina and yelled over the music.

"One more song!" Nina yelled back.

After Drake and Lil Wayne stopped vibrating, Rochelle grabbed Nina's hand and yanked her off the floor.

"Be right back," she said to Vince. The guys took off for the bar.

"Girl, I gotta rest my feet," Rochelle confessed as they reached the ladies' room and she rushed for the next open stall.

"So do I," Nina agreed as she admired herself in the mirror. "Did you see Mystical out there?"

"Mystical? Who is that?"

"Rochelle, you don't get out much, do you? You know who Petey Pablo is but not Mystical?"

Rochelle barged out of the stall and Nina went in. "The fuck I don't! I just don't know who the fuck Mystical is," she admitted with a straight face as she stood in the mirror getting her fine on.

Everyone in the bathroom started laughing. Nina could only shake her head in embarrassment.

"I see that smirk on your face. Hurry up. We gonna go find us a table far away from Vince and Dante so we could do the girls' night out thing," Rochelle said.

"What's the girls' night out thing?"

"You don't know?" Rochelle shrieked. "Get drunk, flirt and talk shit."

Nina could only laugh. She had no clue that Rochelle was this down-to-earth and so ghetto. They headed out of the bathroom in search of a table. The DJ was introducing a special guest performance by the duo Dirty Money. "Oh shit, it's getting ready to get crunk up in the Velvet Room." Nina was ready to get close up on the live performance but the desperate male groupies in the house along with Rochelle grabbing her arm were not allowing that to happen.

Rochelle spotted an empty table and guided Nina over to it before someone else got it. "I know you ain't tired already?" Nina teased. "I wanted to see Dirty Money perform up close."

"I thought we agreed to get our girls' night out thing on," Rochelle said as she slid into the booth and immediately took out her cell and started scrolling through her text messages.

"Rinaldo blowin' you up?"

"Fuck Rinaldo. I am not thinking about him right now. My side piece is who I'm trying to see." She looked at Nina and saw the surprised look on her face. "What? You thought I was some dumb bitch, didn't you? Hell to the nah. I have my own agenda."

Just then the waitress brought over two more drinks. "Compliments of the gentlemen over there." She pointed behind her.

Nina and Rochelle looked over to where she was pointing. Vince and Dante raised their drinks up for a toast.

"Oh shit. Don't tell me we are going to be joined at the hip with them two stalkers for the rest of the night," Nina groaned.

"That is exactly what it looks like."

"Sooooo... Mrs. Rochelle. Let me get back to you. Don't you have a good thing? Why fuck it up? I mean, Rinaldo's the ultimate asshole but it's like being a hustler's wife. You put up with the bullshit to live the lifestyle. You don't fuck that up. You ride that shit until the wheels fall off."

"Nina, the wheels are wobbling. The lug nuts or whatever you call them are loose. I mean, I thought this was different but you hit the analogy right on the head. I ain't no more than a hustler's wife. And we both know that that shit don't last forever. The only advice I can give you is watch your back and I hope you have been building your nest egg." When Nina didn't respond she said, "Nina, I hope you haven't been falling for his spend, spend, spend mentality."

"Well...yes and no," Nina said before being interrupted by Dante and Vince. They dragged them back onto the dance floor.

"We will continue this conversation," Rochelle yelled over the music.

By two thirty they both were past tipsy and had agreed that it was time to go. Especially since they didn't have a designated driver. Their stalkers for the night walked them to the parking lot and they gave them their numbers and made sure they were safe inside their ride. Nina told Rochelle she owed her another girls' night out, since they actually didn't have one, and the next one would be without them having to be glued to the hip with the same two dudes. She told Rochelle she wanted to dance with *everybody*.

"How the hell you going to dance with *everybody*? Girl, you are drunk. Let me get your ass home," Rochelle said while her phone vibrated. When she saw who it was she said, "Let me take this out here."

"Handle your business," Nina told her as she watched Rochelle get out of the Hummer to talk in private and then immediately began whispering and giggling. Nina cracked both windows in an attempt to hear what was going on when she spotted, a few cars down, a brother with dreads giving a not so subtle beat-down to a dude who was leaning against a motorcycle. It must have been his because he was more into protecting the motorcycle than he was into protecting his face from the blows. Nina rolled her window all the way down.

"I swear, man. I'ma get that for you. Just give me a couple of more days," the dude whined like a bitch.

"Yeah, aiight, you got that, my nigga. But only because I want you to spread the word that I'm that nigga. I'm King Muthafucka. You got that?"

"I got it."

King punched him again. "Wrong answer, nigga."

"I got that, Mr. King. I got it."

Nina smiled. King turned her on. Now, that was her kind of man. You don't fuck with niggas like that. You *fuck* niggas like that. She watched his swag as the King kicked the bike over anyway and disappeared into the darkness.

Now that nigga was intriguing. Was it in the power and command of his voice? Or the way he gave that nigga the beat-down? All Nina knew was that he was someone she needed to meet and get between the sheets.

Rochelle finally jumped back into the Hummer.

"We gotta come back here next weekend. You owe me," Nina told her.

"I was hoping that we went somewhere else. I thought you wanted to dance with *everybody*?" Rochelle started laughing.

Nina started to laugh along with her. "Yeah, *everybody* right here in the Velvet Room. Let's go." Nina thought to herself, *Fuck a dance with everybody. I'm on the prowl for that nigga with the dreads.* The King.

As soon as Shawn pulled into the parking lot of the Waffle House and turned the engine off he lit a blunt. He looked at his Presidential Rolex and saw that he had time. It was damn near four in the morning and in a few hours he was going to politic at breakfast with some magazine distributors. He just about had everything in place. He looked up when he saw the gold Hummer pull up in front of him. He put the blunt out and got out. He leaned up against his Benz as she talked on the phone.

Rochelle finally climbed out of the Hummer, sashayed over to Shawn and gave him a nice and slow tongue kiss. When she noticed Shawn's dick stand at attention, she giggled.

"I told you we should have met at the hotel," she purred.

"You know you set those appointments up with those distributors for later on," Shawn reminded her.

"I only need an hour." She handed him an envelope.

"Sheeit. I need more than that." He squeezed her ass. Then his attention went to the envelope. He opened it up and started counting. "How much is this?"

"It's twelve grand like you asked."

He leaned in to kiss her. "I'll see you tomorrow afternoon, aiight."

"Can't wait."

Shawn jumped into his Benz and pulled off.

Shawn was definitely king.

CHAPTER EIGHT

A BAD HABIT

Nina was still riding high off her ladies' night out with Rochelle and couldn't wait until this Friday. As she cruised down Highway 85 heading to Decatur, she pressed the button to open the sunroof. The air was a little brisk but it felt good. All she wanted to do was go home and wash away the day's stench of WMM.

She pressed 1 on her cell phone to get in touch with Cream. *God I hope he changed his mind about wanting to stop by tonight.*

"Yo...baby?" his voice boomed, instantly killing her good mood.

"What's up, Cream?"

"Tryna make this shit happen. You know how it goes. Where you at?"

"On my way home," Nina said with obvious relief.

"Good. I gotta pay this cat for this studio time. How much can you let me hold?"

Nina frowned as she stared at the phone. "Excuse me?" she snapped.

"I gotta pay Tone for this studio time. I need something to tide me over until next week."

"Cream, you didn't even ask me how I'm doing. How was my day, my week, nothing. Just how much can I let you hold?" She mocked his voice.

"C'mon, baby. Don't be like that."

"Oh, I'm like that. I am so sick and tired of you, the job, and I'm acutally getting sick of the state of Georgia. I'm ready to leave all of this the fuck alone!" She spazzed out.

"Damn, baby. I take it that you had a rough day," Cream said humbly.

Actually it wasn't all that bad. But lately whenever she talked to him, he reminded her of WMM and Rinaldo.

"Rough day? How about month? This cracker has now started fining us a thousand dollars if we're late, and a thousand a day for each day that we don't make a sale. I never thought I would be saying this, but I'm seriously thinking about quitting."

"Quit? Why you wanna quit? Just don't be late. And why are you sweatin' makin' a sale? You make a sale every day. You can't quit. We need the money."

"*We* need the money? Is that all you think about? *We?* I've been doing all the paying! You selfish bastard!"

"Selfish?" Cream let out a chuckle. "I'ma let you have that because when a nigga was hooking you up it was *we* this and *we* that. Now that I need you, you tired. Fuck it. Let's keep it funky. You the one talking about quittin'.

How the fuck do you expect to pay all of your bills? I think you need a reality check. I mean, I hooked you up and shit but I can't take care of you. I ain't gonna take care of you."

"Take care of me? Cream, you never took care of me."

"Shit, you forgot how I was hooking you up? How soon *we* forget. I'm even working on some shit now as we speak, so I need you to stay put."

"So, I gotta stress myself and slave until your ship comes in? You got me fucked up, Cream!"

Click. She hung up.

Nina was pissed off and tired of Cream's schemes and scams, which she didn't understand but in which she was a key player.

She glanced at the constant flashing of the cell phone. Cream was obviously blowing her voice mail up but she was done talking to him for now. Then, on top of that, for the past two months it seemed that every week she was giving him three to ten thousand dollars, plus paying her mortgage, insurance, three car notes, lights, gas, water, food. The list was never ending. And on top of that sending money home to her mom. That was even getting out of control. She was doing good for a minute but then shit just drastically started to plunge downhill.

Nina was actually glad that traffic was backed up for several miles. A typical end of the workday in the ATL. She loved the change of pace from her old stomping grounds of New Jersey. The scenery along the GA highways was exhilarating to her. So many restaurants, hotels, office buildings, she even passed by the General Motors plant. She felt recharged every time she rode the highway. *Fuck New Jersey!* The only reason she would leave Georgia was because of Cream.

Jumping onto 285 heading to Decatur. Nina was almost home. Flat Shoals Parkway was her exit. Atlanta was deemed the new Black Mecca and she was feeling right at home. Turning into her cul-de-sac she waved at the cute little Holway twins, Jillian and Dillan. Nina eased into her driveway and hit the remote control. She wished her kids were here to enjoy all of this space to roam around and play with the neighbors, the Holway twins. Just as quickly as that thought entered her mind, she tossed it out.

"Uhhgg!" she groaned as she saw Cream's truck parked. *This nigga was at my house while talking to me and didn't even say anything.* She shut off the engine and groaned again. Grabbing her purse and getting out of the car she decided to leave the garage door open, hoping that Cream would be on his way out.

When she turned the knob and proceeded to open the door, Cream swung it open, pulling Nina with it. Before she could stand up straight he had her by the throat.

"Why the fuck did you call Diamond? What did you say to her?"

Nina's eyes were squeezed shut as she tried to focus on her breathing.

Watching her face turn dark pink, Cream decided to

let her go. She heaved as if she were just held underwater and was suddenly pulled out. "You faggot!" she said between breaths. "Touch me again and I'ma kill yo' ass!" She snatched up a plant and hurled it at him. "I didn't call that bitch! Why the fuck she keeps calling me? Ask the dumb ho that!" She snatched up a lamp and tossed it at him. "I don't give a fuck about her."

Ducking, he took off for her as she ran into the bathroom, slamming and then locking the door. "Faggot-ass punk!" she screamed.

"Come on out and I'ma show you how much of a faggot I am." He slammed his open palm repeatedly against the door. "Nina, don't play games. Stay away from her."

"I'm not playing games. I don't want her. That's your bitch. You need to check your bitch and tell her I'm not the one cheating, you are." They were having a screaming match, separated by the bathroom door. "And stop coming over here. I don't need you and I don't want you."

"You ain't gonna quit that muthafuckin' job! I got you that job. And I ain't hook you up with it just for you to quit because you had a bad day."

"Fuck you, nigga! Oh, so now it's about the job? First it was about Diamond. Now it's about the job. Make up your damned mind. A few minutes ago you was on the phone sounding all sympathetic and shit. Nigga, you got the characteristics of somebody getting high. Mood swings going from one extreme to the next."

"You can't quit that job," he gritted.

"You are not my father and you are not my man. If I up and leave, then what the fuck? I'm the one who goes in and grinds like hell every day. Not you! You ain't got a pot to piss in. All this shit around here I paid for. I worked hard for. That fuckin' truck you driving is mine. I pay the notes. All them fuckin' clothes in your closet, I bought. I don't need you, Cream. You need *me*, so don't forget that." Nina was now pacing back and forth in the bathroom.

"Fuck you and all this shit! If you quit, I'ma kill you, Nina. I mean that shit," he yelled as he began turning over coffee tables, the love seat and the rest of the furniture. "I'm not going to let you fuck up my plans."

"Kill me? Do it, then, muthafucka!" she challenged through the door. "And fuck your plans! I'm sick of this shit!"

When she heard dishes being thrown around she came out of the bathroom. "Cream! What is the matter with you?" She had no idea where this change of behavior was coming from. She ran towards the kitchen and when she saw the mess he made she wanted to *kill* him.

"You said this shit is more important than me, right?" He held his arms out.

"Cream, I am not your woman. We fuck but that is it. Did you forget that? Now get the fuck out of my house!" She grabbed her bag that held her cell phone. "I'm calling the police." She ran back into the bathroom, locked the door and dialed 911. She tried to be calm as she gave them her name, address and explained to them what was going on. The shit was downright embarrassing. The dispatcher assured her that they were sending someone right away.

She knew this was all her fault and accepted full responsibility. She honestly couldn't be mad at Cream because she knew who he was, what he was about and what he was capable of when she got back with him. Leopards cannot change their spots. It was time for her to move on. Him making good on any one of his threats was a chance that she was willing to take. Dealing with Cream, running from Bloods or fighting a murder case in Jersey—it was all the same to her.

She listened as Cream continued wreaking havoc throughout the house. *Damn, I hope the police show up right in the middle of his madness.* Several minutes later it got quiet. She cracked the bathroom door, peeked out and he kicked it open, knocking her flat on her back.

"That's for calling the po-po on me," he spat, and left.

She remained on the floor, tears streaming down her face, staring up at the ceiling. She didn't get up until five-o rang the doorbell a half an hour later. They took her report, inspected the house, gave her some advice and a subtle warning, and then left.

Before the officers got into their patrol car, that's how fast Nina dialed a locksmith to come change all the locks. She had had it with Cream. It was officially over. She ended up cleaning up the house all night and ignoring the ringing phone. Three hours later, she was finally able to ease into her Jacuzzi filled with hot steaming water and apricot bubbles. So much for a relaxing evening curled up in front of the boob tube watching her *CSI* DVDs and eating kettle corn. That was all she wanted. *Was that asking too much?*

She used her big toe to press the on button activating the water jets. The hard force of the jet streams tickled and massaged her body at the same time. "Ooooooohh," she moaned, sinking deeper into the tub with the intention of dozing off. The dude with dreads—his handsome face popped up, causing a smile to spread across her lips. *Man, I hope I run into him again.* She started fantasizing about being with him. She now had something to look forward to.

Twenty minutes later, a groggy Nina was awakened by the sound of her burglar alarm. She sat erect in the tub, snatching up her washcloth and holding it close to her chest. Her heart was beating at a rapid pace. She quickly reached out and turned off the jet streams. She strained to hear any sounds. A lump was caught in her throat as she was frozen with fear. The alarm company was supposed to have called by now. *What if Cream had called Jersey and got in touch with the Bloods? Surely they had Blood members already in Georgia. What if they had sent some soldiers over to kill her?* Then she heard a series of beeps and the alarm turned itself off. She gasped. The killer has to be a professional to deactivate the alarm. The phone rang. It stopped. The house was eerily silent. *Fuck that!*

Nina got out of the tub and grabbed the gun that she kept at the top of her bathroom closet.

"Dear God, take care of my family and forgive me for of all my sins." She heard footsteps but continued to pray. She cocked her piece, and told herself, *It's either them or me and it damn sure ain't gonna be me. But if so, Lord, please let me go out painless and grant me access to your kingdom.* As the footsteps got closer she held her eyes shut tight. "Forgive me, Lord, for not putting you first in my life." She eased out the bathroom and Cream was coming up the stairs.

"Baby, where you at?" his voice slurred.

Nina had almost lost it. She was sweating and hadn't even realized it. "Nigga, I almost blew your fuckin' head off," she screamed before turning around and going back into the bathroom, slamming the door.

Cream came bursting into the bathroom. He came towards her and swept her up into a tight embrace. Whispering, he asked, "Can you forgive me, baby? You gotta forgive me. I've been under a lot of stress lately. I didn't mean to put my hands on you."

"How did you get in here, Cream?" she screamed, mad because he had scared the shit out of her. Even madder that he was able to get in. She turned around and smacked him across the head with the gun.

"Oow, fuck!" he yelled.

"How did you get in here?"

"The basement. We never got that window fixed."

There goes that fuckin' we again.

Nina sucked her teeth and pushed him away from her, not wanting to believe that she went through all that drama earlier for nothing. She was so disgusted with herself she couldn't even speak. She wrapped a towel around her and was tempted to bash his head to the white meat but instead walked away.

"Why did you change the locks?" He trailed behind her, rubbing his head.

She stopped and faced him. "Your drunken ass better fix my basement window first thing in the morning, nigga." She pushed him aside.

"I will, baby. Do you forgive me?" He spoke to her back because she was now heading towards her bedroom.

Ignoring him, she turned on CNN Headline News and proceeded to lotion her body. Cream plopped onto the bed and watched her. "Baby, I'm sorry, all right?" He stood up and began undressing. She continued to ignore him. "You heard me?" He stood there with his dick peeking out of his boxers.

She sucked her teeth and grabbed the remote control to turn up the volume. Before she could take it off mute, he grabbed her hand.

"Why you ignoring me? Say something." Nina punched him in the face and they began to tussle.

"Let me go, Cream," she yelled. He had pinned her down on the bed.

Looking down on her with a smirk on his face, he said, "I love you, girl."

"Get off of me, Cream."

"You lucky I'm high. But don't think you gonna keep hittin' a nigga."

"Cream, get off of me."

He began kissing her sloppily, holding her wrists together with one hand. With the other hand he began massaging her mound.

"Cream...stop. You are...drunk. Get off of me!" She tried to wiggle away but the shit was now feeling good.

Feeling her cream up only made his dick harder.

"Cream, stop," Nina told him, trying to act as if she wasn't aroused.

"You real creamy for Cream."

"Go fuck Diamond and leave me the hell alone."

"I don't want to fuck her. I want you." He had his dick in his hand and it was right at her opening.

"Cream, nooo," Nina moaned as he eased up inside her. She spread her thighs in surrender and took him all the way in. He grabbed one of her legs and put it over his shoulder and went to fucking her like she owed him. "Oh baby, right there. Keep it right there," Nina moaned.

"Right there?" he teased as he stroked her spot.

"Oh...right there, nigga, yes. You know...how I... yess, baby," she moaned and her eyes rolled to the back of her head and she started cumming. He stroked and dug her out until her body went limp. He turned over on his back and helped her slide down on his fat hard-on.

"You love to ride this dick, don't you?" He began moving nice and slow, squeezing her ass cheeks. "Don't you?" He slapped that ass.

"I love it, Cream," she purred. She glanced in the mirror and a picture of Ted Branson was on the TV screen. She froze. Cream continued to grind into her pussy until he busted a nut.

"Shh! Shh!" Nina hopped off of Cream, snatched up the towel as she moved quickly in front of the TV screen, focusing on the closed-captioning.

BARON, THANKS. THAT WAS BARON ZANDER, OUR CORRESPONDENT FROM FT. WORTH, TX., WHERE HE WAS UNSUCCESSFUL AT GETTING AN INTERVIEW FROM RETIRED ENRON EXECUTIVE TED BRANSON, WHOSE NEPHEW WAS FOUND STRANGLED TO DEATH AND SHOT TWICE IN THE HEAD HERE IN THESE VERY BUSHES AT LAKE LANIER. THIS IS SHELLY KRAMER REPORTING TO YOU LIVE.

"Oh shit! Oh shit! Oh shit!" Nina stammered.

"What the fuck is wrong with you?" Cream asked as he lay there on his back, spent, his dick limp.

"I can't believe they killed him. I can't believe that shit."

"Who killed who?" he lazily inquired.

"All he was doing was checking on his uncle. They didn't have to kill him," she spat.

"Who?"

"Rinaldo. He killed him."

"Who?"

"The man on the news," Nina said, still in shock.

"How do you know?" Cream asked.

"He came to the job last week, and Rinaldo said no one will ever fuck with his money. Never! This fool is now murdering people. This cracker really believes he is straight-up gangsta."

Cream's mind was churning and he sat up. This news was the come-up he needed. "Naw, fuck that cracker. I'm from the streets. You from the streets. We hustlers just like him, and you can't hustle a hustler. Look at me." He grabbed her by her chin. "Keep this shit on the low. Act like you don't know shit. I need you to keep working as usual until I get with some people. Do you understand?"

"Nigga, you done lost your fuckin' mind! That cracker ain't nobody to fuck with. He is obviously connected to something, or somebody, for him to dead that customer and then act like nothing happened," she warned him.

"I'm connected too. Fuck that TV *Soprano* bullshit! I'm just as connected as he is."

"How is that? You ain't got a pot to piss in or a window to throw it out!"

He jumped up off the bed and slapped her. Nina fell onto the bed and Cream pounced on her and grabbed her by her throat, again.

"Girl, did you not hear a word I just said? Did you?" he yelled. She nodded her head yes, trying to blink the tears away. She had seen Cream lose it before, but this was scary. He was acting like her getting and keeping this job was life or death, and that had her spooked.

"I need you to continue working until I figure out how I'm gonna get this cracker for a whole lotta cake. Do you understand me?"

Nina nodded her head vigorously. This fool had undoubtedly lost his mind. If the red flags hadn't gone up before, they were all the way up now and waving. And he thought he was going to use her? *Bullshit.*

"You owe me, bitch. You owe me." He let her go, got up, threw his clothes on and left.

At that moment, she was reminded that he was a bad habit that needed to be dropped.

It was going on eight thirty and Shawn had just parted ways with Rochelle. They had linked up at the Hilton by the airport. Shawn was thinking about how good Rochelle's pussy was and was pleased with how much of a freak she was between the sheets. Rinaldo taught her well. Up until now he still didn't see the attraction between the two. Nevertheless, from what he learned from her, the attraction was there in the beginning. Now it was all about what she could get from him, realizing that it was all a fantasy. Nina was right, she was no more than a hustler's wife.

Shawn was flying down 285 puffing on his blunt filled with chocolate. He had a DJ Kay Slay mix CD in. *Damn.*

I miss New York. He had been in Georgia for so long that whenever he called home they teased him about how country he sounded. Shawn took another pull and turned the music up louder. Mix CDs always put him in the zone. He changed lanes and that's when he saw the flashing lights in his rearview mirror.

"Shit!" he yelled out, not one hundred percent sure that they wanted him to pull over. Just in case, he cracked all of the windows in an attempt to air out the car and kept driving as if they didn't want his ass. When he was sure that they wanted him, he pulled over to the shoulder, stopped and prepared for the worst. He quickly sprayed some air freshener but knew it wasn't going to do shit. What he had just finished smoking was the bomb. *How many more blunts were in the glove compartment?* Sweat beads were forming under his armpits. He turned the CD player off. The two officers finally got out and headed for his vehicle, one brother on each side. Shawn rolled the driver's-side window down.

"License and registration please." The officer turned on his flashlight to scan the front seat, his other hand resting on his pistol.

Shawn reached for his paperwork in the glove compartment. He handed the documents to the officer at his side and they headed back to the squad car. Shawn breathed a sigh of relief that neither one of the brothers said nothing about the weed because he knew that they had to smell it. He anxiously waited for the verdict, and the longer they took to run his info, the more he kept stealing glances at them from the rearview mirror. When they finally got out of the car, they walked towards him as if they were on a mission. He mumbled, "Awwww shit. What did they find on me?"

"Mr. Williams, we need you to step out of the car, please," the officer at his door said. The other one was standing behind him, hand on his weapon, fingers twitching.

"What is the problem?"

The officer ignored Shawn and waited patiently as he got out of the car. "I need you to turn around and place both hands on the hood of the car. You are under arrest."

"Under arrest? Arrest for what?"

The officer jerked Shawn around and smashed him down onto the hood of the car. He patted him down before pulling his hands behind his back and placing the cuffs around them.

"I just asked a simple question. Under arrest for what?" When neither of them responded Shawn started yelling. "Excuse me. Can someone tell me what I'm under arrest for?"

"It looks like nonpayment of child support," the second officer said as he snatched him up and led him to the back of the squad car.

"Now was that so fuckin' hard?" Shawn snapped.

"Don't press your luck," the other officer warned. "We smelled the weed."

"I don't owe no child support," Shawn barked before it

sunk in what he just said about the weed. He then decided to tone it down.

"Take that up with the judge," the arresting officer said. "We're just doing our jobs."

"Ain't that some shit," Shawn mumbled.

By the time Shawn was processed and booked it was one thirty in the morning. He called home and told his girl to gather up every child support payment receipt he ever had and bring them down to the courthouse. He still had to wait until morning to see a judge.

Shawn sat up on the concrete bench all night as he tried in vain to block out the noise, funk and all the other bullshit around him. The young cats kept rapping nonstop. All he needed was a cigarette and he would be fine. He stood up, stretched and then stepped over niggas to get to the toilet to take a piss. It had to be at least six by now and if he didn't get a cigarette soon he was going to fuck somebody up, just because. The fools in the cell with him had everything else but a cigarette. Crack. Coke. PCP. Meth.

He went to the cell door made of steel bars and looked at the clock. He was glad to see that it was even later than he thought it was. *Six fifteen.* He was counting the minutes, fuck that, the *seconds* until he got out of this place. His attention went to the federal agents in a huddle down the hall. Them muthafuckas stood out wherever they were. One of them was puffing on a cigarette. Shawn was so desperate for that nicotine he was feeling delusional. Just as he started to yell at him, their huddle opened up and there was Cream. Nina's people. He did a double take to make sure his eyes were't playing tricks on him. *What the fuck is he doing talking to the feds? And in a county jail at six in the morning? He's not even cuffed. And he's talking to them like they all cool, best buds and shit.*

When Cream happened to look in Shawn's direction he wasn't sure if that was him. But Shawn confirmed it. "What's up, man?" he hollered over to Cream. "Let me get a cigarette."

Cream turned his back and acted as if he didn't see or know him. Then he followed the three federalies down the hall and they were gone.

Damn. Cream workin' with the feds? Do Nina know? If she do, is she working with them or what? That was the question. A hundred red flags were now raised in Shawn's mind. He had to do some strategic planning and thinking. Everybody was a pawn in his mind. To see Cream made getting locked up worthwhile. Something was up and he planned to use it to his advantage. Shawn felt as if he were walking on air as he went back to the bench. He forgot all about his jones for a cancer stick.

Mona was at the courthouse at eight thirty with all of Shawn's receipts. He was not called to see the judge until about noon and he was out of there by noon. He got his car out of the pound and all of his blunts were gone. *Fuckin' cops.*

After Mona gave him a hug she said, "This dude named Ock came up to me and said for you to call him as soon as you get out. He said he got a proposition for you." Mona handed him a piece of paper folded with a number on it.

Just as he suspected, Cream was on some bullshit and now the nigga knew he was busted. He probably never figured that someone close to his girl would catch him talking to the feds. He looked at the number and said, "I'm sure he does. Let's get the fuck outta here."

Shawn met up with Cream at Ruby Tuesday around five thirty. They were seated at the bar eating hot wings and knocking down shots of Remy. Cream stared out across the bar, then pitched his spiel. Shawn listened to everything he had to say...his so-called proposition. Once he was finished Cream got up and left, simple as that. Leaving Shawn with a heavy decision to make.

CHAPTER NINE

THE HOOKUP

All during the week Nina could not stop thinking and fantasizing about the sexy and cocky brother with the dreads. He lifted her spirits every time she thought about him. But then immediately her spirits would take a dive at the possibility of her not seeing him again.

When Friday finally came around Rochelle was sitting in front of Nina's house looking in the mirror on her visor, freshening her lipstick and fingering her hair. Her thick jet-black curls hung loosely all over her head. When she looked up Nina was sashaying down her steps heading towards her car.

When Nina got to the curb all she could do was stop and say, "Dayuum."

Rochelle did her one better. She pressed a button and the passenger door raised up. "What you know about that?" Rochelle teased her.

"I can't even front. I don't know shit about this. The fuckin' Bentley? Rinaldo must be feelin' real guilty to let you drive his baby." Nina was honestly in shock.

"Yup, the Bentley. I told you to stack your dough because that is what he's doing. Y'all making him rich. Don't let the toys fool you."

Nina jumped in and the door slid back down. "We ridin' in style tonight! I need this because I swear I just had the week from hell."

When they pulled up to the Velvet Room they decided to take advantage of valet parking. Hell, after all, they were driving a Bentley. Plus, everybody would undoubtedly know that they were definitely on VIP status. When they stepped out of the Bentley, they took a moment to look each other over to give each other the good ole sign of diva approval.

"Shit tight, right?" Rochelle asked with conceit, knowing damn well that they were looking hotter than they were last Friday.

Rochelle was decked out in Proenza Schouler and Nina in Marc Jacobs. They were working *it* and whatever the *it* was it worked. Because when they approached the entrance, they were ushered right past the long line and led into the club to the VIP area called the Velvet Section. There were a few celebs sitting around chillin'. Even though it was only around ten thirty the club was packed. It was ladies' night and they were undoubtedly in the house. The fellas had to be on cloud nine there were so many different flavors to choose from. The waitress brought over the first set of drinks for Nina and Rochelle compliments of Big Boi from OutKast. The ladies raised their glasses to him in appreciation while trying not to be starstruck.

After the first two drinks, Rochelle was ready to get her party on. Nina sat there constantly scanning the room for Mr. King, disappointed that she hadn't spotted him yet.

"You seem preoccupied tonight. What's the matter?" Rochelle asked her.

"I'm okay."

"Good." Rochelle jumped up and damn near snatched Nina out of the booth. "C'mon, let's get our dance on. That will keep you occupied. Let your hair down."

"My hair is down. Haven't you noticed?" Nina joked and Rochelle laughed.

"Stop talking shit and get your ass up!"

Nina slowly got up and went with the flow. They both hit the dance floor, joining a group of ladies dancing with each other. After about a half hour Nina stopped dancing, went back to the booth and sat down. If she was to be out on the dance floor, she wanted to be dancing with or for *him*. Her mystery man.

She ordered a White Russian and went back to scanning the club, refusing to accept the possiblity that she may not ever see him...again. Her gaze landed on Rochelle, who was tipsy as hell but obviously enjoying herself. She was dancing all wild, acting as if she hadn't been let loose in years. Nina smiled as she went back to sipping on her drink, while wishing she had a joint to go with it. She couldn't believe she was tripping over some nigga she didn't even know, but it was something about him and she could not shake it. Just then Rochelle fell into the booth, damn near crushing her.

"Girl, why are you acting so bougie tonight? What's up?" Rochelle was all in her face.

"Bitch, please. Move over. As a matter of fact, go sit over on your side."

Rochelle started laughing and moved to the seat across from Nina. "Damn, I just want you to lighten up. I invited you out to have a good time. This VIP shit got you twisted. You sittin' over there, pinkie out, sippin' on your little drink, nose all up in the air. Miss Boujwa!"

"Boujwa? There is no such word."

"Well shit, it is now."

They both started laughing. "Rochelle, stay your drunken ass right over there. Ain't nobody trying to act bougie. I'm trying to enjoy my high. There's a time and a place to be wild."

"Be wild? Bitch, from what I see you ain't got no wild side." Rochelle cracked on Nina.

"If you only knew," Nina mumbled.

"Sheeit. Oh, I know. But in case I don't, put your money where your mouth is," Rochelle challenged.

"What's your offer?" Nina sat up, eyebrow raised.

Rochelle recognized that look and knew that she had her. "Now that's what I'm talking about. Loosen your tight ass up."

"C'mon, bitch. Make me an offer."

"All right, all right." Rochelle thought about it for a minute. "Okay. I got it. I bet you won't go up to one of these dudes and grab their dick, and not a quick grab either. You know, the ten-second rule." Rochelle leaned back and stared at Nina, waiting for her response.

"Don't threaten me with a good time. How much? And I see someone right there."

"Five hundred and, oh no, Miss Thing, I get to pick him." Rochelle scanned the room with her arm outstretched and finger pointing. "Let me seeeeeee," she sang. "You thought this shit was gonna be easy. Didn't you? How aboouuuut him. Him right there."

When Nina looked up Rochelle was pointing right at Mr. King. Her eyes almost popped out of her head and her stomach took a dive to her feet. *It's him. Oh my God. He's here. He's here. Oh shit. What are the fuckin' odds of this?*

"Don't get scared now. You was staring me down and all brave and shit a minute ago. What? You thought I was going to pick some little square muthafucka? Or a celebrity? Nah, that would have been too easy. But I hooked you up. He looks like he might be your type. Hurry up. Get a move on. And while you're at it, bring me back the same thing you're drinking. If you get him to buy it, I'll throw in another hundred. But shit, you better hurry up before I keep my money and go get me handful of that dick myself." Rochelle had to smile at that, even though she was serious as a heart attack.

Nina looked at her as if to say, "Bitch, I'll break your arm," before sliding out of the booth. But not before picking up her drink and turning it all the way up.

"C'mon now, we ain't got all night," Rochelle pressed.

"Bitch, I'm going." Nina stood up, adjusted her dress and boldly started walking in King's direction. *What are the fuckin' odds?*

"Yeah! Yeah!" Rochelle shouted in the background, hyping her up even more. "Nina! Nina!" she chanted.

Nina was taking small steps as she kept her eyes glued directly on him. Her intense gaze snagged his attention and she sped up her strut. He looked as if he saw a ghost and now she was about to panic. But luckily the rest of the White Russian kicked in and it heated her up from head to toe. When she got up close to him he was still looking into her eyes. Nina gave him a sexy grin before reaching down and rubbing his dick...nice and slow.

"You better be careful. I don't have him on a leash tonight," he whispered into her ear, causing her to blush. The exchange was electrifying.

She acted as if she didn't hear him and as if she didn't just feel him up, and moved around him and headed for the bar. She stood in line trembling, not believeing what she had just done, as she ordered Rochelle's White Russian.

King came up behind her and pressed his semi-hard dick on her ass. Nina jumped. He put his mouth to her ear and said, "Don't get scared now. I thought you wanted to meet lil' King."

Shit. Ain't nothing little about him. She amused herself
as she then felt his warm hand on her thigh. She stood
frozen in place. Scared to move.

"Now it's my turn." He skillfully slid his hand up her
thigh between her legs and past her thong. His fingers
roamed her neatly shaved pussy and began massaging
her clit. Nina's heart rate rose to the ceiling as she gave in
to what she hoped was going to be a finger fuck.

"Do you make it a habit of going around waking people
out of their sleep? What am I supposed to tell lil' King now
that you done woke him up?" His mouth was pressed to
her ear as he continued massaging her clit, getting her
hotter and wetter. "You feel him? Let me introduce him
to you now that he's fully awake." Then he adjusted her
waist so he would be positioned right between her ass
checks. And continued to assault her clit.

The shit was feeling so good, Nina had to open her legs
a little wider. She was giving him all the room he needed
to get her off. Her nipples began to protrude as his fingers were moving faster and faster over her clit. She knew
that she was on the verge of getting one off, standing
right there at the bar. All of her body weight was leaning
back on him and her pussy began twitching and jumping. She was no longer in control as she closed her eyes,
not caring who saw her or that there was cum oozing
down her thighs. Nina let out a soft moan. King looked
up and saw the bartender staring at them and holding
Nina's drink in his hand. He was apparently impressed by

what was going on with the couple standing right there in front of him.

"I got her drink," King said to the bartender. He wasn't letting her go. As he watched her face in the mirror behind the bar all he could think was what just happened was magical. "You didn't answer me. What do you want to tell him?"

"Tell him to excuse my hands." She leaned forward and grabbed Rochelle's drink and took a sip. She made an attempt to pull away but he wouldn't let her go and she didn't really want him to. What she wanted was for him to lean her over, spread her thighs and put lil' King deep inside of her. "You can move your hand now and thanks for the finger fuck."

"Anytime. Can I get a name?" He slid his hand from between her legs but kept it rested on her thigh. His big dick was still pressed to her ass.

"Nina. Nina Coleman," she told him. "Why were you looking at me as if you saw a ghost?"

"You remind me of someone...a lot."

Nina grabbed a stack of napkins, turned around and faced him, checking out his features, and she was not disappointed. His chocolate skin, she wanted to lick. His sparkling eyes were hard to turn away from, and his defined cheekbones—everything about him told her that, yeah, he was that nigga. That strong nigga who would hold her down under any circumstance. He pulled her close so that she could feel his hard-on up close and personal. His hand slid over her ass. He had a look in his eyes that said, "I will eat your ass up." That made Nina imagine him lifting her up on a barstool, her reaching down and grabbing his hard, long dick and guiding it inside her. She would then wrap her legs around his waist and start riding him as he simultaneously hit her G-spot and rubbed against her clit.

She moaned at the thought. "What would *she* say if this *someone* knew what you do to strange women in clubs and how good you make them feel?"

"Don't worry about what she would say."

He took his time admiring her beautiful skin and luscious breasts. Whatever was playing in the background he began swaying to that beat, firmly holding on to her ass, causing her to grind up against him. Nina's hand eased to his shoulder to hold on as she seductively wound her hips, enjoying lil' King. Before speaking he licked his lips, then said, "A nigga needs to be tasting your juices right about now."

Ooooh. The nigga eats pussy. Nina got chills at the thought. Then she was brought to reality with the thought of him having *someone special* waiting on him. Hell, the good ones always do. With that she broke away from his grip and walked away with a throbbing and wet pussy. Leaving him standing there with cum all over his fingers and his dick standing straight out.

When Nina returned, Rochelle was shocked as hell. "Bitch, no the fuck you didn't! What took you so long? Damn, did you fuck him? I was breaking my damn neck trying to see what was going on."

Nina smiled as she placed her White Russian down in front of her.

"That's what I'm talking about!" She high-fived her. "I can't believe you went through with that shit."

"The pleasure was *all* mines. And I mean that literally," Nina said, fanning herself. "Now give me my money." She held out her hand.

Rochelle went into her Dior clutch bag and pulled out six crispy hundred-dollar bills. She handed them to her one at a time.

King was in the cut watching the whole thing.

"You ain't get that nigga's number?" Rochelle was looking at her like she was slipping.

"Nah. It's all good. He'll find me just like I found him," Nina said with conviction.

"Oh bitch, there you go with all that conceited and boojie shit."

"Sheeeiit, I ain't conceited. I'm convinced."

When Nina got home in the wee hours of the morning, Cream was waiting for her. When he asked her where she'd been, she told him. He started tripping about her hanging out all night at what he said was a strip club. Then he started accusing her of stripping. She simply tuned him out. She had just made her fantasy a reality and she was not about to let him ruin it. Nina got undressed, then went into the bathroom. She locked the door and took a nice hot bubble bath, letting the thoughts of big and lil' King take her away.

*   *   *

"Rochellllllle," Nina whined. "I didn't get his number. I could just kill myself." She groaned, not wanting to believe that she was sweatin' a nigga like this and calling the boss's wife at home. *Damn. Will I ever get a man of my own?* Reflecting on the answer to that question drove Nina's spirits down to the ground.

"Look, Nina. Cheer the fuck up. If the nigga was all into you like you into him, you will run into him again. You will just have to go back to the club every Friday night until you do. I told you to get his number." Rochelle started laughing. "I'm sure he'll be there sooner or later. But I won't be able to hang with you this weekend."

"Why not?" Nina asked in disappointment. "Mr. Asshole ain't going to let you?"

"No. He claims he is going to be home all weekend. But we shall see. I'll let you know. Now get off my line and go do something to lift your spirits." She tried to hurry Nina off the phone.

"I am. I'm getting ready to check the one o'clock movie schedule. I can take a hint. I know when I'm getting kicked off the phone." Nina hung up but couldn't help but smile. She looked at the movie section of the Sunday paper. There were several new flicks that she wanted to see so she put on her sneakers, grabbed her purse and was out the door.

There was a new theater that just popped up over in Lithonia and Nina was behind on her movie watching so she said, "What the hell." Instead of moping around an empty house, on yet another Sunday, she figured she might as well get out and enjoy the day. Plus, she hadn't seen *Why Did I Get Married Too?* or *Karate Kid.* Maybe she would see them both.

When Nina pulled into the parking lot she was shocked at the sight of all the people standing outside and inside the theater. She figured that everybody had delcared Sunday afternoon as movie day. Plus, it was beautiful outside. It was sunny and at least seventy degrees. She still couldn't make up her mind on which movie to see, so she bought a ticket for each and then got in line to buy popcorn, lemonade and her favorite candy, Raisinets.

What she didn't know was that King was standing in the cut watching her every move. He took the opportunity to admire her ass in those tight jeans and smiled at the pair of tiny Gucci sneakers on her feet. Her small frame matched Kyra's to a tee. But *damn.* He thought that he was the only one who came to the movies by himself. Was she with somebody? He scanned his surroundings to see if somebody looked as if they were posted up or waiting for her. He didn't see anyone and she wasn't looking around or at her watch as if she was anticipating some company. He hoped she wasn't.

Friday night at the club, after he played in her pussy the scent that was left on his fingers was intoxicating. It was so sweet he vowed that he would never wash that hand again. Then when he realized that he didn't get her number he could have kicked himself, especially when he went to find her and she had already left the club. He wasn't too worried because, worst-case scenario, if he had to he would get his boy that worked in security to pull the videotapes that covered the parking lot. That way he could at least get a license plate number. But shit, put all that to the side because today was his lucky day.

After Nina paid for her snacks he watched her disappear into the *Married Too* theater. His ticket was for *Karate Kid* so he went and bought another one. He made his way to the back of the theater and sat down. When his eyes adjusted he scanned the room for her. She was not getting away from him. *Not this time*. When he spotted her she was still sitting by herself.

He got up and moved to the row behind her. As soon as the previews finished and the lights went off he took the opportunity to lean up and whisper in her ear. "When am I going to get my share?" He was referring to the money he saw her collect from Rochelle the other night at the Velvet Room.

Nina abruptly turned around and saw that it was *him*. The man who she had been stressing over for the past thirty-six hours. He was sitting right behind her. She smiled to herself and mouthed "Thank you, God." In her mind she was doing cartwheels. After she calmed herself down she turned slightly and said flirtatiously, "Whatever it is you want, I'm quite sure I can't give it to you from back there."

"Well you met him. He specializes in reaching a little sumthin' sumthin' from the back." He flirted right back.

The mere thought of his big dick hittin' it from the back made her coochie tingle. "That may be true, but some things are best done from the front, real close and slow." Nina was enjoying their little wordplay and getting hot at the same time.

"Aiight now. I'ma come up there, but don't hold me responsible when you get *a...dick...ted.*" He stood up, climbed over the seat and sat next to her.

"Don't hold me responsible if you get pussy whipped," Nina teased. Their flirtatious banter went on for almost a half hour, turning them both on and causing them to forget that they were there to watch the movie and ended up in the parking lot.

She looked up at him.

"Why do you look at me like that?"

"Like what?"

"It's not lustful or anything, it's like...I don't know. Like you are looking at a long-lost lover."

Damn. She's right on point with that assessment. "I'll tell you about that when the time is right. But let me ask you something. I can tell by the way you talk that you are not from here. Where are you from?" King asked, trying to lead her away from Kyra.

"I'm a Jersey girl. Born and raised."

Damn. So was Kyra. "Then what brings you all the way to GA?"

The smile on Nina's face slowly faded. Nina took a deep breath and said, "I was in a desperate need of a change of atmosphere. And when my brother and best friend were killed, that was the straw that broke the camel's back. Soooooo, I packed up all my things and was GA bound."

"Damn. I'm sorry to hear that. Violence these days is the order of the day."

"Tell me about it. Now, I just do all I can to let the past go and not let it dictate my future."

"I heard that. What do you do for a living? The clothes and jewelry you wear ain't the small shit. Is that all you or is there some nigga that I need to be competing with?"

"I work my ass off. This is all me. But mainly I'm trying to stack my paper, go back, get my kids and live happily ever after," Nina said as if she was reading a fairy tale.

"Wow. You have little ones you left behind? That takes guts."

"It was hard but thank God my mom is holding on to them for me. Even though she was never there for me, she is there for my kids and for that I'm grateful. I send her money and everything but I know it is long overdue and time for me to put my family back together."

"I hear you. You come off to me as a strong-ass woman."

"I don't know about all that. I have just been surviving and playing the hell out of the cards I have been dealt. So that's my story. Now what's yours? Your accent doesn't scream, 'I'm from the South.'"

"I'm not. I'm from the West Coast. I too needed a change of atmosphere."

"Well, how long have you been around here?"

"Long enough to run into you."

"Okay, Mr. Very Vague. Why are you being so stingy with the information?"

"I'm not being stingy. I'm trying to get *into* you. Later for me."

"What do you think I'm trying to do? A nigga done played all up under my skirt and I can't ask where he is from and what's he doing here? You done pulled me out of my movie, got me all hot and bothered and I don't even know your name."

He flashed that gangsta smile. "My bad. I'm Rick, you met lil' King and *we* want to take you out tonight. Can I have your number? You had my head so fucked up that I let you get away from me the other night. But not this time." He passed her his phone. "Put your number in here." Nina did and passed it back. She pulled out hers and asked for his number. She wasn't allowing him to get away neither.

"Can I call this number anytime or is there some bitch that *I* have to compete with?" Nina was trying to fish for the same info he was after earlier.

"Ma, you gots no competition."

Nina figured she would let that go for now. "Okay, soooo... now what?" she pressed him.

"Let me pick you up later on."

"To go where?"

"I got that. Just be ready around seven. I'll call you and get the address when I'm on my way."

"There you go being all vague again. So how do I dress?"

"It doesn't matter. Just don't wear a skirt. Me or lil' King might not be such nice gentlemen as we were the other night."

Shit. I might not want y'all to be nice gentlemen. I ain't had no different dick since Reese and that was almost two years ago. And Cream was no longer puttin' it in. Nina didn't respond out loud to his come-on. "All right. I'll catch *y'all* later." And she went to her ride.

At seven o'clock sharp, Rick pulled up in front of Nina's condo and called her. "I'm out front. You ready?" he asked in anticipation. He was actually very excited to be taking her out.

"I'll be right out."

Several minutes later she came out and locked the door. A smirk appeared across his mouth as he watched her slowly come down the stairs. She had on a pair of tan stilettos, a tan miniskirt and a sheer white blouse. Rick was drooling at the mouth. *Oh, she really wants to try a nigga.* He got out, went around and opened the door to his pearl-white Escalade and watched her get in.

When he got in the driver's seat, Nina had started to ask him what's up with the smirk on his face but changed her mind. She had a feeling it was because she had on a short-ass skirt, fuck-me stilettos and a see-through blouse. Yeah, she was sending a message.

"So, where are we going, Mr. Vague?"

"You better stop calling me that."

"Not until you fill in the blanks. Now, where are we going?"

"Since it was my fault that you missed your movie, I'm taking you to the drive-in." He glanced over at her creamy thighs and thought, *Damn, I can't wait to get in between those.*

"Oooh, nice move. You get some cool points for that because I haven't been to a drive-in since I was a kid." Then she frowned. "But I have on stilettos."

"You won't have them on long." He flashed a real slick grin. He saw her blush. "Don't worry about it, I got you. I packed us a picnic basket with everything that we'll need."

"I'm not worried I'm just trying to protect my eight-hundred-dollar shoes." She laughed. "All I remember about drive-ins are the rocks on the ground, the hot dogs and cheap-tasting popcorn. Have you ever walked in stilettos over a sea of rocks?"

"Can't say that I have. But don't worry about that. I told you I got you." When they arrived, they were pleased to see that *Karate Kid, Why Did I Get Married Too?* and *Salt* were playing.

Rick found a spot to park. With the back of the truck to the screen. He got out and flipped the last row down, then proceeded to get everything situated. When he was done he then headed to Nina's side. Nina watched as he walked around to her. He opened her door and reached for her hand, then he lifted Nina from the front seat and put her in the back, where he had a blanket, pillows and a picnic basket that opened up to a little tray. He had brought sandwiches, snacks and a bottle of wine.

Nina started giggling.

"What's so funny?"

"You must be a professional drive-in attendee."

"Oh, so you got jokes?" He got in and shut the door. He grabbed a little travel bag, opened it and took out a joint. He lit it, took a few pulls before passing it to her. After she took a few pulls and passed it back he put it out. "That's all you need of this here." He slid next to her and took a minute to admire her fineness. He loved what he saw. Her petite frame was just like Kyra's, and her curves were in all the right places. She was beautiful, and as an added bonus she had the body to match. Now he had to get into her mind. He was lost in thought.

She had kicked off the stilettos.

"I told you, you wouldn't have them on long," he teased.

"Whatever. You are looking as if you like what you see."

"I do. But I told you if you wore a skirt me and lil' King might be tempted to get *into* something." He leaned over and lightly brushed his lips against her neck. Nina melted. "Why are you around here tempting a brother? You know we ain't got no discipline when it comes to a beautiful woman."

"Did the thought ever occur to you that maybe I might want y'all to *get up and into* something?" she purred, and lil' King jumped.

"I think he heard that. The thought did occur but I didn't want to assume anything." He took her hand and placed it on the head of his dick.

She rubbed it and then rubbed the length of him and it got harder. "Oh, he heard me...loud and clear." She kept rubbing him and he stretched all the way out. Her pussy was on fire and the only thing that would put out the fire would be some good, long and hard fucking. Fuck being a lady and not giving it up on the first date. She needed to be fucked and she was getting ready to take lil' King for a test-drive. Just then his lips met hers for the very first time. She felt his strong hands grab her and lift her up onto his lap as their tongues continued to slow dance. His hands slid her skirt up over her ass as he squeezed and rubbed on her juicy cheeks.

"Baby girl, I'm about to nutt. If you gonna ride you better hop on." Nina slid back, giving him enough room to whip his damager out. He slid his jeans and boxers down in one move.

Nina looked down and saw that he was throbbing. Precum was oozing out. She rose up, he slid her thong to the side and guided her onto the head. Nina contracted her pussy muscles and squeezed it before sliding down a couple of inches and then sliding back up to the head. That was her favorite teaser. She did that same move again and Rick groaned as he damn near tore open her blouse. He had been anticipating sucking on her breasts and nipples. He wanted to swallow them whole.

Nina then slid all the way down his dick and went to riding him hard. She took charge as she bounced up and down, around and around, trying to find her spot. Before she could find it, Rick did and began hittin' it and hittin' it. She leaned back, squeezed her eyes shut and grabbed on to the back of the seat as he held her down and gave her the fuck that she needed and was hoping to get, hittin' her spot, going in deep as he could as his face was smothered between her breasts. If anyone was looking at the truck, it was rocking.

When Nina felt that first contraction, she grabbed on to the ceiling as if she could climb away. He held her tighter and got his grind and fuck on as she started cumming. Her pussy muscles were massaging the length of his dick in all the right places. He grunted and came right behind her. She was limp as a wet noodle as he lifted her off him. All she could do was lie back against the window. Her legs were spread and Rick couldn't resist the urge to lean over and give her some head.

"No, wait," she whispered. Her pussy was still sensitive and still twitching and popping from that monster orgasm. "Oh God. No, Rick."

His tongue was already sucking and licking on her clit. Her pussy tasted good and she unwillingly began grinding into his face. When she started coming again, he didn't let up until she forced him away.

CHAPTER TEN

THE NEXT LEVEL

Houser was sitting in his office with his partners, Agents Radcliff and Parker, flanking him on his right. On his left were four FBI agents: Melissa Korn, his brother-in-law T.J. Rhodes, and Detectives Rick Brown and Bill Graveney. This was the team spearheading the WMM case.

The room was silent because T.J. Rhodes had come and done what he said he was going to do. He had just told Houser in a way that was impossible to not understand, to back off of WMM. He had heard about the little stunt he pulled with calling the girl down to the headquarters. He couldn't chance his two-year case getting botched at this late stage in the game. And especially not by some damn local agency like the GBI. Houser had always been jealous of him, just because *he* wasn't FBI material.

"Botched? What do you mean botched? I've been doing investigations when you were still wet behind the ears." Houser's face was beet red.

"You want me to use another word? Are you familiar

with ruined? Bundled? Fucked up? Houser, when we move in to make the arrests, I'll be sure to extend some courtesy and make sure you guys are there. But Danny, we got it from here. You calling Miss Coles down here could have jeopardized the whole operation. We've been on this for too long. We—"

"If it wasn't for me, you wouldn't have known anything about WMM, T.J. How dare you come into my office and discredit what me and my colleagues have done. Hell, if it wasn't for us, your ass wouldn't even have a case. You lazy sons of bitches!" Houser spat.

"I'll ignore that last comment, but Danny, we are not trying to discredit you. I was only informing you personally to fall back. The bureau has it from here. I figure I would do it informally to save you some embarrassment. Hell, you oughta thank me for that."

T.J. then headed towards the exit. He held out his hand, offering Radcliff a handshake. Radcliff just looked down at it. He went to Parker, and Parker did the same thing. When he stood directly in front of Houser, the GBI agent hauled back and punched T.J. square in the face, spinning him around and causing him to fall back into Detective Brown's arms.

Before Houser could get off another punch, Radcliff and Parker rushed over to subdue their boss, while Detectives Brown and Graveney sudued theirs.

I don't believe this shit, Detective Brown thought. "C'mon, Rhodes. What's gotten into you? Y'all muthafuckas talking about how professional y'all are. I can't tell. Why are we even wasting our time explaining shit to these punk-ass muthafuckas?" Brown asked him. "If you ask me, this was a waste of goddamned time. We run this shit. We outrank these low-level muthafuckas. He was the newest member on this team and was very rough around the edges. He had been transferred from California, where he was the ruler among his elements: gangs, drugs, drug dealers and beautiful women. And where he also almost lost his life on many different occasions. He felt that he didn't lose his life physically, but he did lose a young lady that he actually fell in love with and he left behind a new friend who reminded him of his brother. The force faked his death just to get him transferred against his wishes. He hated the South and he hired an attorney to get him back to Cali. So far he was on his second appeal. He was fighting it because he left his mother in California, and she refused to move. Slow-ass Georgia was the last place he wanted to be. Now here this fool was getting ready to fuck up the investigation just because he didn't like his brother-in-law. *Country-ass muthafuckas.*

His thoughts went to Cali. Damn he missed the West Coast. Kyra. Why couldn't she leave that dope fiend mutha-fucka alone? Why did she have to go play captain save-a-nigga? He thought about the day she had snuck away and met him at his mother's house. He was deep inside of her looking into her eyes and was telling her how much he wanted her.

"Kyra." He stroked her slow and deep. "Tell me you want me as much as I want you, baby." He felt her nails dig into his back "Rick, don't do this now. Let me enjoy this, please."

He was deep inside the pussy. It was hot and moist and he had never felt like this before, not even with his wife. "Kyra, let's go. Pack your shit and the baby and let's go."

"Rick," Kyra moaned. All she needed was to enjoy this moment and get a nutt. When she was with him she didn't want to think about anything else.

"Kyra." He could feel that he was losing her. "All you gotta do is say yes." He slid his dick out and went to sucking on her nipples.

"Baby, no. Don't do this right now." Tears were streaming down her cheeks. "I need a little more time. I want to give him one more chance, like he gave me. That's the least I can do."

He let her nipple go with one last kiss and rolled off her to allow what she just said to sink in.

Kyra went that next night to save her marriage, to save her dope fiend husband and got her brains blown out.

The killers had caught Rick, who had been following her that whole day. They caught him slipping and he was unable to save her. Next thing he knew he woke up in a trunk. He wished to this day that he was gone instead of Kyra. He couldn't wait until the time was right to go back to Cali and kill all of those muthafuckas, including her dope fiend–ass husband.

He led Rhodes quietly out of the building. He could hear Graveney and Korn behind him snickering. They had won the bet. They already knew that once T.J. got in there with Houser, sparks would fly. Plus the female agent, Korn, was admiring Detective Brown's ass. He was the new kid on the block and all the women had their bets in on who would get to fuck the brother with the dreads first. He was the topic of watercooler conversation and even the white chicks were on him. The sisters were trying to play it cool but shit was getting ready to get ugly if he didn't choose somebody soon.

"No need to apologize," Brown said to Rhodes as he started the car.

"Apologize for what? Me going off has nothing to do with the investigation," Rhodes told him.

"The fuck it don't! Your family in there could blow this thing intentionally if he wants to. All he has to do is gather a team and pay WMM a visit, make a phone call or send the media over there or anything. I'm sure he could get creative, if it means fucking your day up. Damn, y'all some stupid muthafuckas." Detective Brown spoke freely, not giving a fuck.

"He's right, T.J.," Graveney added.

"Y'all know that's bullshit. Rinaldo is not going to up and shut down his whole operation because of the media or fuckin' GBI. His operation is too sophisticated." T.J. started coughing. Once he started up it took him forever to stop. Rick made a mental note to get a TB test.

"He's right, Rick. It's going to take a lot more than the GBI to move Rinaldo. It's been two years. I say we go ahead and move on in, just to be sure," Korn added. She was upset with Rhodes as well. She had been on WMM with him since day one.

It was Tuesday morning and everyone was seated in Rinaldo's office for his staff meeting. He and Shawn were going at it because he fined him a thousand dollars for missing work. Shawn kept telling him that he was in court for child support but Rinaldo wasn't trying to hear it. Now he had turned his attention on Nina.

"Well damn, Alexis, what's the deal with you? Is it that time of the month?" Rinaldo asked and all eyes turned on her. "You look stressed and you're very quiet. You usually have something to say, and you usually are focused at these meetings." Rinaldo looked her over.

"Yeah, I'm bleeding, muthafucka, so what? Are you my gynecologist now?" she snapped.

"Well excuse the fuck out of me. I hope that bitchiness gets me some money today." Rinaldo looked over at her and then continued with his sales meeting.

He began reading some passages out of a book Michael Jordan wrote on being the best. He closed the book, set it aside and stood up.

"All you muthafuckas need to wake up, step up and make the most of this opportunity. Every one of you has obviously gotten too comfortable. If I were y'all, I'd be pounding on these phones trying to make as much money as I could. Y'all don't know how long this shit is going to last."

"What are you saying, man?" Milt wanted to know.

"I said it! If I were y'all, I'd be trying to make as much money as I could. I mean, let's face it. There is no place as sweet as this, where you can make this kind of money, every week and do it legally. Hell, y'all pull in more than some of these rap stars Shawn wants to be like."

"Y'all see that he got something personal against me, right? I'm over here minding my own business. Why you gotta always single me out, man? For your information, I ain't tryna be no damn rap star. I'm launching a hip-hop magazine and I'm doing it with your money. Get that shit straight."

Rinaldo waved Shawn off. "Listen, y'all, I ain't going nowhere, I'ma be here. But shit, I could drop dead tomorrow. Then like a flash this would be over for everybody. I'm expecting a hundred grand from every one of y'all by Friday. This meeting is adjourned."

He pressed the intercom button and yelled, "Deanna, you heard from Simeon yet?"

"Not yet," she sang.

Rinaldo looked at his watch. "Damn. It's nine ten. Looks like he's on one of his crack binges. Y'all get on them phones. I'ma have to go babysit the beginning salespeople."

Shawn smirked. "Are you gonna fine *him*?"

"Or give away *his* clients?" Nina chimed in.

"I got this," Rinaldo said as he put on his suit jacket. "Let's go!" He held his office door open for the Platinum Sales Team. "Make a sale!" he yelled into each one of their faces as they glided past him.

"Man, go 'head with that," Shawn snapped.

"You the only muthafucka that got something smart to say. And you'll probably be the only mutherfucka that don't make a sale," Rinaldo screamed at Shawn.

"Whatever, man." Shawn nonchalantly waved him off.

Rinaldo headed to the back of the building to babysit the beginners while Nina and Milt headed to Shawn's office and shut the door. These three had to have a meeting.

"You hear that shit?" Milt spoke in hushed tones.

"Something's up. I don't know what the fuck it is, but something's going down, in the Keys or here. I just know something's up, talking about make all the money we can make. What kinda shit is that?" Shawn spoke with conviction and as if he already knew something.

"I know the deal. But y'all can't say shit!" Nina warned, giving both of them a serious look.

"Spill it, girl. You should have said something," Shawn told her. "Have us all hemmed the fuck up. What's up?"

"Rinaldo said if I told anybody he was going to kill me."

"C'mon, Nina. He told you that? He had to be joking," Milt stated, sure that Nina was overexaggerating.

"Joking? Ask Mr. Branson's nephew. Rinaldo said no one or no thing is gonna come between his money. And he's dead. Found in a wooded area of Lake Lanier strangled to death and two bullets to the dome. Don't y'all watch the news or read the newspapers? He was just here a few weeks ago and Rinaldo took the Branson file from me and gave me specific instructions not to call him. So no, I'm not joking."

Both Milt and Shawn were speechless. The only sounds were the distant ringing of the phone lines in the receptionist area.

"Damn!" Shawn finally exclaimed. "Are you sure?"

"Yeah, Nina, you talkin' about murder," Milt said, playing the interrogator. "You have to be sure. How do you know?"

"Cmon, y'all, the signs are pointing towards him. Y'all ignore the signs if you want to, but I got something y'all can't ignore." Nina stood up and placed a hand on her hip. "We're under investigation."

Shawn just stared in space repeating, "I knew something was up." *But is she down with Akil?*

Milt said, "Well, I'll be damned."

"Yeah...and I know because the GBI hauled me into their offices. They played tapes and the whole nine. They tried to scare me up and told me to cooperate or else."

"What!" Shawn stood up, knocking his chair backwards. "And you're just now telling us? What the fuck?" He paced back and forth, slamming his fist into the palm of his other hand. "I ain't going to prison for nobody, man."

"Calm down, money. Don't jump to conclusions." Milt

made a feeble attempt at trying to calm him down. "Nina, you should have told us about this."

"I don't know why the fuck y'all surprised. This ain't exactly the post office we are working for. I'll talk to y'all later. I hear his keys!" Nina and Milt hurried to their offices and jumped on the phones. Rinaldo unlocked his office, set some files on his desk, returned to the hallway, locked his door and began to make his rounds. He peeked in Shawn's office, Milt's, Pete's, Jeff's and Nina's. Everyone was on the phone working as he headed back to babysitting the beginning salespeople.

When they felt the coast was clear Nina and Milt dashed back to Shawn's office.

"Nina, tell us what the fuck is going on? Did you make a deal with them or what? Did they ask about me?" Shawn was up in Nina's face trying to see if she was going to lie. She pushed him out of her face.

"Shawn, calm down, we aren't doing anything wrong. This is a legitimate place of business." Milt was doing his best to assure them that they had nothing to worry about. "All we do is come to work, clock in, do our jobs, clock out and go home. On Fridays, we pick up our check. So being under investigation, I wouldn't worry about it. We aren't doing anything wrong."

"Bullshit, man!" Shawn bellowed. "These crackers paying us in cash, what you talking about a paycheck? The clients complain and shit about not getting enough gold. We make the client a business owner, even though they don't have a business. I keep telling him he has to give the clients more. Nothing to worry about? He is so fuckin' greedy and his greed's gonna take all of us down. And how do the GBI know so much? Who the fuck is they anyway? That fuckin' Jeff! I told Rinaldo, dude was hot! I felt that shit!"

Milt and Nina couldn't say anything.

"We going down, y'all," Nina concluded. "We don't know how long they've been investigating, how many tapes they got, how many inside snitches are coming in here every day. And the worst part is, we can't up and quit. We are in too deep. It's too late to walk away. How much money y'all got saved?" When no one answered, she said, "He has us right where he wants us."

The next morning it was clear to everybody that Rinaldo was up to something as he herded the Platinum Pros into his office. "We are going to have to make this morning's sales meeting quick. My crackhead sales manager is somewhere still sucking on that glass dick, so I gots to do his job again today. He took home about six grand last Friday. So I should have known then his ass would be smoking until all the money was gone. What can I say? Anyway, for yesterday, on a Monday everybody did well except for Pete. Loopy Pete, what the fuck is this baby forty-five-hundred-dollar sale? Even lazy-ass Shawn got a sale bigger than that!"

"Can you believe this guy?" Shawn looked around the room. "See. Here he goes again. Why you gotta always use me as an example?"

"'Cause you lazy, man. I expect so much more from you. You got the skills."

"And what's the matter with forty-five hundred dollars?" Pete feigned shock. "It's something."

"Loopy, you far away from a hundred grand. Oh, what, you forgot the goal? You're ninety-five grand short," Rinaldo snapped.

"It's only Monday, man, and watch that Loopy shit!" Pete growled.

"Monday my ass. It's Tuesday. You so looped you don't even know what day it is. Anyway, good job for the rest of the crew. I'm up front working the shit out of the beginners. I'm generating some really nice leads for y'all. But listen up. We're about to take this to another level. Y'all down or what?" Rinaldo leaned back into his chair.

Jeff shrugged his shoulders. Everyone else just stared blankly, anticipating what good ole Rinaldo had up his sleeves this time.

Milt asked, "What do you mean?"

"Well, you know how some of you have clients that are lonely, horny, bored and all that shit?"

Nina had a frown on her face. "And?"

"Well," Rinaldo continued, "they'll be able to use our services. We will be very accommodating. Of course, for a fee that is. And a very hefty one." Rinaldo rubbed his hands together greedily. "For example, Nina. Mr. Cohen has been trying to get you to visit for how long? Well for twenty thousand dollars his dream can come true!"

Rinaldo stated with conviction, obviously quite pleased with his new program.

"What?" Nina was looking at Rinaldo as if he just sprouted another head.

"You can finally go and see him and check out the old man behind the voice and the owner of all that money." He was hoping to entice her to go.

"Finally go? What the fuck are you talking about? You done really lost your mind for real now. I ain't trying to go and see none of these fucking clients," Nina snapped. "You got me fucked up."

"Why not? Twenty grand, that's a lot of cash!" Rinaldo couldn't believe that she wasn't jumping for joy and embracing his new scheme as he was expecting her to.

"Twenty grand for who? I can make more than that over the phone. Then how much of that do you keep? I ain't no fuckin' ho. You not about to pimp me out," Nina rattled off.

"Nina. Now you know I would not insult you like that. I am not calling you a ho. I would never disrespect you like that. I'm just trying to put more money into your pockets."

"And your pockets," Nina shot back. "You better send some of them chickens you got working in the back. Or better yet, you want somebody to sell some pussy, tell your wife to do it." Everyone started snickering.

"Those are *your* clients, Alexis. How we gonna send somebody they don't know. These clients have been sending you their money. They know *you*," Rinaldo pressed.

"Oh shit!" Nina gasped in disbelief. "You *are* seriously crazy. These old white men think that they are talking to a young white girl. I sound like a white Yankee over the phone. I can see me ringing the doorbell and saying, 'Hi, I'm Alexis, your sales rep from WMM.' I'ma either get shot or somebody's gonna drop dead."

The whole room erupted into laughter. "Man, you can't be serious, can you? That *is* rather dangerous," Milt, the levelheaded one, stated. "You know if these old-timers knew they were sending all of this money to somebody black, they would fall into cardiac arrest."

"Martin Luther, you mean to tell me if old lady Lipscoe wanted a date with you for twenty grand, and thirty if you lay the pipe down, you wouldn't take it?" Rinaldo challenged.

"Ewwww," everyone blurted out. They all were disgusted at the thought of old lady Lipscoe—who was old, shriveled up and looked like the Crypt Keeper—naked and legs spread. But she was crazy about Milt. She sent him gifts, flowers and pictures of herself on the first of every month.

"Hell, thirty grand? I'd honestly have to think about that. That would cover several semesters." The whole room erupted into more laughter.

"See, that's what I'm saying. This is a huge untapped market. One of your clients might want to go dancing, one may want to go to dinner, and some just want to meet you in person. They are lonely and need some excitement in their lives. And we are gonna give it to them. It ain't about the color anymore."

"Man, outta twenty grand how much do you keep?" Milt wanted to know.

Nina did a double take when Milt asked that. She couldn't believe that he was actually contemplating Rinaldo's crazy-ass scheme.

"The twenty grand is yours except for twenty percent. Plus, we charge an extra ten, fifteen percent for setup-slash-administrative fees, but in return you can get a bald-headed blow job."

"A what?" everybody said in unison.

"Damn, y'all dumb. You never had your dick sucked by a bitch with no teeth?" Rinaldo cracked up at his own joke. "Okay, okay, seriously. Twenty grand for a weekend. Straight up."

That got a bunch of "ooh"s and "uh-huh"s out of the room. Except from Nina.

"That's crackhead money to me," she snapped. "I ain't no crackhead ho."

"But understand, people, what was just said in this office, stays in this office because this is only for my Platinum sales force to participate in. Travel can only take place on weekends. I need y'all here during the week to work those phones. And this is a package deal. Meaning, if you are a Platinum Team member you are expected to be here Monday through Friday working the phones. If you are a Platinum Team member you are expected to take these weekend assignments as they come. Being a Platinum Team member, the seven-day workweek is now a mandatory package."

"Mandatory?" Nina screeched.

"C'mon, money," Milt added.

"Man, you crazy," Shawn barked.

"Mandatory!" Rinaldo said with pride. "Whoever doesn't want to take part in this opportunity of expanding their pockets as well as the company's, maybe they should go back with the beginning sales force." Rinaldo issued the obvious but subtle threat.

"Now who's in?" Rinaldo passed out celebratory cigars. Nina got up and walked out.

CHAPTER ELEVEN

IT'S ALL ABOUT THE BENJAMINS

Cream was waiting on the porch with a bouquet of roses when Nina pulled up in front of the house. He motioned for her to stop in the driveway instead of going into the garage. She rolled her eyes at him, turned the engine off, grabbed her purse and a container of food from Yasin's and stepped out of the car.

"Hey. I've missed you and I figured we could go out to eat tonight. These are for you." He held out the roses for her. She looked at them, then at him, and went into the house. He followed her.

"You choke me twice, threaten me to keep a job that I hate and then show up here and expect me to accept your cheap-ass roses and go out to dinner with you? I don't think so."

"I got something for you." He pulled out a manila envelope. "Here's ten thousand dollars. I plan to have more for you soon. I do appreciate how you've been holding me down. That girl group that I got is about to blow up. They came in first place in that talent show last night," Cream stated with pride.

"You keep the ten grand. Use it to take care of your baby and baby mama. I want you out of here. Get all your shit and go," she told him as she went inside the house with him right on her heels.

"Nina, why do we gotta fight all of the time?"

"Because, Cream, I am not your woman. We are not a couple. You have somebody." *And I hope to have some-body named Rick.* "It is over. Our little fuck-fest is over." She was pushing him towards the door.

"Don't do this," Cream pleaded. He was trying to put the envelope of money into her hand. "What about us?"

"Us? There is no us. You forgot you got a girl and a baby? That means you have a family, Cream." She allowed the envelope to fall to the floor. "It's been all about you and whatever it is you are trying to get out of my damned job. There is no *us*. Let's keep it real. And I didn't even see it until you threatened me to keep it. You don't give a fuck about me. Like I said, it's all about you, and it's always been."

"That move was about us. Your job is gonna be my come-up. I meant to say *our* come-up. You won't have to work anymore. I'ma take care of you. I promise. But you gotta trust me and give me a little more time. I got the right people already working on it."

"What people, Cream? What are you planning on doing? I'm still clueless to this day."

"I'll let you know when the time is right. I just need

you to keep working as if everything's everything." He picked up the envelope. "Here, Nina. Seriously, I want you to have this."

"Cream, listen to me. I don't know if I can do this. Rinaldo now wants us to go trick off with the clients."

"Trick off? You ain't 'bout to do no trickin'."

"I know I ain't."

"Damn, that cracker is greedy as fuck. But listen to me, baby, I ain't for you trickin' off with no damn body. I just need you to go to work a little while longer. I also need you to place this under his desk." He held out what looked like a simple magnet.

"What is that?" Nina jumped as if he was handing her something toxic.

"It's a recording device."

"Nigga, are you trying to get me killed?" she shrieked.

"I'm telling you, baby, that cracker is setting y'all up. And this is going to protect you."

"Protect me how? Cream, what have you gotten me into?"

"Nina, I'm telling you. If you trust me on this, you can walk away from this shit, free and paid. It's getting ready to get real ugly. My sources say that your man has been under investigation for almost three years now. That whole operation is going down. The feds already have a secret indictment cooked up."

"Where are you getting this information from, Cream? Are you working for the feds? If you are that's your business, but I'm not a fuckin' snitch." Nina was beginning to see how serious Cream was about bringing Rinaldo down but still didn't understand why.

"Hell naw, I ain't workin' for the feds! You should know me better than that. It's some people who your boss happened to piss off and I happen to know them, be in the right place at the right time, with the right info. I'm telling you. It's bigger than the feds. I am about to hit the fuckin' jackpot. They gave me twenty g's last night. I split it in half with you. Now I just need you to hang in there a little while longer. Can you do that for me? For us?" He stared at her with begging eyes. "Let me use this opportunity to prove to you that I got your back like you've always had mines."

Nina for once was at a total loss for words. This was not happening. She knew that he was a piece of shit, but this? He outdid himself this time. Place a recording device under Rinaldo's desk? What if she got caught? Rinaldo didn't hesitate to take out Ted Branson's nephew. What the fuck did Cream think he would do to her? Give her a slap on the wrist?

"Hell to the no! Plus, you would have to give me a whole lot more information than what you been giving me. Rinaldo ain't no fuckin' lame in the streets and he damn sure ain't nobody to fuck over."

"My sources ain't neither. But the less you know the better. And yes, my sources are well connected and assured me that nothing would happen to me or you."

"Hell no, Cream. Get the fuck out!"

*   *   *

Nina was dying to tell Rick about her job, Cream and all of the drama in her life. But something kept telling her not to. To wait until the time was right. They had been hooking up just about every other weekend and going to the drive-in. With him she always left everything at the office or in Jersey.

She had finally stopped fucking with Cream, changed her cell number, and he seemed to have gotten the hint because he had stopped coming around.

One month later...

Nina and Rinaldo had been constantly at each other's throats. When he saw that he couldn't persuade her to go meet clients like everyone else, he threatened to kick her off of the Platinum Team and put her in the back with the Intermediate Sales Team. He told her he would give away all of her clients and made sure Simeon gave her the shittiest leads. He even went as far as to not tell her that the private detective called, the one she had hired to find her daughter. The relatives Jatana stayed with moved and now they were back at square one. She found that piece of information out from Rochelle. When Rochelle told her that, Nina declared all-out war against Rinaldo.

Last week when Shawn and Milt told her how much money she was missing, how much money they were making, she still wasn't about to be pimped out by Rinaldo on these weekend excursions.

"Congratulations to everyone. This is working out better than I expected." Rinaldo was handing out his favorite cigar for the week, Bolivar, to his Platinum sales staff. "This is one of the best sales meetings I've had in a long time," he exclaimed while handing Nina a cigar.

"I don't smoke." She fanned him away.

"Well, give it to your man. These are expensive." He shoved the cigar into her hand, then went back and sat at his desk. He put fire to the Cuban and took a long drag. "God, I love these things! I really think that these are my favorite. They are as close to natural as you can get. They taste good because they are aged longer than most brands. That's how the old-school growers do it. This *is* a premium cigar."

That got several grunts of approval from all the men flunkies in the room, including Shawn, who were all now puffing away.

Nina went to his desk and turned on his smokeless ashtray. "Is this a sales meeting or a cigar convention?"

"Both, Alexis," Rinaldo told her. "Don't forget this is my world and you're just a squirrel trying to get a nut."

"Now back to you guys." He nixed Alexis off. "Why hasn't anyone been willing to share any stories or escapades with your favorite clients? I mean, what's the big secret? I thought about taking pictures and hanging them up on the board. What y'all think?"

"It doesn't matter what we think. You gonna do what you want to do anyway." Nina's voice dripped with sarcasm.

"Alexis, since you haven't been participating in our very profitable extracurricular activities, your opinion doesn't count. However, I am feeling rather chipper on this Monday morning. And I'm not going to let you spoil that for me. We took in almost a million dollars last week. I've been working that shit outta the beginners. Now if we can just stay on that track, I'd be one thrilled mutha-fucka. Y'all feel me? And I know that y'all are just as thrilled to be making a shitload of easy, extra money."

Everybody agreed.

"Now back to what I was saying. Tell me how your clients like their outings. Let us start with you, Nina. Oops," Rinaldo teased. "I forgot. We have to start with somebody else. Because you haven't been a team player." He smiled at her. "But, I gotta tell you this. If you don't participate this coming weekend, then it's back there in the cheap seats you go. *Comprende?*"

"It doesn't matter to me. You wanna know why? Because I can sell, Rinaldo. You can put me in the garage, it don't matter. You obviously forgot who the fuck I am."

"Yeah, I know because I'm the one who taught you how to sell," he reminded her. "So tell us, Martin Luther, how was your very first date?" He turned his attention to Milt.

"All the Howells did was take me out to dinner and tell me how much money they made back in the day, their children, blah, blah, blah. It was actually quite boring."

"Boring? You made a quick and extra fifteen grand. See, Alexis, what you been missing out on all these weeks? Looks like you are no longer my top salesperson anymore. Is this Friday's check gonna be boring?" Rinaldo asked Milt.

"Hell no!" Milt said, and everyone started clapping.

"Now see. Was that so hard? Here you was rebelling, acting like I was pimping you out or something. Who else got something to share? Anybody got a freaky customer?" Rinaldo looked around the room at his tight-faced sales team. "Milt's little outing wasn't exciting enough for him. What's the matter with y'all?" He reached into his back pocket and pulled out a platinum money clip. "All right. I'm going to make this interesting." He began throwing one hundred dollar bills onto the desk. "Here go a thousand! I understand the game is to be sold not told. Who got something freaky?"

Pete jumped up, beating Jeff to the desk. "I got this!" He went to snatch up the money.

"Hold up," Rinaldo told him. "You do have something freaky to share with the class?" Rinaldo put both hands over the cash, cigar dangling from the corner of his mouth.

"Yeah, man." Pete lifted Rinaldo's hands, grabbing up the grand.

"This is crazy." Shawn chuckled.

"Get that money!" Milt encouraged.

"Let's split it. I got a story to tell too," Jeff pleaded.

"Nah, nah, you too late," Rinaldo teased. "Let's hear it, Pete."

"Cagan." Pete shook his head back and forth as if he didn't believe what he was getting ready to say.

"Who? Henry Cagan? The ex-lieutenant governor–slash-congressman? I'll be damned! The lieutenant governor is a freak? What did he say when your black ass showed up at his front door? I would have paid anything to be a fly on the wall!" Rinaldo and everyone else were laughing. Nina had crossed her legs and was now sitting on the edge of her seat. Pete had Shawn and Milt's full attention as well. They all knew that these clients were positive that they were sending their hard-earned cash money to their people, white people. These older white clients would not have it any other way.

"Yeah that's him. And I must say...he was shocked. He said, 'Dick, by golly, I thought you were Caucasian!'" Dick Garner was Pete's phone name. "I said, 'Henry, by golly, I thought you were black!'"

The room erupted in laughter.

"You're lying, Pete," Jeff said in disbelief.

"No, I'm not. I swear on my great-grandmother." Pete placed his right hand up in the air.

"So what happened next?" Rinaldo prodded. They were all dying to hear the rest of this escapade.

"We shook hands, and he invited me in. He gave me the tour of his crib. Even though his house is small the tour took forever. He walks with a cane. We then sat down and had a few drinks. He wanted to know the inside scoop of WMM, and how much I wanted for sharing info on how he can get the biggest share of the gold coins. At that point he didn't see me being black. I was all gold." Everyone started laughing again.

"I knew he was a true player. What did you tell him?" Rinaldo questioned. "Did you take the bribe?"

"I told him some bullshit about me getting in trouble for insider trading, and that shit just hyped him up even more. He was rubbing his palms together and literally drooling at the mouth. I could not believe it. It's amazing to me how these clients are so into this gold."

"All right...all right...get on with the freaky shit!" Rinaldo pressed.

"Hold up, man. Be patient. I got you." Pete used this opportunity to remain in control. "We then went to the golf course and played a few rounds. He even brought me all new golf gear. You were right, these muthafuckas are lonely as shit! After golf, we went to dinner and he got pissy-ass drunk. When we got back to his house, his driver and I had to hold him up and walk him inside."

"Driver?" Rinaldo and Nina blurted.

"Yeah. I know you ain't surprised. He is seventy-two. He does not drive anymore. We then downed some black coffee, ham sandwiches and Danishes and that's when he popped the question." Pete looked around at everyone in the room.

"C'mon, man. Popped what question? He wanted to marry you?" Shawn joked.

"Naw. He asked if I would give him a sponge bath!"

"Oh my God!" Nina shrieked. "How fuckin' sick!"

Rinaldo was laughing so hard he was choking. Shawn and Milt were bent over laughing as well.

"Man. I know you didn't do that?" Jeff did not find that request funny at all.

"The fuck I didn't! It's all about the Benjamins, homeboy. I got a four-grand cash tip for that shit!" Pete proudly stated.

"And it gets freakier." Pete leaned back into his chair, placing his hands behind his head with a smirk on his face.

"What, man?" Rinaldo urged.

"The game is to be sold not told," Pete reminded him.

"I don't know if I really want to hear this or not," Nina said, and Jeff was in agreement.

"Oh you *want* to hear this!" Pete teased. "Trust me."

Rinaldo pulled out another grand and placed it on the desk. Pete got up and swept it up. "Keep talking, muthafucka!"

"He then asked me to play in his ass!"

"*Illlk!*" Nina screamed. "He's seventy-two for crying out loud. He can't have any sexual desires!"

"Aww hell to the naw!" Shawn was up and out of his seat pacing back and forth.

"Aww, money. I know you didn't go there, did you?" Milt looked at him, hoping that he was going to say no.

BANG! BANG!

"What the fuck?" Rinaldo jumped up to see what the commotion was.

"They back there fighting," Nina yelled after Rinaldo. "It is too early in the damn morning!" she snapped. "So much for being a respectable place of business." She smiled.

"He should let Simeon handle that shit. That is what he pays him for! Plus, I wasn't finished telling y'all the rest." Pete didn't want his fifteen minutes of fame to be over just yet.

"It's a raid, y'all," Rinaldo calmly stated as he came back into his office.

"What?" Milt asked.

"Call Charlie, Deanna," he yelled out. "It's a raid." Rinaldo picked up the phone to call his lawyer.

BOOM! The front door came down. FBI, ATF, DEA agents and local police clad in dark blue khaki uniforms, black helmets and black boots swarmed the office, all yelling at once, guns pointed.

"FBI! Get on the fucking floor! Now! Everybody! On the floor, hands behind your head."

CHAPTER TWELVE

SHE SAW HIM

Nina sat alone in the backseat of the unmarked fed vehicle. She was relieved that the handcuffs weren't tight. She assumed that she was sitting in a car by herself because she was the only girl. She kept hearing them ask, "You got the girl?" as if she was some sort of prized possession.

None of the Platinum squad had been brought out yet. She was watching as all the beginning and intermediate salespeople were jumping into their cars and scattering like roaches being exposed to light, including Pete's fiancée, Jill.

Twenty minutes later, out strolled Rinaldo. He appeared to be calm as they placed him inside one of the unmarked vehicles. Then all the men on the Platinum Sales Team were led out in cuffs. One by one. They too were put in separate vehicles. Nina tried to read the expressions on everyone's face. The only one who was sweating was Pete.

The female agent, Melissa Korn, jumped in the front seat of the vehicle. "I have your purse and I wrote down everything that was inside of it."

"Thank you." Nina was wondering why she was being so helpful, when an hour ago she was pointing a shotgun to her head.

She looked back at Nina, jumped out and opened the back door to fasten the seat belt on Nina. Then, just as quick, she was back in the driver's seat. "We're on our way down to the Federal Building." Nina nodded as she anticipated what fate awaited her.

All types of thoughts were running through her mind. *What is this about? Will I spend the night in jail? Did Cream know about this? What about Rick? What would he say if he found out? Will I have a job tomorrow? Now what?*

When they pulled up to the Federal Building, Nina was taken to an underground garage and then escorted onto an elevator. This was her first time being arrested and undoubtedly she wanted it to be her last time. The elevator door opened and Agent Korn led her by the elbow down the corridor through some wire mesh gates that enclosed several holding cells. She was then uncuffed and placed into a cell with another female who actually looked like a dude. She was stretched out on the wooden bench, looked Nina over and then turned her back towards her, obviously intending to get some sleep.

Nina looked around the cell at the writing on the walls. JIMMY WAS HERE, THE FEDS AIN'T SHIT!, FUCK THE LAW!, DOWN WITH SNITCHES, TAMEKA AND SHELLY FOREVER! The cell smelled as if they had just waxed the floor. It was clean. It was quiet. Something she had not expected. Well actually, she didn't know what to expect. She did know that her adrenaline level was extremely high. The anticipation of what was going to happen next was killing her.

Finally, she heard keys jingling and stood up. When Agent Korn unlocked the door she told her to step out and follow her.

"What about me?" Nina's cell mate yelled out, jumping up off the steel bunk.

"Not yet, Turner," Agent Korn told her.

"Why not? What the hell is taking so long? Y'all mutha-fuckas think everything is a game."

"Come on, Miss Coles," Korn told Nina, who followed her around a corner, then went down three steps and was buzzed into the room where the sign on the door read, PROCESSING. As Nina stood in the doorway, she looked around the well-lit room. It was spotless and smelled like fresh wax just like the holding cell. There was a small radio in the back playing jazz.

That was when Nina saw him. *Rick*. She literally stood there holding her breath. He felt her gaze, stopped what he was doing and looked up. His gaze locked on hers. Both obviously surprised.

Agent Korn said, "Right this way, Miss Coles. We gotta get your fingerprints on file."

Nina could not stop looking at Rick. He could not stop looking at her.

"You all right, Nina?" Milt asked her. He was standing at the sink washing off the black fingerprint ink. "What, you know money over there?" he asked, referring to Rick. He witnessed their exchange.

"Where is everybody else?" she asked Milt.

"They already been through here. We are the last ones." Agent Korn pointed her towards the fingerprinting stand.

"Don't I get a phone call?" Nina asked nobody in particular, but was looking at Rick.

"Yeah, you get one. I had mines," Milt said, then went back to talking to Detective Rick Brown. Milt was refusing to sign one of the documents that Rick had given him and he was explaining to Rick why.

"You can have your phone call as soon as I get you processed," Agent Korn assured her.

Nina did not know who to call. It was not like she had a whole lot of options. She didn't have any friends, only a casual relationship with Rochelle, and she was the last person she needed to be calling at this time. The only choices were Cream, her mom and her oldest brother, Peedie. After thinking it over, she decided not to call anyone. Korn took her mug shot and fingerprinted her. She gathered all of the required intake forms for her to fill out and showed her to a chair. "Start filling these out and I'll be right back." Korn then whispered something to Rick and then she left.

Nina began filling out the forms but she kept looking up at Rick.

Damn. Nina Coleman. Nina Coles. How could I not make the connection? Rick tried to shake the thought as he walked past her, leading Milt out of the processing room.

When he came back he was in there alone with Nina. He saw the pictures of the leading lady of WMM but they were not crystal clear. They didn't look like Nina.

She got in his face. "A cop? I'm fucking a cop?"

"Lower your voice. And I'm a detective, Nina."

"Cop, detective, five-o, po-po, it's all the same."

"So what? You got a problem with *fucking* the police?"

"*Fuck* you, Rick. You could have at least been honest with me, *Detective*," she said, sarcastically emphasizing "detective."

"You didn't care who I was when I was deep under-cover in that pussy." He shot her a sexy grin.

Nina sucked her teeth and rolled her eyes at him. "Does this appear to be the time for fucking jokes?"

"Well aiight then. What about you, *Nina Coleman*? That ain't even your fuckin' name."

"Not right now." She waved him off. "Don't try and flip the bullshit. You the one privy to all the information, *Detective*," she snapped.

"Look, let's put this shit on the fucking table. Do you have a problem with fucking the police? Because it damn sure didn't feel like it when you were ridin' my dick and screaming my name."

Nina sighed. At this moment she didn't know what or who she had a problem with or what she had gotten herself into. She gritted her teeth and said, "I don't know. I thought you did something else. I didn't know I was fucking the enemy."

"Something else? Enemy? Who the fuck did you think I was?" Rick was now beginning to get pissed.

Nina was embarrassed to say who she thought he was. Then she thought about his deceit and said, "Nigga, I thought you was a hustla!"

"Hustla?" Rick chuckled. "What gave you that idea?"

"You just came off to me as a hustla."

Rick chuckled. "Nina, don't tell me that's the life you want. Because if it is—"

"I saw that exchange you had in the parking lot with that dude on the bike. That's just the impression I got and it stayed with me."

"Well, you got the wrong impression. I was working."

Nina was dumbfounded. Then she replayed the scene from that night in the parking lot: *"I swear, man. I'ma get that for you. Just give me a couple of more days." The dude whined like a bitch.*

"Yeah, aiight, you got that, my nigga. But only because I want you to spread the word that I'm that nigga. I'm King, muthafucka. You got that?"

This nigga is a cop. Then her stomach took a dive. "So wait a minute. You knew about all this here shit and didn't tell me? You were using me all this time?" she strongly accused Rick. "Was fucking me a part of your job too?"

In a twisted way Rick was actually turned on by her little tantrum and the fact that he was busted. "You couldn't tell by the way I was touching you that it was more to us than just my work?" He reached over and ran his thumb across her erect nipple. "Bitches, I don't care about. I don't make them cum the way I had you cumming," he said while gazing in her eyes. "But I care about you. About us."

Nina pushed his hand away.

The only sound in the room was the faintness of the jazz station. This whole scenario was awkward.

Rick finally spoke, "Look, I ain't no hustla, not anymore. And I wasn't using you. That's my word. I didn't know."

At that moment, Nina almost gave in. But she decided against it. She knew these muthafuckas would use whatever, even their own mamas, to get their man. And now her fucking freedom was on the line. She glared at him and gritted, "Rick...did...you...know...about me?"

"No, I didn't know, *Nina Coleman*. Remember, you gave me the wrong fucking name. I didn't put the pieces together until they hauled your ass up in here. I would have eventually, but I mean, what are the odds of us hooking up like we did?"

"There are no odds, nigga, you knew all along." Nina felt hurt and betrayed, refusing to believe that he didn't know. "You knew," she said with finality.

"Believe whatever the fuck you want to believe." Rick was now ready to slap the shit out of her. He gave her a dirty look and said, "Are you done filling out the forms? They're waiting for you."

Just then, Agent Korn barged back into the room, interrupting their heated exchange.

She finished up the last document and held them out to

no one in particular. Rick took the forms from her and she watched him place them in a folder and walk off. *A fuckin' cop*, Nina said to herself as she stared out into space. Her trance was interrupted when Agent Korn tapped her on the shoulder, shooed her out of the room and pointed down the hall. They turned the corner and stopped at the big brown door. Agent Korn tapped lightly, someone with keys on the other side unlocked it and Nina walked into a full courtroom that was already in session. She was seated at the table with the rest of the Platinum staff. Rinaldo sat close to the WMM attorneys that Nina recognized as Matt Stone and Mack and David Abramoff.

"What's going on?" she leaned over and whispered to Milt.

"Shh!" he hushed her, smacking her lip with the back of his hand in the process.

Embarrassed, she looked around to see if anyone had caught the exchange. Mack and his team were shuffling through papers as the prosecutor was talking. The judge then said for counsel and government to approach the bench. Both sides handed the judge some paperwork. She scanned through all of it as she continuously pushed her glasses up on her nose. After several minutes, she gave the paperwork back. She then set another hearing for thirty days and released all of them on their own recognizance.

And just like that, everyone was free to go.

Nina looked towards the back of the courtroom for Agent Korn. She needed her purse. She didn't see her. But her heart skipped a beat when Rick held up her belongings and motioned for her to come over to where he was.

"Call me as soon as you wrap this shit up," he hissed. She could tell that he was beyond pissed. He gave her her belongings and started to say something else but Rinaldo started yelling and he turned around and left.

"Alexis!" He yelled out her phone name as if they were in the office. "Come over here with everyone else instead of fraternizing with the enemy."

"Rinaldo..." She decided against saying what was really on her mind. Instead she sat down and was acting as if she was making sure that everything was in her purse. But she was really collecting her thoughts. Her knees had felt like rubber and her head was spinning as she wondered if shit could get any more interesting at this point.

Rinaldo and the attorneys gathered everyone together. Matt asked if everyone would rather go to their offices or to a restaurant. Everyone said restaurant, jumped into the three attorney vehicles and headed to the Cheesecake Factory.

After everyone was seated and the waitress took everyone's order, Nina was the first to speak. "Okay. In layman's terms, why did they arrest us?" Nina directed her question to Mack.

She watched him pour sugar into his already-sweetened lemonade. Then he looked around at all of the Platinum members and began to explain. "In June, the grand jury returned an indictment, charging you and the Platinum

Team with multiple counts of mail and wire fraud and conspiracy to commit money laundering. In April, the grand jury turned right back around and returned their first superceding indictment. This one is charging you guys with conspiracy, multiple counts of mail and wire fraud and conspiracy to commit money laundering."

"Two indictments?" Milt questioned.

"Yes, two," Mack said.

"This is ridiculous." Nina sighed.

"Trust me, y'all. You guys have nothing to worry about," Rinaldo cut in. "We're not doing anything wrong."

"Then why the fuck did they arrest us?" Shawn spat.

"Because they *think* that they have something. The more shit they throw at us, it raises their chances of making sure something sticks."

"I saw that guy Houser from the Georgia Bureau of Investigation sitting in the courtroom. Do you think he was behind this?" Nina wanted to know, since she was actually clueless to the whole arrest, indictments and the entire court process.

"Well actually, that's where these types of cases usually get started. That is, after the Better Business Bureau starts to get repeated complaints, the attorney general's office and the GBI will step in. Plus, we're talking thousands of dollars per complaint coming from your firm. So someone is going to eventually pay attention," Matt, Mack's partner, explained to her.

"Fuck the BBB, GBI, attorney general, FBI and whoever

else," Rinaldo ranted. "WMM is a legal enterprise and we have done nothing wrong," he stated matter-of-factly. "Fuck them all!"

The waitress was back and everyone was silent as she placed their meals in front of them. As soon as she left, Matt continued.

"Rinaldo," Matt said as he sliced his steak. "You guys gotta lay low. It's no going back to work in the morning, no conducting business as usual."

"Why not?" Rinaldo snapped. "They didn't shut me down. I don't have a cease and desist order."

"They didn't issue you one on paper, but believe me when I tell you, if you take your ass back and continue doing business it's only going to compound the problem." Mack glanced at everyone seated around the table.

Rinaldo is such a greedy asshole. Nina shook her head in disbelief.

It was as if Shawn was reading her mind because he was shaking his head as if to say, "He sure is."

"He's right," Matt chimed in.

"That's what the fuck I pay y'all for, to allow me to continue to do business," Rinaldo huffed in arrogance.

"I've heard enough," Milt mumbled. "Look, Rinaldo, we have just been arrested and indicted on money laundering, mail fraud, wire fraud and I don't even remember the rest. This is serious, money."

"You look, *money*." Rinaldo pointed in his face. "I'm talking to my attorneys. This is between me and them."

"Between you and them?" Shawn, Milt and Nina said at the same time.

"Fuck that! This is between *us* when you puttin' my freedom on the line," Shawn snapped and was now standing up.

Dave grabbed his elbow. "Calm down, big fella. I understand that this is a stressful time for everyone. And right now I know it's kind of difficult to even think straight."

"This is bullshit! Rinaldo, you better stop playing, man. This is my freedom you fuckin' with!" Shawn warned him.

"C'mon, money." Milt had grabbed both of Shawn's shoulders.

Nina stood up as well. "We can all share a cab. I know how to reach you, if I need to," she said to the attorneys. Nina could not help but notice how Matt had been looking at her the entire time as if she were a chocolate-covered cherry. *Let me find out Matt has jungle fever*, she said to herself.

"Take my card." Matt stood up and placed it gently in the palm of her hand. "Any questions or concerns, don't hesitate to call me. We'll talk some sense into this guy's head right here. He'll be all right." He shot a nasty look at Rinaldo, who was sitting there looking like a madman. His ponytail was coming loose, his face was beet red and sweaty and his usually neat clothing were all in disarray.

"Thanks, Matt." Nina smiled at him.

"I'll see you all at the office tomorrow," Rinaldo yelled. "Nine sharp!"

"Later, Pete. Jeff," Milt called out as they headed out of the restaurant. Both Pete and Jeff remained seated at the table.

"Damn. They just up and left all of this food," Jeff said to Pete.

"Ain't nobody thinking about food," Pete told him. "We about to go to prison. How can you be hungry?" Pete got up from the table and walked out too.

CHAPTER THIRTEEN

IT'S ON NOW

On the ride to the office to pick up their cars everyone was trying to talk about what happened and what they were going to do now. But all Nina could do was think about Rick and that he was a damn cop. Questions kept crossing her mind. Did he set her up? Was the whole relationship a decoy to get info for his case? It couldn't have been because she never told him where she worked or what she did. They never talked about her job. Hell, he claimed he thought she was Nina Coleman. She didn't know what to believe. Nina knew that she and Rick shared something special but the thoughts of sitting in a fucking cell for ten to twenty years scared her to death. But when she set eyes on the man she was falling for in the courthouse, he did not sit right with her.

"Nina, why are you so quiet?" Her thoughts were interrupted by Milt.

"I'm just trying to plan my next move, that's all."

After the taxi dropped off Shawn, Milt and Nina at the offices of WMM, they stood in the parking lot stunned at what caused them to be standing there. None of them wanting to believe it. Each one of them thinking about the coulda, woulda, shouldas. A few minutes later a taxi pulled up and it was Pete. They all watched as he rushed to his ride and jumped in.

With a nonchalance Shawn said, "That nigga got the shakes. His jones is calling him."

"What a waste. All that talent," Milt commented.

"What about today, y'all?" Nina brought them back to why they were all standing there in the first place, in the middle of the parking lot looking lost. "Can you believe it? Here I try to do the job thing, stay legal and this is what I get. A case? I mean, what the fuck? Where do we go from here? Are y'all coming to work tomorrow?"

"Hell no!" Shawn spat.

Milt said, "We haven't done anything. How can we catch a case? All we do is get on the phones and sell the customer a product. We don't twist their arms and force them to buy. How can they arrest us for that?"

"Dude, they just did!" Nina belted.

"You damn fuckin' right they did. But ain't no fuckin' jury gonna convict us," Shawn spat.

"I don't know about that, y'all. The feds had Rinaldo on their radar for almost three years now. Plus..." Nina caught herself and decided not to say what she had started to say.

Just then Pete joined them. It was obvious that he was talking to his fiancée, Jill, on the phone. As he was cussing her out, they could hear her screaming and crying on the other end. When he hung up, he spat, "That bitch got me fucked up! But listen, y'all, I don't know about y'all but I'll be here in the morning. It's time to stack as much paper as we can."

"Man, you crazy! It's too late for that shit. You should have been doing that all along," Shawn snapped. "Did you hear them muthafuckin' attorneys? Them muthafuckas instructed Rinaldo to not open and to shut this shit down! How you gonna not listen to them?"

"Yeah, that's what they said. We don't need to be back up in here," Milt reasoned. "At least not until they get things straightened out."

"Shit, Pete. You talking about stackin' dough. The feds froze the muthafuckin' accounts!" Shawn yelled.

"Y'all know Rinaldo got stacks put away. The nigga pays us in cash," Pete reminded them. "He better pay me my muthafuckin' money, I know that."

"Well, Pete is right, y'all. He definitely got a stash," Milt said.

The Atlanta temperature was beginning to drop, causing Nina to shiver. She had had enough for the day. She was overwhelmed. "Look, I'm out. I'll holla at y'all tomorrow." Nina left the guys standing there and went to her car.

"Call me if you need me, Nina," Milt yelled out. He could tell she was shook from the day's events.

"Thanks, Milt. I will."

She hopped in her ride, shut the door and rested her head

back on the headrest. She took a deep breath, then grabbed her purse and looked for her cell phone. She had mixed feelings and couldn't decide if she should call him or not. She started the car and started out the parking lot. She opened the phone and saw she had five messages and the first one was from Rick. She stopped so that she could listen to them.

"Nina, I don't want to fight with you. I care about you too much. You have to believe me. Call me. I need to talk to you." *Shit.*

"Hey, Nina. This is Reese. I haven't talked to you in a while. I am just checking on you. If you ever need me I'm here. And for what it's worth, I'm missing you like fuck." *Oh really?*

"Where the fuck are you. Why you ain't home yet. Call me back when you get this message." Cream sounded pissed off. *What the fuck does he want?*

"Nina, call me when you get this," Rick said. *I can't.*

"Nina, it's your mother. Call me when you get this." *How much now?*

Nina threw the phone in the seat next to her and drove home in silence. Twenty minutes later when Nina pulled up in front of her condo, the garage door was open. She eased into the garage and was surprised when Cream appeared at the back door.

"Now what?" She exhaled, as she asked, not even getting out of the car good, "Cream, I am not in the mood. And you said you didn't have any more of my keys. How did you get in here?"

"I only came over to check on you. I know what happened, baby. How are you holding up?" He came down the garage stairs, grabbed her and pulled her close, giving her a huge hug. This was the closest they had been in almost two months. Nina got comfortable in his arms as he gently rubbed up and down her back.

"I'm sorry," Cream whispered. "I'ma make sure that you're going to be okay. I promise you that."

"I knew I should have quit when my gut was telling me to." She disgustedly pushed him away, blaming him for getting her the job. "I was fingerprinted, handcuffed, had a shotgun poked at my head. I now have an FBI file and the federal government wants to lock me up for ten to twenty-five years. So how can you make sure I'ma be all right? Then, on top of that, I no longer have a job, but I still have a mortgage payment, car notes, credit card bills, utilities and insurance...I don't believe this. This has been one of the worst days of my life."

"You don't see it now, but you will. I told you I got you," he assured her.

"How? You gonna get them to drop all charges against me? Give my fingerprint cards back? Get them to issue me a public apology saying they made a mistake today? And that I wasn't supposed to get arrested? I don't think so, Cream."

Cream's cell phone rang, saving him from her ranting. He answered it. "Yeah. Yeah, she's here. A little shook up, but she's okay. I got it. I got it, man." He hung up. "I gotta make a run."

"Who was that?" she snapped, and was appalled and felt defeated that she didn't know what he had going on.

"My peoples I was telling you about."

"Why were they asking you about me? And who are these people, Cream? You better fuckin' tell me something. And I mean now."

"Just hang tight. I'll be back in a couple of hours, and trust me. My peoples said you ain't got anything to worry about." He pulled his keys out of his back pocket and jetted out of the garage, once again leaving Nina in a total state of confusion.

"Cream! Cream!" she screamed after him. She cursed him out under her breath. As soon as she walked into the kitchen, the phone rang. The caller ID said it was her mother.

Nina snatched the phone off the wall. "Hey, Mom, how's the kids?"

Her mother was quiet for several seconds. "*Me* and the kids are fine. What's the matter with *you*?"

"Let me speak to them, please."

"They went to church with the deacon."

"Ma, who is this man that you keep sending my kids to church with?"

"Deacon Rutherford."

"Don't make Daysha go if she doesn't want to."

"Don't tell me how to raise these children. And don't forget, they belong to the Lord not you. What is your problem?"

Deciding not to tell her mother what happened, Nina said, "I'm tired, Mom. I've had a very long day, that's all."

Telling her mother that she got locked up would send her on a verbal tirade and would only confirm in her mother's mind that much more as to why she has Nina's children and Nina was living in Georgia.

"Well, you sound terrible. I've been calling your cell phone all day long."

"I've been busy, Mom. But I'm here now." *How much do you need this time?* Nina said to herself, eyes rolling. "What's up, Mom?"

"Why did you stop payment on that last five-thousand-dollar check you sent me? You could have at least called me before I deposited it."

"Stop payment? I didn't stop payment on no check. What are you talking about?" Nina was baffled.

"When I went to the bank to withdraw the money, it wasn't there. I went to my bank manager and she said that you had put a stop payment on it. Are you doing that bad down there?"

"Mom, let me call you back."

"Are you doing bad down there?"

"No, Mom. I am not doing bad. Let me call you right back."

"Wait. Then how soon—"

Nina hung up without waiting for her mother to finish her sentence and went over to her computer. She powered it up, wondering what was going on. As soon as she logged in, she went to her bank's website. What she saw had her mouth hanging open. Wire transfer after wire transfer. "What the fuck? This has gotta be a mistake. All of my accounts have less than two thousand dollars!" she screamed. She was going through the accounts looking at the amounts that were transferred out: *$7,500, $6,200, $9,700, $5,400.* "This has got to be a mistake." She needed to talk to someone at that damn bank. She needed answers. And she needed them now. She began pacing the floor as she called the bank.

As soon as the customer service recording came on the line, it hit her like a ton of bricks.

Cream.

She hung up the phone.

Cream. That snake bastard! Oh shit! My safe!

She rushed upstairs to her bedroom closet. Remembering how her brother had stolen all of her cash, she slowed down with each step she took. Actually it was her brother's thievery that catapulted her to being in Atlanta.

She opened the closet door, slid the clothes back and let out a sigh of relief when she saw that the safe hadn't been tampered with. She opened it up. The envelope with the ten grand Cream gave her was there but it felt lighter. She opened it up and counted thirty-five hundred dollars.

Cream. How did he get the combination to my safe? My pillow talk ain't like that . . . is it? She thumbed through her stacks of gold coins. She never counted them so she didn't know how many she actually had. Her other stacks of money felt the same. She had at least forty-two g's stashed outside of the hundred grand left from the keys. *Why didn't he touch the other money? And my jewelry?*

Nina remained on her knees staring at the safe for almost an hour racking her brain trying to figure out what Cream was up to. *How was he able to go into my accounts? Especially since he's not a signee? How did he know the combination to the safe?*

The phone in the background had been ringing. It stopped and began ringing again. Wanting the noise to go away, she dragged herself up off the floor to answer it. "Hello."

"I asked you to call me as soon as you were done." It was Rick. "We need to talk, Nina."

"I'm just getting in and I have to make a quick run," she lied. "Let me call you when I get back." She hung up without waiting for his response. She didn't want to talk to him because she didn't know what to say or what she wanted to do. Just then the phone rang, startling the hell out of her. Her stomach flipped. She looked at the caller ID. *Cream.* She frowned.

It's time for me to do what I should have done a long time ago. It's on now! She was going to have to kill Cream.

Twenty minutes later Rick called again. "Rick, I'm not home yet. I'll call you when I get there."

"Nina, you never left out. I'm getting out of my car now. Come open the door."

Shit. She ran and looked out her window, phone glued

to her ear. Sure enough he was getting out of the white Escalade. She was busted.

"Come open the door, Nina."

She hung up and went downstairs to open the door. She didn't know what she was going to say to him. When she opened the front door and set eyes on him, she knew he would never set her up. Rick didn't give her a chance to say a word. He grabbed her and started to kiss her. Nina was caught totally off guard. The next thing she knew she was standing in her bedroom being undressed by Detective Rick Brown and wasn't trying to resist. Nina loved everything about him. Within minutes, Rick was lying on top of Nina preparing to get him some good loving.

"You still don't like fucking with the police?" Rick asked her between kisses.

Nina moaned. "Arrest me, Officer."

"I couldn't do that."

"Well, tell lil' King his boss needs to take him real deep undercover," she purred as she wrapped her legs around his back. And Rick did just that, stroked her long and deep.

They then spent the rest of the night strengthening their relationship. When they got up in the morning, they began planning what they were going to do to get Nina out of this bullshit.

CHAPTER FOURTEEN

A SUICIDE MISSION

The next morning, the sun glaring through the bedroom window woke Nina up. When her eyes popped open, she tossed the sheet over her face. She didn't even remember going to bed. The last thing she remembered was getting *a...dick...ted*. As the fog cleared her mind she did remember Rick kissing all over her breasts and nipples and then saying goodbye. A tingling sensation surged through her body. It immediately went away when she reflected on the arrest, the charges, the courtroom, the meeting at the restaurant and her bank accounts.

Rinaldo.

A text coming across her cell caused her to throw the sheets off her face. She reached over to her nightstand and grabbed her BlackBerry. She had already missed three calls. The text was from Rinaldo: IF YOU WANT YOUR CHECK ON FRIDAY BE HERE AT TEN. The hairs on her arms stood up. *He is such a prick.*

She called Milt.

"Good morning," Milt's voice boomed. "I called you earlier. Did Rinaldo call you?"

"I'm sure he did. I just read his pompous-ass text message. I overslept and was sleeping hard. I usually wake up at six. No later than six thirty."

"Well, it's almost nine thirty. But hey, you must have needed it. Especially after yesterday. Shit, I ain't mad at you. I couldn't sleep at all."

Nina groaned. "Don't remind me about the nightmare that I wish it was. Y'all going in?"

"I'm on my way now. I need my money. Plus, I need to hear what he has to say. We can play his little game until Friday," Milt told her.

I'ma play the fuckin' game all right. I'ma play every-body's fuckin' game.

"Nina, you still there?"

"I'm here."

"Just until Friday. I need my money. You don't need yours? You got a stash that long?" Milt let out a chuckle.

"Please!" Thinking about Cream, she said, "You don't know the half of it. I may be a little late, but I'll be there."

Nina checked her voice mail. Cream had the nerve to call saying he would be there in a couple of hours. The other two messages were from Rinaldo and her mother. Rinaldo told her to be there at ten or come and clean out her desk. *What desk? The feds shut them down. He is so disillusioned*. She got up, showered and threw on a pair of sweats and some sneakers and headed to the office.

Nina eased her Benz into her parking spot. The parking lot was full as if it was a regular working day. Knowing Rinaldo, he probably called every employee and told them to come to work, there was money to be made. She knew that the entire parking lot was not there to clean out their desks.

The door inside the waiting area was off the hinges. The time card slots were empty. Deanna the receptionist had a phone glued to each ear. The next thing Nina noticed was their big white money board was gone. She assumed the feds would use that as evidence.

"Nina, here." Deanna shoved about six or seven messages into her hand. "Please call Ed Simmons. I had to stop writing his messages down. He's been calling every half hour it seems."

"Thanks, Deanna." Nina balled up the messages and dropped them into the first trash can she saw. She had no intentions on calling anyone. She slowly eased the door open to her office. She didn't know what to expect. All of her motivational Post-its were gone. The ones that said, I GOTTA MAKE 10,000 A DAY, and DON'T TAKE NO FOR AN ANSWER, and YOU GOT THE MONEY! And several others that kept her focused on her job. Her sales log was gone, but other than that, she didn't notice anything else missing.

"Hey," Jeff said as he invited himself in. He gave her a

hug and she was tempted to push his ass onto the floor. He had tears coming down his face. *Bitch-ass nigga!* "You okay?" he asked her.

She gently pushed him away. "I'm all right. Thanks. Where is everyone?"

"They're around here somewhere." He quickly wiped away his tears.

She walked around his bitch-ass leaving him standing in her office. Rinaldo and the rest of the Platinum crew were coming out of the lounge area.

"Alexis, good for you to join us. We were just on our way into my office." He pulled out his keys and opened the door. "Have a seat, everyone. I'll be right back. I need to go check on the beginning salespeople."

"Beginning salespeople?" Nina said in disbelief, staring at Rinaldo. He looked as if he had been up all night.

"Have a seat, Alexis!" Rinaldo turned around and left.

"I know it's not business as usual," Nina stated in disbelief as she turned to face her co-workers. They were all seated around Rinaldo's office, casually dressed in jeans and sneakers. Everybody looked as if they had a rough night.

"That's what it looks like," Milt said.

"You don't know this cracker by now? I keep telling y'all he crazy." Shawn sucked his teeth, laid his head back and closed his eyes.

"Hey. You gotta do what you gotta do," Pete said.

Moments later Rinaldo burst back into the office. "When it rains it pours. But you know what? I ain't gonna let these muthafuckas stop me! They obviously don't have a fuckin' clue of who I am." He sat down and glared at every one of his Platinum sales staff.

"I just want to congratulate everyone on how they handled the raid yesterday. Y'all did good. All we gotta do now is keep our mouths shut. I spoke to the attorneys and they said we could get back on the phones. They got our backs."

"Man, you crazy!" Shawn couldn't hold back that outburst. "We sat there and heard them say it would be suicide for us to get back on the phones."

"Yeah, money," Milt interjected. "Now you're trying to tell us it's cool to get back on the phones? I think we need to lay low until this shit blows over. I mean, *we* all got families to think about."

"I can't believe you want us back on the phones," Nina stated.

Rinaldo stood up. He leaned over his desk, looked everyone over and sighed. "How y'all gonna punk out now? The *judge* didn't say we couldn't get on the phones. That's who y'all need to be scared of. Not the fuckin' attorneys! They work for *us*."

"Well, it was said, man," Shawn snapped. "I sat there and heard them. What you think, we stupid?"

Jeff raised his hand.

"We ain't in school, fool. Say what you gotta say." Rinaldo was growing more agitated by the minute with his Platinum Sales Team. He expected more loyalty than this. "You down with me or what?" he snapped at Jeff, daring him to say no.

"Get the lawyers on the speakerphone," Jeff pleaded, "and if they say we straight, then I'm down. I'm with Milt, I got a family at home."

"Look. The lawyers already told me they would be in court all day. So talking to them right now would be out of the question. Now I told y'all these muthafuckas ain't got nothing!" Rinaldo lied as he looked around at the faces of his Platinum Sales Team. "If they did, they wouldn't have released everybody on their own recognizance."

"Rinaldo, Simeon just pulled up," Deanna announced over the loudspeaker.

Rinaldo looked at his watch. "Here it is eleven thirty and this muthafucka is just coming to work, knowing what we just been through." Rinaldo hit his intercom button. "Tell him to come into my office." He turned back to the sales team. "Any questions? Or are y'all still scared shitless?"

"Scared? This is the feds, Rinaldo!" Shawn spat. "If a muthafucka ain't scared he obviously high off something because he definitely ain't in his right frame of mind. What muthafucka you know is *trying* to go to prison?"

"Ump, ump, ump. Scary-ass Shawn. I expected that to come from Alexis. The girl of the crew. Not a big, bad-ass wannabe rapper."

Rinaldo yanked the plug out of the wall that was attached to his favorite wooden lamp. He took the lamp-shade off.

"But Rinaldo, the attorneys specifically said *do not work*," Nina reiterated.

"If y'all say that shit one more time," Rinaldo snapped. "Look, y'all muthafuckas are either with me or against me. And I hate to bust y'all's bubble. Even if they did have something, it's too late to back out now. And in case y'all already didn't know, if I go down, y'all go down. I ain't in this shit by my damn self." Rinaldo looked around at everyone's shocked expressions. "Yeah, I said it. Y'all got me fucked up. Y'all ain't showing me any loyalty. How the fuck y'all expect me to show y'all some? We made money together, so we go down together."

That's all I needed to hear, Nina said to herself.

Simeon knocked on the door and then pulled it open. He stepped inside Rinaldo's office with a big ole smile on his face as if he just came back from a long vacation. Rinaldo smashed the lamp across his head and began beating his twin brother with the lamp.

Nina jumped out of her chair and moved across the room. Everyone else in the office had jumped out of their seats as well. They were all once again...shocked.

Simeon was screaming at the top of his lungs, asking Rinaldo what was the matter with him and pleading with him to stop. Once again, the secretaries and the salespeople from the back had migrated to the always-action-centered front office.

"Don't...fuck with my...money! Don't anybody fuck with my mu-tha-fuckin'...money! Your ass was supposed to be here before everyone else making sure I had bodies on every phone." Rinaldo had sweat all over his face and was beet red as he beat his twin brother down.

"This cracker is crazy," Nina said out loud.

"Hell, yeah," agreed Pete.

"Man, fuck this shit!" Shawn spat. "I wish he would come at me like that. I know y'all ain't falling for this wack-ass scare tactic."

Jeff stood there scared shitless, unable to utter a sound.

Milt finally went over to Rinaldo and snatched the lamp out of his hand. Rinaldo appeared to be just getting warmed up. Simeon was lying in a fetal position. Rinaldo began kicking him.

"Get up!" he screamed, and kicked him again.

Simeon forced himslef up on all fours and began crawling around in his Armani suit and custom-made shoes, scuffing them up.

Rinaldo stood behind him, ran his hands across his head and yelled, "Everybody, get on those phones. I need some deals closed within the next sixty minutes. I'm doubling the commission for the first person to get a sale! Platinum Team, back into my office." He then walked away and headed straight for the beginning sales team.

When he came back, he closed his door and sat at his desk. He grabbed a cigar and lit it. "Okay. Where was I?" Acting as if he had not just completed an assault. "Oh yeah. I'm upping the commission another ten percent and will pay daily in cash. Pete and Nina, y'all got appointments to go see clients. I know y'all ain't gonna let that money go. Y'all in or what?"

"An extra ten percent *and* paid daily?" Nina needed to make sure she heard him right.

"That's what I said."

She thought about it. It was tempting but then decided it was not worth the risk. "I'm out. I'm chillin' until further notice," she said.

"I'm in," Pete said. "Fuck it!"

"Okay, good. So let me get this straight. Pete is in. Alexis is out. Shawn, what's up, man?"

"I'm out." Shawn stood up.

"Why am I not surprised? What about you, Martin Luther? I guess you're wimping out like Shawn?"

"Count me out," Milt said with finality.

Rinaldo turned to Jeff, who was having a change of heart. "An extra ten percent? I'm in," he stated before Rinaldo could say anything.

Rinaldo stood there puffing on his cigar as he looked around at his staff that he had been getting rich off of for the past two and a half, going on three years. "I can't believe y'all going out like this. After all I've done for y'all. When we come across a little speed bump y'all jump out the car!"

Shawn, Milt and Nina started laughing.

"Speed bump?" Milt repeated.

"If looking at a conspiracy, money laundering and a fraud case is a speed *bump*, then I hate to see what constitutes a *hill*," Nina stated matter-of-factly.

Rinaldo looked at Shawn. "What you got to say?"

"Man, ain't nothing to say but what I've always said, you crazy. I need my money so I can bounce." Shawn pulled out his car keys.

"What money?" Rinaldo looked at Shawn as if he was the crazy one.

"For the sales I made that came in. That's what money!" Shawn snapped.

"Me too. I had two come in as well," Nina added.

"Well I don't know how the fuck y'all expect to get paid when the accounts are frozen," Rinaldo smugly stated.

"Money, come on and don't play games with your people. You got it," Milt said.

"Well, my *people*, I'll tell y'all what. All of y'all got messages. Clients are begging to send in some money. Sell to these hungry-ass clients this one last time. Get them out to the banks today to pick up the checks and have them in here by the morning and I'll pay y'all on them in cash, tomorrow afternoon with an extra ten percent. Is that a deal?" When nobody responded, he pleaded, "C'mon, can't y'all do this one thing for me? If y'all don't feel safe using these phones, then go to a pay phone or use your cell phones. Can y'all at least do that? If not, then I won't be able to pay y'all. But, if you do, I'll have cash for y'all tomorrow afternoon."

Pete ended up at a client's home in Laguna Hills, California. It was his only black client, Marilyn Dobson. She had her luscious red painted lips wrapped around Pete's dick when her husband, Jonathan, stepped into the den. He heard his wife talking in the kitchen and headed that way.

"Oh, Peter. Mommy's been a bad girl," she paused to tell Pete in her British accent. Pete ignored her as he took a snort of heroin. He wished she would shut up and go ahead and get her nutt because he definitely wasn't coming anytime soon. He actually was ready to bounce.

Jonathan's pale white face turned crimson red as he watched his wife of fourteen years do something to this man whom he had never seen before, and he couldn't get her to do it to him. And on top of that, how she was talking to this…this negro stranger. He wondered who the stranger was, how long they'd been having this affair— and in their very kitchen—and if they met like this every Friday night. *There must be an explanation. Obviously this strange negro is forcing her to do this*, he told himself. He slowly backpedaled out of the den to their emergency spot in the living room. They kept a gun in a secret compartment over the fireplace.

He retrieved the weapon and began to pace back and forth. He looked at Marilyn's beautiful picture resting on the mantel. *Oh, what beauty.* It was rare and subtle and now it infuriated him. He marched back towards the kitchen, and what Jonathan Dobson, founder and owner of the largest PR firm in the state, saw at that moment was unforgivable and would forever be etched in stone on his mind. *She assured me that my impotency was no problem. Now I see why.* His lovely wife, Marilyn, was bent over their grandson's high chair screaming out in obvious ecstasy as Pete watched and amused himself sliding in and out of her asshole.

"Oh, Pete, you tiger you!" she screamed. "Oh yyyyessss," she squealed out as her body shook and trembled in the quaking orgasm that she considered was long overdue.

Click! Click!

The unmistakable sound of a bullet entering its chamber caught Pete's attention. He froze in midstroke.

"Marilyn?" Jonathan questioned as if he wasn't sure it was her.

Marilyn's face, clad in layers of makeup, turned an impossible shade of pale. "Jonathan, what are you doing home?" She tried to catch her breath as she stood upright, and eased the silk dress over her thighs. Pete slowly backed up.

"How could you?"

"Jon, I..."

BOOM.

"Whoa, man!" Pete held his hands up high in the air as his gaze shot from the gun to his dick, which was still sticking straight out. Marilyn's body twitched in a pool of blood on the floor. The bullet had struck her neck. Blood was gushing out of her mouth and neck.

"Nigger, put your pecker away. Now!" Jonathan yelled, since Pete was moving in slow motion.

Nigger? What the fuck you think your wife was? That

statement damn near fucked up his high. It should have been the gun and bullets but, no, it was the *n* word. Pete grabbed his now limp and shriveled-up member and shoved it inside his pants. Then, in a swift motion, he picked up and tossed the high chair at Jonathan Dobson and ran for the door.

The Dobsons lived on top of a hill. Pete ran as fast as he could, before tripping and tumbling down the hill onto the road.

"Come back here!" Jonathan ordered. *Pop. Pop.* He shot at him. He was skilled at running down this very hill. He had done so a million times as a young boy.

Pete got up and began waving frantically at an oncoming Chevy dump truck. The trucker slowed down but then spotted the white man with a gun and he immediately sped up.

Pete began running down the road. Mr. Dobson was not giving up. "Stop it now! I demand that you stop!" he yelled, out of breath. He knew that the curve at the bottom of the hill was a dangerous one.

Pete, spotting the white dump truck coming towards him, ran out onto the road, waving.

Screeeeccchhhh. The driver slammed on the brakes, skidded sideways, knocking Pete almost three feet up into the air. His body came down with a spill and then a splat... onto the road.

CHAPTER FIFTEEN

INTERTWINED

Nina cut the ringer off on her phone, ignoring the constant calling from Rinaldo and Cream. She needed time to herself. She did something she did not have the luxury of doing in a while, and that was just drive. She found herself driving up and down the Georgia interstate, stopping at various shops, and even did a little grocery shopping at the farmers' market, and it felt good. She wanted to cook Rick an intimate dinner.

Cream.

She never gave him the combination to her safe or her bank account passwords. He better have a damned good explanation. The only reason she hadn't taken action was because she wasn't sure of what action to take. Call the police? Confront Cream, who would only lie? To date the bank hadn't contacted her at all. Shit, up until that point she didn't know what to do. Well, now she did. Nina got off the first exit, jumped on Interstate 85 and made a U-turn. She was going to the bank.

*   *   *

Rochelle was working up a sweat as she pushed her son, Raymond, on the swing. She was jet-black, with skin as smooth as silk. Her five-foot-seven frame was well toned and the navy Tory Burch stretch pants she had on looked as if they were painted on. As she pushed Raymond her thoughts flashed to Rinaldo. She had been with Rinaldo three whole years before she got pregnant with their son. Even though Rinaldo was six years younger than her, she couldn't help but acknowledge his relentless drive to acquire wealth. It didn't matter to her that he was white. All she knew was he was always hungry and there was no doubt in her mind that he was going places. She too had been dreaming of going places, and he would be the vehicle to get her there, undoubtedly.

She was the secretary at a telemarketing room in Vegas and he was a sales rep, selling home security systems attached to a sweepstakes. He immediately outsold all the other salespeople, and naturally, Charlie, the owner and man to know in Vegas, took an immediate liking to the young kid. Rinaldo went from team leader to supervisor to manager to business partner. He was young, poor, fat and white. Her family had no understanding of the fascination that she held for Rinaldo. She didn't care. But she saw something in him. Every day that he came to work, she saw *it*. And she wanted to be there when *it* took him to the top.

But now those same qualities she loved about him she despised. Of course, she was living like a queen. Five-figure shopping sprees, boob job, liposuction, house with a pool, travel anywhere she wanted to go at any time. She even survived his coke habit. But to end up lonely? What's all of that money when you don't have a loved one to share it with? What is the fun in boob jobs, lipo and an ass lift when you don't have a man to enjoy it and tell you how nice it looks?

She was now feeling much happier that now she had someone who appreciated every inch of her body and he makes sure that he tells her that. Even though it wasn't all of the time, it was more than what she was getting at home. When daddy is away, mommy will play. The S-man, she nicknamed him. Why? Because he is Superman between the sheets. The fact that he doesn't like it when she calls him that made her smile. But that is exactly what he was in bed, super!

Her heart skipped a beat as the forest green Mercedes S500 pulled up into the driveway.

"Who is that, Mommy?" Raymond asked.

"A friend of your father's." She lifted him off the swing. "Go play in your sandbox," she instructed Raymond. When he took off running she sauntered over to the car.

"Hey," he said.

She loved his gruff voice. It was so masculine to her. "Hey back." She grinned sexily at him.

"You have everything ready? We want to make our move right before the feds make theirs. Hopefully that will throw them off. My man Akil is about ready. How much is in Florida?"

"At least sixty mil. Give or take five or ten." Rochelle said it as if it wasn't nothing.

"You sure?" Shawn was trying to be cool and hide his excitement. This was unbelievable.

"I'm sure. When are you going?" She didn't want Charlie's and Rinaldo's people coming after her, that's why she got Shawn to take the risk. She didn't mind splitting it. That way if Rinaldo goes away, which she knows that he will, she can be with Shawn a little bit more and she damn sure won't be broke. She'll still be there for Rinaldo but Shawn'll be able to freely do her.

"We'll be leaving within the next two weeks."

"Why so long? I thought the feds were getting ready to swing by?"

"We thought so too. With Rinaldo opening back up, I think they are going to let him go ahead and dig his hole a little deeper. Plus, I gotta make sure everything is in place after we pick it up. Every move we make needs to be done at the same time."

"Are you sure you can trust this Akil guy to do the pickup?" Rochelle asked him.

"Yeah, he straight. I told you already, he got connections to them muthafuckas. Plus, don't forget, I'll be with him the whole time."

"All right, it's your call. Keep an eye on my little man and I'll be right back."

"I got him." He watched her as she disappeared into the house. Looking over at Raymond as he filled up a sand bucket, his thoughts went to his own children. *After this, they will not want for nothing. I wish I could see Rinaldo's face when he realizes that I used his wife to get his money.* Just the thought caused him to chuckle aloud.

"When do I get the privilege of seeing you again?" Rochelle sauntered down the front porch steps and placed a manila envelope in his hands. She wished she could take him in the house at that very moment.

"Combination, keys and addresses?" Shawn asked as his face was buried inside the envelope. He was more concerned with the matter at hand than her flirting.

"Everything's there."

He then looked up at her and said, "As soon as me and ole boy get back I'll call you." He turned and jumped into his ride and pulled off. Leaving Rochelle hoping that she was doing the right thing.

Nina turned into the shopping center on Flat Soals when she spotted them. Her brow furrowed. She was confused. In fact she was very confused. She pulled up next to a van and watched Petra the bank manager as Cream opened and held the door for her. They were getting into her silver Jag. Where was Cream's truck? *That bitch! That sneaky-ass bitch! They're both in on this shit. Stealing her money.*

Nina's pride was flattened. The only way she was able to hold her head high was to tell herself that at least he wasn't driving the chick around in the truck that she got for him. She watched as the Jag left the parking lot and then noticed Cream's truck parked off to the side. It was stashed away, as if he knew he wouldn't be back anytime soon to get it.

Muthafucka! "He got me fucked up," Nina gritted out loud.

Nina sat there and tried to figure out what was going on and how long was *it* going on. She and Rick came to the conclusion that Cream was working with somebody but mostly himself. This plot was definitely thickening. Cream and WMM. Cream and her banker. Cream and the record label. Cream landing in Georgia…of all places. Who was he? What was he? She honestly didn't know. But one thing she did know was she was not going to take this lying down. "Y'all got me fucked up!" Nina spat as she called Tony.

"Yyello!" Tony answered in his signature greeting.

"Tony, this is Nina from WMM."

"I know who you are. How's it going? You ready to make a trade already? Or add something new? I swear, I need to be working for Rinaldo." He started laughing.

"Neither. I have to downsize. Sales are rough. I will no longer be able to pay for a truck that I'm not even driving."

"I see." Tony knew that she got the truck for her boyfriend. "You want to put him into something less expensive? Something smaller?" Tony was a salesman. He never took no for an answer and especially not the first time around.

"Hell no! If you want your truck, I suggest you come and get it right now, or you might not never get it. I'm not paying on it anymore."

"Say no more. I understand."

Nina told him where she was and hung up. She started up her ride and drove over to Cream's truck and parked. She popped her trunk, got out and went to clean out the truck. She unlocked the truck with her remote and got in on the passenger side, where she opened up the glove compartment and took everything out, including the two blunts. She checked under the seats and found almost ninety dollars, some chick named Donna Halsey's welfare ID and some coke. She took the ID but left the coke for Tony. She was sure he would enjoy that. The pockets behind the seats had baby toys, flyers of his upcoming show and another blunt. She disconnected the DVD player and took out all four flat screens. They were hers. She took everything she gathered so far and put them into her trunk. She then went to the back of the truck and opened up the rear doors. She unzipped the gray duffel bag. There was a change of clothes, condoms, DVDs, CDs and more condoms. There were two boxes, a briefcase and a small travel bag. Nina opened the two boxes. They were full of CDs and more DVDs. She put them in her trunk.

When she came back she stood staring at the briefcase. She tried to open it but it was locked. She picked it up and shook it. She placed her ear close to it and shook it again. It was light and there was light movement. It felt like money or papers. *My fuckin' money.* She snatched up the travel bag and stacks of small cassettes fell out. She picked one up. WMM. The briefcase fell to the ground. She examined another one. WMM. And another one. They all had WMM written across them. Nina's heart rate sped up. She quickly put all of the cassettes back in the travel case and slammed the doors. She picked up the briefcase and decided that her mission was done here. *Everything happens for a reason.* It was no coincidence that she made a U-turn and came to the bank. Placing the briefcase and travel case in her trunk, she decided to put the key under the mat. Akil aka Cream and this truck was a closed chapter in her life.

She was embarrassed to have to call the locksmith...*again*. His number was saved in her cell phone. But hey, even a fool can eventually come to his or her senses. After she spoke to the locksmith, she sat drumming her fingertips on the steering wheel. She called Rick.

"Hey, baby. You all right?" Rick answered.

"I need to *see* you. I need to talk to you and I need you to check out some things." She was talking about the tapes.

"Actually I was just getting ready to call you. You free to hang out tonight?"

"Hang out where? You mean while you do your police work?" She frowned.

Rick laughed. And his laugh felt as if a warm blanket was wrapping around her. She liked that feeling and wanted more of it. He was too sexy to be a man of the law.

"Naw, baby. I gotta run to New York for an engagement."

"New York?" She lit up.

"Yeah, New York. The City. The Big Apple? It's Friday.

You want to talk to me tonight or would you rather wait until I came back? I was hoping that you would hang out with me."

Nina began to stammer. "New York...I...when...umm." She wasn't ready to go north. At least she didn't think so.

He picked up on her hesitation. "All we gonna do is fly over and catch a red-eye back. I got you. Get yourself together. I'll be over there in a couple of hours." He hung up, leaving Nina stuck on stupid. But only for a minute. She called the locksmith and told him to hurry up and made sure that he knew to change all of the locks, including the garage door and to put a new lock on the basement window.

CHAPTER SIXTEEN

FLAMES

Rick pulled up exactly two hours later. Nina stood staring at him out of her front door window. His dreads were pulled back in a neat ponytail, he had on baggy jeans, a white tee, a black leather jacket and what looked like some black timbs. He had a huge diamond-encrusted eagle hanging around his neck.

He came up the front porch and their eyes locked. They stood there for a minute just staring at one another.

"You coming out or what?" he mouthed through the window separating them.

Nina opened the door. "Were you just thinking about her? I want to know because you stare at me as if you've just seen a ghost. What's her name?"

Rick smiled. "What? If I don't tell you, you're not coming with me?"

"I didn't say that. I just want to know."

"Her name was Kyra. I told you y'all don't look alike, but y'all have the same mannerisms, spirit and build. She was murdered."

Nina gasped. "Murdered? Damn! Were you in love with her?"

"Yeah. I was."

Nina locked the door, feeling a little jealous as she followed behind Rick down the stairs.

By the time they landed at JFK Nina felt as if she had just been born again. The first thing she did was go into a bathroom and cry. Since the death of Michelle she had no one to talk to. No one to share her thoughts with. No one to give a damn about her. Now here was Rick. She had just unloaded everything off her mind onto him. During the entire two-hour-and-fifteen-minute plane ride, Nina talked. She started with telling Rick her entire history with Cream all the way up until today with him stealing her money out of the bank, to her giving the truck back and the tapes that were labeled wmm. She told him all about her and Supreme's relationship, the relationship with her mother and oldest brother. She even went as far back as the jacking of the girl named Canada and her mother, which led to her brother getting killed. She told him about Reese and Wicked. She told him about the murder of her client's nephew. And throwing caution to the wind, she even told Rick about the night she became a murderer. There. It was all off her chest. Whatever was going to happen next, she would leave it up to him. She felt safe with him. She trusted him. Trusted him with her life and knew from her past relationships she was taking a huge chance but she did not care. She was going for broke.

After she dried her eyes, she came out of the bathroom. Rick was standing there waiting. He had stopped by Nathan's and bought them some cheese fries and lemonade. "We gotta roll or we are going to be late." And he started walking.

Nina practically had to skip to keep up with him. "Where are we going?"

"You'll see."

When they got outside, Rick hailed a taxi and they got in. Nina was back up north. New York, New York. Her heart smiled.

They turned onto a narrow dark street and pulled up in front of a club on East Third Street called Verses. It was starting to drizzle. Groups of people were scurrying down the block. People were walking their dogs as they pulled up their collars as if it would protect them from the drops. There were several people standing out front smoking cigarettes, dro and talking. They had formed a line to get into the club. Rick and Nina were standing behind this tall light-skinned dude who looked to be about six-foot-five and he was holding a drum.

"Sooooo...we are here to watch a band?" Nina questioned.

"No, this is open-mic night."

"Open-mic...meaning?"

"Meaning, poets get on stage and do their thing."

"Oh. I see." Nina frowned. "You came all the way to New York just to watch some poets?"

"A good friend of mine, Helena, runs the show. And don't tell me you've never experienced an open-mic session?"

Embarrassed, Nina said, "No."

"Well, I'm glad to be your first." He grabbed her hand and led her inside. The place was small and cozy. Behind the bar an older Latino guy nodded at Rick and Rick gave him twenty dollars for them to come in. To their left was a partition housing a DJ booth. The DJ in the back was mixing some neo-soul sounds.

Rick led her to the front of the room and pulled her chair out for her. He told her he would be right back and then disappeared. Nina looked around and checked out her surroundings. The place was simple with high ceilings, an upstairs and a stage. People were now rushing through the entrance. She spotted Rick talking to a brown-skinned woman with dreads. He was holding two bottles of Corona. Nina took a minute and closed her eyes. She was so glad she called him. He was her salvation. Her new knight in shining armor.

"Hey. You all right?" Nina opened her eyes to find Rick and the brown-skinned woman were right up on her. He leaned down and kissed her lightly on the cheek and whispered in her ear, "You all right? You want to leave?"

"I'm fine. I was just thinking. Thanks for asking."

"Just checking. I want you to meet a good friend of mine." He turned to Helena. "Helena, this is Nina. Nina, this is Helena."

"Heyyyyyyy, gurrl!" Helena said in a high-pitched screech and she leaned over and gave Nina a big warm hug, filling her with surprise.

Nina couldn't help but smile. "Nice to meet you."

"Gurll, you are in good hands tonight! Anything you want, let me know. I am so glad to see Rick. You are in for a treat. Rick, I'll see you in a few." And just like that she was gone.

"She's a live one, isn't she?" Rick asked Nina.

"Yes, she is."

"Here. I brought you something to loosen you up."

"What, you trying to say I'm stiff?" Nina eyed him, daring him to say yes.

He leaned over and kissed her on the cheek. "I just want you to relax and enjoy yourself. Leave the state of Georgia behind. Can you do that for me?"

Nina thought about it for a few seconds and said, "Yeah, I can do that."

"Good."

"What about you? Can you do it? Leave Georgia behind?" She returned his question.

"I'm a pro at it. I do it all of the time."

Nina took a sip of her Corona. She wasn't a beer drinker but hey. She was stepping outside her comfort zone tonight. She looked around and the place was now packed. Packed with people of all ages, colors and genders. Helena was moving swiftly down the aisle and jumped on stage. A bright spotlight went on her and the music was lowered.

"Good evening, ladies and gentlemen. My name is Helena Lewis and welcome to Verses." Everyone clapped and whistled vigorously. "I am your host for tonight and, boy, do I have some treats and surprises for you. To name a few, we got Jamaal St. John in the building!" The crowd went wild. "We got Sean360!" The crowd went wilder. "And ladies and gentlemen, we have...the one...the only, in the building tonight, Fiyah!"

The adrenaline rush of the crowd coursed through Nina's veins. She was pumped up and ready for the show to get started. She had never heard of none of these poets. The first poet that went up was a scrawny, white dude. He talked about the year 2012 and how we need to get prepared. The next poet, Saleh, got up and did a piece on gang violence and how the violence killed a mother of two small children. Nina enjoyed that one. A tall poet/model by the name of Sean360 got up and he had introduced his band. They were awesome. Then Helena called up who Helena was overly hyped about...Fiyah. Nina gasped as Rick got up and walked to the stage.

"Good evening, everybody. This poem, along with feeling that sexy lady right there with the white blouse, has helped me get through a real tough loss and also rejuvenated my spirit," Rick confessed as he waited for the applause to subside.

Rick stood back, took a deep breath, and locked his gaze on Nina. At that very moment it was only the two of them in the room.

Flames

A married woman should be every man's taboo but
every time I saw her she gave me
Flames
Hey, pretty lady, whenever I see you all I can think is
how I want to feel you,
Taking a chance every time I take a glance at you.
I know you belong to him, but he doesn't deserve you
Because, baby, I do
And, like a moth to a flame, I could not contain my
attraction to you.
I guess it's something about what you can't have that
makes you need it more, and then I swore to myself
that I would just leave her alone.
But, it was something about her eyes, black like onyx,
white like pearl, both, deep and cool at the same
time, and when she stared back at me she gave me
Flames
The mere sight of her ignited my soul
Oh baby
I want to drink from deep down inside of you.
Watching you walk and that curve of your back
damn
I don't know how to act around you.
And when you give me that smile with that sexy
attitude
Oh baby, I know what to do with that attitude.

I am haunted with thoughts of what is she thinking?
  Does she want me like I want her?
Damn I want to penetrate your mind, so I can find a
  way to define this passion I'm feeling for you.
Then one day I looked up and I was alone with you.
The heat of her breath, intensity of her touch, my
  heart is beating like an ancient drum, awaiting the
  moment of deep pleasure of emergence, and then
  I was inside of you, I have to keep the rhythm slow
  so I can enjoy you, each stroke was paradise born.
  Wrapped in her angelic embrace, watching the plea-
  sure on her face, wanting that night to be my forever.
And, that night, she made me a man.
Because she fucked me from the tip of my toes to the
  palm of my hand, and now that hand that used to
  open full closes empty.
And I could only envy God, because he felt he needed
  you more than me.
And like a dove you floated in my life, and then out, I
  lost the bout with fate, damn karma is a bitch,
Because now I don't see you, and I can't breathe, I
  wake up thinking was she a dream? Was she real?
  Or was she too unreal for reality, or maybe she
  became my fallacy of guilty pleasure that one day
  all went up in

                    Flames
But then I looked up one day and saw you, and you
  remind me of a perfect replica of her, and don't

mistake the gaze, I'm not trying to replace you
for her, just trying to find someone who can be
adjacent to her.
And my heart aches and mourns, because I know one
day I will feel fire but never again will I feel
Flames
Be my air, Nina. Help me breathe.

"Thank you."

The crowd erupted. Nina's face was flushed. Rick walked off the stage and held out his hand for Nina. They stared in each other's eyes as Helena took the stage. "Let's hear it for Fiyah!" The crowd erupted once again.

Rick blew Helena a kiss. He took Nina by the hand, pulled her up and they left the club.

Neither of them spoke as they held hands while walking up the narrow block. Rick was trying to hail a taxi. Everyone was trying to go somewhere and in a hurry. It would have been impossible to imagine that Rick was going to pull that off tonight. He was one giant surprise. Finally a cab stopped. Rick took a moment and asked Nina, "So you still think I set you up?"

Nina pulled him close. "I'm sorry."

He kissed her forehead. They jumped into the backseat and before they could slam the doors, the driver pulled off. *Only in New York.*

"Where to?" the cabbie asked, looking at them through his rearview mirror and driving at the same time.

"Are you hungry?" Rick looked over at Nina.

"Wow" was all Nina could say as she admired the brother who was sitting next to her. "I'm speechless."

"Well, I'm hungry. What do you have a taste for?" When he saw that food was the last thing on Nina's mind he told the driver to take them to the nearest Dallas BBQ's. A stop he made ritually every time he came into the city.

"What am I supposed to say?" Nina asked him as she snuggled up to him.

"It's too late now. You had your chance. I already picked the spot. My favorite spot."

"I'm not talking about food, silly. I'm talking about *her*...*me*...and the *flames*." Nina couldn't even hide it. She was floored at this point. Totally blown away. "First of all, I was shocked when she introduced 'Fiyah' and you got up and went on the stage. I was saying to myself, 'A thug detective doing poetry? *And* with so much passion?'" She squeezed his hand. "But when you said my name, I couldn't move. No one had ever done that to me before. You know, put me on the spot like that. And when you started talking about *her*, I got a little jealous. I asked myself, 'How can I compete with *her*?' But then you said the part about 'You remind me of a perfect replica of her, and don't mistake the gaze, I'm not trying to replace you for her, just trying to find someone who can be adjacent to her,'" Nina recited word for word. Then she whispered, "You had me."

Nina was talking nonstop. But Rick was listening to his own thoughts. He hadn't planned to get up there and recite "Flames." His plan was to recite a piece he had been working on called "Justify." "Flames" wasn't even finished yet. But from the very first time Nina was in his presence, it was as if Kyra was back. And that scared the shit out of him. He hadn't been able to shake the feeling. Hell, shake California. He always thought about Kyra, Trae and Tasha. He was hoping that Georgia would make him forget, turn him into a different Rick. A plain regular-joe Rick. But when he thought about Cali, Marvin and how he destroyed Kyra's life...King Rick fought to come out. The bureau was even trying to make him go to counseling for that shit.

"Are you all right?" Nina nudged him. "You look like you are visiting some real dark place."

He looked over at her and thought to himself, *I couldn't save Kyra, but I'm going to save you and at the same time save myself.* "I'm good."

The taxi stopped on Amsterdam. "Fourteen dollars please."

Rick paid the driver. "C'mon. Let's get something to eat." He grabbed Nina's hand.

New York. Nina could hear Alicia Keys singing the hook as she looked around at all the bright lights. Even though it was late, people were moving about as if it was twelve noon. Even the Laundromat was open. Nina looked around in amazement. *Damn, I need to get out more often.*

They stepped inside of Dallas BBQ's and it was a nice crowd. She had never been there but could smell the burgers and saw a few of the patrons chowing down on some of the biggest, juiciest burgers and chicken wings she had ever seen. Up until now she wasn't hungry. Now her mouth was watering.

As if Rick could read her mind he said, "Oh, now it ain't all about me anymore. It's all about the double burgers and big wangs you lusting after. I see you slobbing over there," Rick joked.

Nina punched him playfully on the arm. She couldn't help but laugh. Something she did often around him.

After about forty minutes, they were seated at their table and had ordered double turkey cheeseburgers with everything on them, fries, a tray of Hennessy chicken wings and margaritas. They were enjoying themselves, talking as if they had been the best of friends for the last ten years.

Rick leaned over and wiped some ketchup off Nina's cheek. She almost had a heart attack when he told her that since they were up this way, she needed to stop by and check on her children. Nina got quiet and now Rick was having a one-sided conversation.

"Talk to me, Nina. Ever since I mentioned going to Jersey, you became distant. I'm not going to let anything happen to you. We'll go, see the kids and then leave."

"I'm scared and not really sure why. I left the same day

my best friend and brother got shot down, and days after my brother died."

"I know why you left, Nina."

"I just up and left my kids, Rick. And what if they don't know who I am?" Her eyes were getting watery. "What do I say when they ask me why did I leave them? That is, if they even know me. Then I have to face my mother. She always said I shouldn't have brought any children into this world. And ever since I've been gone, I've been starting to believe that."

"Well, I suggest that you look at it like this: It's never too late to make a thing right. The longer you wait the harder it's going to be."

"I know. But at least allow me to plan for it. And when I do go to see them it won't be just for that day. I'm bringing them back with me. And that's where you come in. I need your help."

"Nina, I'm here for you," Rick assured her.

"I know, but still, think about it...think about it while I go to the bathroom."

Nina excused herself, loving how exhilarated she felt being around Rick.

When she walked into the bathroom she heard someone in one of the stalls ask, "Can someone pass me some tissue please?"

One lady barged by Nina and left the restroom, slamming the door. Two other ladies were looking at the stall and giggling. They left as well.

"Helllooo," the voice sang. "Can someone please pass me some tissue?"

"Girl, bitches can be so petty," Nina said as she went into a stall to get some tissue.

One lady was standing in front of the mirror acting as if she didn't have a clue.

"Here you go." Nina passed the tissue under the stall.

"Thank you. I appreciate it. I can't believe them bitches wouldn't pass me any fuckin' tissue. Like they had to put a quarter in the machine and fuckin' pay for it."

"I know. Bitches are a trip and it's still one out here that act like she got a stick up her ass."

"The ho better be gone when I come out of this stall," the voice threatened.

"You want me to hold her?" Nina looked over at the woman.

The lady in the mirror heard the threats loud and clear. "I know y'all ain't talkin' about me. I don't work in this bathroom." She threw her makeup in her purse and sashayed out.

Nina started laughing. "Only in New York."

The bathroom stall flew open; the sister took one step forward, stopped and said, "Oh shit." She turned around and started hurling into the toilet bowl.

Nina frowned as she grabbed a few paper towels and wet them. The sister sounded as if she was emptying her guts out and it was beginning to make Nina queasy.

"Oh God," she heard the sister say as she flushed the toilet. "Oh my God." She groaned.

Nina went over to the stall. "Here's a couple of wet paper towels." The sister turned around and grabbed them, then patted her face.

"Thank you. Thank you so much."

"No problem. I was all caught up in your shit, I didn't do what I came in here to do and that's use the bathroom." Nina's bladder felt like it was about to burst, so she rushed into one of the stalls.

"You got tissue in there?" the sister teased.

Nina laughed. "Yeah, I got some."

When she came out of the stall the sister was brushing her teeth. Nina checked her out from head to toe. She reeked of money. She either was the wife of a major hustler, a hustler herself or just flat-out rich. Nina could smell it and wanted to know which one she was.

"Are you okay? Was it something you ate out there?"

"I wish that's all it was. I'm a few weeks pregnant."

"Oh!" Nina squealed. "Congratulations. Is this your first one? Are you excited?"

The sister started smiling. "Girl, this is baby number four."

"Four?" Nina gasped. "Oh shit."

"My sentiments exactly. I have three boys, that includes a set of twins."

"Twins?"

"Yes, twins. What about you?"

"I have three also. Two girls and a boy." Nina beamed.

"Let me see your little ones and I'll let you see mines." Tasha said as she pulled out a diamond-studded GoldVish cell phone.

Nina's eyes almost popped out of her head. The only place she had seen one of those was in a *Robb Report* in Rinaldo's office. Those muthafuckas started at twenty-five g's. She was so intrigued by the diamonds she was barely looking at the pictures.

"These are my twins, Shaheem and Kareem. And this is my baby, Caliph," she cooed.

Nina drooled over the three handsome boys. "I can tell that's your baby. He looks just like you. And the twins must look just like their father. All you did was carry them."

"I know." She beamed with pride. "The twins *belong* to their father. They look just like him and act just like him."

"You have a beautiful family." Nina was now ashamed to pull out her wack-ass BlackBerry, but she did and pulled up a few pictures.

"Awww, they are adorable. Now, they all look like you. I wish I had at least one daughter."

Nina pointed to her stomach. "That could be your daughter right there."

"Girl, please, I don't even know if I'ma keep this one."

Nina gasped. "For real?"

"Girl, it's a long story."

"Well, it's your body. It's your choice. I ain't judging."

"I like you. You cool as hell. What is your name?"

Nina started laughing. "I'm Nina. And yours?"

"I'm Tasha. And if you are ever in California look me up. Let's exchange numbers, give me your phone." Nina handed over her cell. "Cool." Tasha locked her number in. "Promise you'll look me up."

"Hell yeah. As a matter of fact, I'm looking forward to it. Rodeo Drive, here I come!" Both of the ladies started laughing.

Rick looked at his watch. Nina had been gone for almost twenty minutes. Way too long for someone to have to freshen up. *What the hell they got in there? A shower?* He stood up and headed for the restrooms. When he got there another brother was standing there knocking on the door.

"Shorty, you all right in there?" he yelled out.

"Be right out." The voice came from the other side of the door.

He sighed and stepped to the side. Rick cracked the door. "Nina, what's up?"

"Here I come."

Rick heard the ladies giggling. "Man, they in there socializing."

"I see. They been in there for almost a half hour," the dude waiting for Tasha said.

Rick looked at him closely. He looked familiar to him, but then he quickly nixed it off when the bathroom door came open and both ladies stepped out.

"Shorty, you aiight? I was getting worried."

Rick watched as the dude asked his boy's wife lovingly,

and then took her by the hand as if she was his most prized possession.

"I threw up...again," Tasha whined. Then she looked over at Nina. "Nina here was making sure I was all right. Nina, this is Kyron. Kyron, this is Nina." She then looked at the dude that was standing next to Kyron. She squinted. When they locked gazes, she gasped as if she had just seen a ghost. Her hand flew over her mouth as she slowly backed into the bathroom.

Rick followed her.

Kyron was right behind Rick.

Nina was behind Kyron.

"Tasha, what's the matter?" Kyron had eased his hand over his burner. "Is there a problem?"

Tasha couldn't speak.

Kyron went around Rick and stood between him and Tasha. He placed his hand up to Rick's chest and pushed him back. "Man, step out for a minute. Let me talk to my shorty."

Rick slapped his arm away. "Hold up, my man. Tash, what the fuck is you doin' with this nigga?" He tried to step around Kyron but Kyron kept Tasha blocked.

"I'm not going to ask you again. Step out of the bathroom, yo," Kyron gritted. He turned to Tasha. "Shorty, who is this nigga?"

"I'm just a friend of the family," Rick said, hoping to relax Kyron. "Tasha, tell him."

Tasha remained in shock and hiding behind Kyron.

Rick's attempt at peace obviously didn't work because Kyron pushed Rick back again. Nina grabbed his arm and pulled him out of the bathroom.

Kyron turned around and faced Tasha, who was visibly shaken. "Who is that nigga, Tasha? You used to fuck with him or something?"

"He's dead. A dead cop," she mumbled.

"A dead cop? What the fuck are you talking about?" Kyron grabbed her by the shoulders but she was still mumbling. "Let me get you the fuck outta here so you can tell me what the fuck is going on." He grabbed her hand and they barged out of the bathroom.

They almost knocked over Rick, who was pacing back and forth. "Tasha, let me explain," he pleaded as he went after them.

"You need to back the fuck up. Can't you see she don't want to be bothered?" Kyron barked as he waved his burner.

"Don't wave that if you don't plan on using it." Rick regretted those words as soon as they came out.

Kyron stopped dead in his tracks. He cocked his hammer and gritted, "You don't know me, muthafucka."

Rick held up his two hands in the form of surrender. "I don't want no trouble, man. It's all good. I come in peace. I told you I'm just a friend of the family. *Trae* was like a brother to me and I was just wondering, what the fuck are you doing with my man's wife? You know how that is."

"Don't worry about what the fuck I'm doing and who

I'm doing it with." Kyron spat as he put the safety back on his burner, tucked it into his waist and proceeded to take Tasha out of the restaurant.

Rick paused. *This muthafucka must be crazy. Do he know who the fuck I am?* Rick was right on their heels. Nina could barely keep up and she was confused as hell. "Tasha, what are you doing with this nigga?" Rick yelled after them. "And where is Trae? Let me talk to you. Just give me a couple of minutes. Fuck that nigga," Rick ranted as he followed them outside.

Kyron once again stopped dead in his tracks. He was torn between the idea of killing this nigga in front of everybody with Tasha with him or just walking away. He then turned to Rick and said, "Another place, another time." They jumped into a taxi and pulled off.

"Shit!" Rick ranted as he pounded the hood of someone's car.

"Rick, why are you stressing? I have her phone number," Nina said soothingly.

"What I need to say can't be said over no telephone, Nina."

"So what do you have to say? Enlighten me, Rick. Because I don't know what the fuck just happened."

"Not now, Nina. Let's get out of here."

By three o'clock that morning Rick couldn't believe how such a perfect evening turned into shit. Everything was perfect except for that run-in with Tasha. That freaked him out and he was sure it freaked her out as well. Never in a million years did he see that coming. That was something that he would have to handle, first chance he got. He gave Nina a partial story about Trae and Tasha and was glad that she didn't press the issue any further. But the run-in really opened up some old wounds for him.

Even though he had a lot of feelings for Nina, his heart was still with Kyra. He was also now glad that they made him transfer to Georgia. Maybe he would cancel the lawsuit against them... *Nah, fuck that! Them muthafuckas ain't gettin' off that easy, forcing me to leave the state,* he said to himself. He just wished that Nina wasn't caught up in the web of WMM, especially since his new partner, Rhodes, was determined to put everyone at WMM away for life.

Rick glided the Escalade into Nina's driveway and turned off the ignition. They had driven the majority of the way from the airport in silence.

God, I don't want this moment to end. Nina looked over at Rick, who was looking at her. "So, now what?" she asked him. "Ever since you ran into the girl, you been trippin.' Can you leave New York behind?"

"I'll do my best." He placed his hand gently behind her neck and pulled her towards him. Nina took over from there. She placed her hand behind his head and began teasing his lips with her tongue. Rick closed his eyes and savored her sweet taste.

"Don't leave. I need you to stay with me," she pleaded.

Nina's breathing was heavy, which only made his dick hard.

"Are you sure about that?" He was now kissing her neck and rubbing the inside of her thigh.

"I'm sure." *I ain't never been so sure in my life.* Nina kissed him one more time before getting out of the truck. Rick didn't waste a second getting out behind her.

Nina fumbled with the lock before remembering that they were changed. She went to the mailbox and felt underneath it and unraveled a taped envelope. She and the locksmith had done this many times before. Rick waited anxiously as she came back up the stairs. When they stepped inside the house, Nina told Rick to make himself at home. "I'm going to take a shower and slip into something comfortable."

"What about me? Can I shower and slip into something comfortable?"

Nina turned around and said, "I'm not going to be long. Make yourself comfortable. I got something special planned for you." She disappeared up the staircase.

Rick took off his jacket, felt inside for his burner and laid it across the couch. He never really took the time to check her place out. He was always in her bedroom and out. He sat down and scanned her living room. Her home décor was very modern. She had great taste. The sofa was split suede and leather in a rich chocolate brown. The plasma TV was encased by a mirror. When the TV wasn't on it looked like a mirror. The end tables had marble throughout the smoked-glass tops. The paintings on the walls were bright, colorful and abstract. He nodded his head in approval.

When he stepped into her kitchen he looked around before going into her refrigerator. He poured two glasses of Krug and headed back for the living room. As he was sitting down, Nina was coming down the stairs. Her feet were bare; she had a diamond anklet dangling around her ankle. His eyes gleamed with approval at her shapely legs and rested on the booty shorts she was wearing. Her pussy print was staring back at him. She had on a tank top, and her luscious-looking breasts were damn near spilling out the top. Her ponytail was pinned on top of her head. He fired up a blunt as she stood there teasing him.

"I see you got something to drink. Was I that long?" She took the blunt from him and took a couple of pulls before putting it out.

"Come here." He held his hand out for her. When she grabbed it, he guided her small frame to straddle his lap.

"Thank you," she whispered as she kissed him lightly on the lips.

"For what?"

"For everything up to now and for everything to come." She rocked subtly on his dick, making it harder. She was already on fire and was ready to ride that pole. They began hugging and caressing each other. Nina leaned in for a kiss and he started easing the tank top up over her head. She raised her arms and he tossed it on the floor.

He licked his lips as he admired her breasts and juicy dark nipples. He leaned in and began teasing one of her nipples with his teeth as she massaged his neck and released sexy moans in his ear.

Knock! Knock! Ding! Dong! The bell rang. "Nina!" Cream yelled. "Open the door, baby," he slurred.

"What the fuck? It's damn near five o'clock in the morning. Why is he here?" Rick spat.

Knock! Knock! Ding! Dong! Cream was banging and pressing the bell again.

Rick slid Nina off his lap. She bent over and snatched up her tank top and put it on. Rick had already grabbed his piece and was at the door. He was pissed, his dick was hard as hell but it wasn't deep up in some pussy. Rick mumbled to himself, "I'm about to fuck him up."

Nina dashed over to where he was. He stopped and turned to her. "You said ain't nothing up between y'all, right?"

"Nothing," she firmly stated. "But what I told you on the plane, he knows about it and he's been threatening me with exposure."

"Then let me handle this."

Nina backed up and sat on the couch.

Cream was still banging and ringing the bell. Rick looked out of the window. "This nigga got flowers, a bag of groceries and he's holding a stack of papers. It looks like mail or something. This fool is crazy."

"He's probably high off something, Rick."

Rick unlocked the door and as soon as he yanked it

open, he pounced on Cream and started beating him down with his burner. Groceries, mail and the flowers went everywhere. Cream didn't know what or who hit him. He went down after the second blow to the head, tumbled down the steps and stayed down.

Rick started towards the house but he stopped. Nina was standing in the doorway. "You want any of this shit?" He pointed to the groceries and everything else on the ground.

"My mail. I need my mail."

Rick grabbed up the mail that was scattered around and came back into the house.

"Should I call his boy Mo to come get him, or the police? You didn't kill him, did you?"

"Call his boy. He'll be aiight. I just put my foot in his ass. One for interrupting us and two for giving you all that grief. He had that shit coming." Rick slammed the door shut.

Nina called his boy Mo and told him to come and get Cream. Rick passed her the mail. "He must have been taking my mail for a while. Look at all of this stuff. Some of this is two, three weeks old. This is why I didn't know about my mother's check bouncing. That bastard!" she spat as she thumbed through the mail. When she came across a large green and white first-class envelope she started shaking. Rick noticed her drastic attitude change and came over to where she was.

"Oh my God. Oh my God. This can't be what I think it

is." She was tearing frantically at the envelope but couldn't get it open. Rick took it out of her hands and opened it for her and handed it back. Not before checking out that the envelope came from a private investigation firm, being the detective he is.

Nina sat down on the couch like a robot, took a deep breath and dumped the contents out onto the coffee table. Just as she anticipated, pictures of Jatana at the house, at another house marked BABYSITTER and shots of her playing in the front yard. "My baby." She started crying. "Jatana. Look how big she's gotten." She sat there crying as she looked at the pictures.

CHAPTER SEVENTEEN

THE DECISION

The Suburban cruised down Calhoun Street. Nina's mother just recently moved into a new condo. With the help of Nina, of course. Trenton was building new condos in several areas and Nina was impressed.

She couldn't wait to see the look on her mother's and children's faces when she announced that she was here to take them with her. They flew down to Philadelphia and rented a truck to drive the kids and their things back.

The GPS instructed them to turn left and their destination would be on their left on Louise Lane. Nina squeezed Rick's hand. She wouldn't have wanted to share this moment with anyone else but him. He leaned over and kissed her cheek. "Everything's going to be all right."

Her mother's condo was the third one on the right. Nina looked up and saw that a male figure was walking towards the same house where she was headed. He was holding the hand of a young girl.

The Suburban came to a stop and Rick deaded the engine. Nina's eyes were glued to the back of her daughter's figure. *Who was this man?* She sat there staring out of the window.

"Are we getting out or what?" Rick asked her.

Nina's mother came to the door and let the man and the young child in. The three of them disappeared inside.

"What's up?"

"That was my daughter," Nina mumbled. "She has gotton so big." Nina's heart was fluttering.

"Is that the house? These are nice," Rick commented. The entire block was brand new.

Nina got out of the truck, took a deep breath and started walking towards the front door. Rick jumped out, shut the door and caught up with her.

"Who was the man with your daughter?"

"I have no clue. But I'm getting ready to find out." Nina took another deep breath and rang the doorbell. She was excited, nervous and full of anxiety all at the same time.

The door flew open and Nina's mother stood there. She looked at Rick and then back at Nina.

"Nina, is that you?" She opened the screen door. "Nina?"

"Hi, Mom." Nina stood there unsure of what to do next. *How is everyone going to receive me? Shit, why am I so fucking paranoid? Will she put up a fight when I tell her I am taking my kids?*

"Lawd! Lawd! Lawd! Come on in. Children!" she yelled out. "Look who's here. It's your mother. Lawd! Lawd! Let me call your brother. The prodigal child has returned." She grabbed Nina and gave her a hug.

Rick stood there watching the exchange. Her mother was an older Nina with a little more weight on her. Her hair was long and twisted up into a bun on the back of her head. She looked to be around forty-five.

"Deacon Rutherford, this here is my daughter. This is Nina."

Deacon Rutherford stood up and came over to Nina and gave her a hug. "My, my, my. Emma, she looks just like you. And that youngin' you got looks just like her mama."

Nina cringed. Deacon Rutherford was creepy.

"Why didn't you tell me you was coming?" her mother asked.

"I wanted to surprise you and the kids. Plus, it was sort of a spur-of-the-moment thing." And that was true. For the last couple of days Nina had been having funny feelings. Call it a mother's intuition but Nina got a strong urge to come right then. The original plan was to leave in two and a half weeks when everything else was in place. But her gut was saying go now.

Jermichael was at the dinner table throwing down. At first he didn't bother to look up. Nina stood there watching her son eat. He looked just like his father. So handsome, and he obviously had his appetite. When he finally glanced up he froze, mouth hung open, and then he jumped up, knocking the chair backwards. Nina couldn't help but laugh. He ran and jumped into her arms, yelling, "Mommy, Mommy!" She rained kisses all over his face and then they hugged each other. Tears streamed down Nina's cheeks.

Then she noticed she didn't see Daysha. "Where is Daysha?"

"Daysha," her mother yelled out. "She's in the bathroom. She stay in that bathroom. Go right there and turn left. Let me call your brother."

Nina went to find the bathroom. She tapped on the door. Daysha didn't answer. "Daysha, it's Mommy. Can I come in?"

Daysha cracked the door and said, "Mommy?" as if she wasn't sure. Nina pushed it open.

"Hey baby, you all right?"

"Mommy!" Daysha screamed and jumped into her mother's arms.

Nina couldn't stop crying, so glad and relieved that they were glad to see her. "I'm sorry, baby. Mommy came to get you."

Daysha reached back and locked the door. "You mean today?"

"Yes, I'm here to get you today."

"Now? Because I don't want to stay here anymore." She was whispering and peeking around Nina as if she thought that someone would come in any minute.

"Why were you with that man in the kitchen?" Nina knew something was wrong. Now all she needed was confirmation.

"Grandma makes me go with the deacon."

Nina stiffened up. "Why don't you like going with him?"

Daysha shrugged her shoulders, obviously hesitant to say what she was thinking.

"Did you tell your grandma you don't like going with him?" Daysha nodded her head yes. Nina could tell she was scared to death. "What did Grandma say?"

"Don't tell nobody and she gonna pray on it."

Nina tried her hardest to remain calm. All she could see was red. "Daysha, tell Mommy what the deacon do. Does he touch you?"

Daysha shrugged her shoulders.

"Daysha, you can tell Mommy. I won't tell your grandma. Plus, you are leaving here tonight."

Daysha stood there, head hung low. Nina could tell she was trying to figure out if she should trust her or not. "Daysha, please, just tell me why you don't want to go with him." Nina knew but deep down she didn't want to hear it but at the same time needed to hear it.

"He touched my poo poo."

Nina hugged her daughter tight. *Oh my God.* "Everything's gonna be okay. Mommy isn't going to let anything happen to you again." Nina mustered up a smile when she really wanted to throw up. "Go to your room and pack whatever you and Jermichael are going to want to take with you. Don't pack a lot. Mommy is gonna buy you all new stuff."

Daysha smiled a huge smile and headed for her room.

Nina dropped her fake smile and headed straight for Rick. When she got in the living room, her mother was in the kitchen.

Nina snatched Rick by the arm and took him outside. He noticed that she was shaking like a leaf. "Give me your burner, Rick!" She pushed him towards the car.

"What?"

"Rick, you heard me. Give me the fuckin' burner. I'ma kill that muthafucka," she gritted.

"Who? What the fuck is the matter with you?"

Nina burst into tears. "That fucking preacher been touching my daughter."

"What?" Rick was hoping that he heard her wrong.

"Rick, I can't let the shit go. No. I can't." Nina started pacing back and forth. "Hell no."

Rick thought about it. "We need to take her to a hospital."

"I gotta get my kids."

"Does your mother know?"

"Yeah, that bitch know. She probably selling her for price," Nina spat. "Rick, give me your burner, I'ma kill both their asses!"

"No, I'm not gonna do that, Nina. Think about what you're saying."

"Rick, I know exactly what I'm saying. Just give me the fuckin' gun!"

"And again, I'm telling you no. Your emotions have you thinking illogically. What you gonna do, march in there and kill them both? Then what? You're going to jail and the kids are gonna be a part of the system. And what about Jatana? I'm telling you. Think about it for a minute."

Nina paced back and forth like a tiger in a cage. Rick could see that she was not trying to hear what he was saying.

"Aiight look," Rick gave in. "Your brother is on the way over here, right? Aiight. Look. I'ma go ahead and bounce, but I won't be far away, I'ma make sure the preacher doesn't get outta my sight. You take the kids and go with your brother. I'ma call you when I got the preacher somewhere and you can handle him. But you gotta let your mother go, Nina."

When Nina didn't respond, Rick said, "It's either my way or no way. I know how you feel and you're gonna get the preacher, but you gotta spare your mother."

"We still gotta get Jatana," Nina said, her anger finally subsiding.

"We are going to get Jatana. But first we deal with the preacher. You with me or what?"

"I'm with it. But it doesn't mean I have to like it. My mother is just as guilty as the preacher. You go ahead and bounce. And you better call me when you have him."

CHAPTER EIGHTEEN

THE TAKE AWAY

What started as a lovely family reunion trip to pick up her children turned into a battle. When Nina's brother Peedie arrived at her mother's, Nina and the kids packed his car with their things and went to his house. But not before Nina went back into the house and repeatedly slapped the shit out of the woman who brought her into this world. The deacon had to tear her off of Mama Coles. Nina knew that this would be the last time she would see her mother. Her mother felt it as well because she didn't so much as attempt to protest. But deep down inside she knew she would have to live with her guilt forever.

Rick was camped out in his ride, waiting for Deacon Rutherford. After he spent time consoling Ms. Emma he finally said good night and got into his Cadillac and left. Rick followed him and was happy when he stopped at a liquor store, and in the hood of all places. When he came out Rick got behind him, hit him on the head and dragged him into an alley.

"Let me go!" Deacon Rutherford yelled. "Somebody help me!"

"You like raping little girls? It's bitches out here who will fuck for free." Rick was contemplating on whether he should break the preacher's neck or simply blow his brains out. But that would be breaking his word to Nina and denying her the right to avenge her daughter.

"What? What are you talking about?" Deacon Rutherford protested.

"You know damned well what I'm talking about, you filthy muthafucka. The gig is up, holy man."

"I don't know what you're talking about," the preacher pleaded as he stared into Rick's eyes. "You got the wrong person. I swear to God, you do."

"Leave God out of this, preacher man. You didn't invoke his name when you were molesting that little girl. Besides, I'm not the one you have to convince. C'mon, you're taking a ride with me. If you try anything on the way to my car, I'ma kill you. You got that, preacher man?!"

"You got the wrong person." Deacon Rutherford couldn't stop trembling.

The taxi let Nina out one block away from Cadwalder Park. When she got to the entrance, she pulled out her cell phone and dialed Rick's number. He picked up on the first ring.

"Start walking towards the back of the park. Count four poles. It's dark as shit so—"

"I'll find you." She hung up.

Rick, dressed in dark clothes and long dreads loosely swinging as he moved, wasn't hard to spot. Nina approached and saw that the preacher was on the ground, handcuffed and gagged. As soon as she saw his eyes pleading with her, the fire that burned inside her the night she killed Darlene returned and it roared and crackled as if it could sense a meal. Immediately, Nina started kicking the preacher.

"You like feeling little girls on their coochies, huh? You sick, perverted muthafucka! Take whatever that is out of his mouth."

Rick pulled out the dirty rag that he had found from the man's mouth.

"Please! Please...I didn't do it! I didn't do nothing! I..."

"If you would've been reading your Bible more and touching my child less, you wouldn't be in this situation. So you can save the innocent plea and the tears. Tell it to God...better yet, the devil when you see him."

"Cuff him in the front. Then put the gag back in his mouth and turn him over onto his stomach."

Without saying a word, Rick did as Nina asked.

Nina reached under the now struggling preacher and undid his pants. Then she snatched his pants and briefs down until they were around his ankles. With one foot on the preacher's back and one on the ground, Nina put the burner between the man's buttcheeks. She shoved the barrel of the gun until she figured it was as far as it would go. The rag in his mouth muffled his agonizing scream.

"My daughter told me to tell you, Fuck you!" Nina pulled the trigger repeatedly until she was sure the preacher was dead.

She smiled.

When they pulled up in front of Supreme's aunt's house it was obvious that no one was home. They sat there for almost an hour. Nina was crying uncontrollably. They weren't going to bring Jatana home. But around twenty minutes later, just when Nina had given up, a Volvo station wagon pulled into the driveway. The trunk popped open and they could see the grocery bags. Supreme's aunt let Jatana out of the car and she ran straight for the sliding board and started playing in the dark. While his aunt was distracted unloading the trunk, Nina jumped out of the Suburban and ran over to Jatana and took her. They got into the truck and Rick pulled off. Supreme's aunt was left standing there. She pulled out her cell phone and began dialing. She already knew who had just taken Jatana.

Nina had put her house up for sale, tied up all loose ends and was on her way to Florida with the kids to wait for Rick. Rick would meet up with her once he took care of some things on his end. If everything went as planned they were going to take a long vacation on somebody's tropical island. But for now she was anxious to get out of Georgia, paranoid that Supreme would show her how far his hand could reach.

The WMM tapes had a lot of info on them, way too much. The tape that had Rinaldo and Charlie talking about their stash spot and their case were the only tapes that Rick kept. The rest of the tapes he turned over to Rhodes in exchange for his resignation letter, along with the classified info on everyone involved in the WMM case and walking papers for Nina.

With Nina and the kids tucked safely away, Rick was able to move around and do what he did best, get grimy with it. He learned that Shawn was fucking Rochelle, Rinaldo's wife. *Some bitches ain't shit! Just like his ex-wife.* A nigga can work hard as hell to get a bitch the way he wants her and the next nigga will move in and reap all the benefits, his woman, his pussy and his money. Rick was on a mission and would have to call in a few favors; his hookup with the bureau got him the pertinent flight information he needed. He thought that only Shawn was going to Florida, but as luck would have it Cream was going too, two birds with one big-ass rock. He wasn't quite clear on the connection but vowed to be right there when the shit unfolded. This was the type of shit he lived for.

CHAPTER NINETEEN

THE END

Since Nina and the crew left, a completely new Platinum Team except for Frank and Pete was in place and grinding on the phones. Simeon was still working the rest of the sales force, enabling Rinaldo to clear another eight million dollars in two short months.

Charlie, Rinaldo's partner from Florida, was now sitting in Rinaldo's office. Charlie looked like an older James Bond. His six-three frame towered over Rinaldo's desk as they argued back and forth. His thinning hair hung across his sweaty forehead. His steely blue eyes were pinned on Rinaldo.

"Let's take our losses and close up shop." He tried to reason with Rinaldo.

"Why we gotta close shop? We never ran from these fuckers before, why start now?" Rinaldo tried to rationalize with Charlie. "You are getting soft, old man."

"Soft? I already did one bid. I ain't trying to do another one. Hell, I'll be fifty-nine next month but you got your whole life ahead of you. We've made millions together, man. You got to know when to walk away. That's the sign of a smart man, Rinaldo. I know I taught you better than that. You can't be too greedy in this business. If you do, you're going to end up wearing football numbers. Charlie made another attempt to school his young protégé.

"Char, I just need you to hold it down up there a little while longer," Rinaldo pleaded. "I'll take the weight if need be and you know that. Just give me a couple more months."

Charlie shook his head in disbelief, grabbed his briefcase and stormed out of Rinaldo's office.

Rinaldo ran behind him. "What, man? You gonna give me two more months or what?"

"Rinaldo, I know you. Two months will turn into four, four will turn into eight. Then where are we?"

Rinaldo needed Charlie because the Florida address was where all the money was sent and all of the products were shipped from and administrative duties were handled. Charlie had always controlled all of the administrative and banking issues. Rinaldo only needed just a few more months.

The Florida Keys...

With Rick's plan in motion he had to show up a day before to get his props. He borrowed a uniform and an unmarked vehicle, for a hefty fee, of course. Everyone has their price.

He learned that a long time ago. He had visited the address to their stash spot and almost shitted on himself when he saw that it was a huge cemetery. He was convinced that it was no way they would stash millions in a damn cemetery. He was mad as hell and tossed and turned all night because he had looked and looked and came up empty. He didn't know the exact spot.

The next morning his gut told him to go back and squat. And as always his gut was right on point. A little after noon, just when he was about to give up, he got excited and yelled, "Bingo," when a dark blue Chevy Tahoe pulled up. The two passengers wasted no time jumping out. They both were wearing dark shades and were looking around nervously before heading to the huge mausoleum, which had a combination lock on it. *These muthafuckers.* Rick couldn't help but laugh to himself. *Soft-ass niggas trying to be gangsta.*

After about twenty minutes Cream came out with a suitcase. Shawn followed with another one. They then went back and returned carrying a suitcase in each hand. And this time they were grinning from ear to ear.

They got in the Tahoe and pulled off. Rick started his ride and pulled off, keeping a safe distance. He followed the Tahoe for a half hour when they turned off onto Route 7.

He immediately cut the siren on and pulled them over.

"I told you to slow down, man!" Shawn barked. "Now look. We came all this way to get pulled over for some dumb shit. Slow down, man."

"Fuck that shit. I'm going out with the goods or I'm going out blazing," Cream spat as he patted the head of the gun that was tucked down in his waist.

"Ain't this some shit," Shawn mumbled while looking out the rearview mirror.

They sat waiting.

"What the fuck is he doing? It don't take this long to run muthafuckin' tags," Cream spat.

Rick was indeed sitting there waiting. He needed a break in the traffic. When it finally slowed down he put on his dark shades and adjusted the hat on his head. He got out, hand on his burner, and walked up to the Tahoe.

"License and registration please, sir," Rick instructed. The night that Rick beat his ass, Cream was so drunk that he didn't even get a good look at him.

Cream started to buck but Shawn cleared his throat, reminding him to don't even try it. When Cream leaned over to reach into the glove compartment, Rick pulled out his taped-up .38 and shot him in the back of the head. Before Shawn realized that this was the same nigga who fingerprinted him, Rick then aimed at Shawn and popped him twice in the dome. He snatched the keys out of the ignition and went to the trunk. He opened it and took out all of the suitcases one by one and placed them in his trunk. When he finished he got in his vehicle and pulled off.

He called Nina. "Flames, I'm good."

"No problems?" She held her breath.

"No problems."

Yesss! She exhaled. "You're on your way here?"

"I'll be there in about an hour."

Nina was on the other end jumping up and down. The kids started jumping up and down along with her and had no clue as to why.

As Rick drove across the bridge, he tossed the gun and keys out into the water. When he arrived at the hotel, his contact was there to pick up the police car. Nina and the kids had the minivan packed and ready. He went inside of the hotel room.

The first stop was to cash in the gold coins. When they opened up the suitcase with the coins, Nina's knees got weak. "Gotdamn! Gotdamn! Rick, do you see this shit?"

"I see it, baby. This is the fuckin' jackpot." He opened up one of the money suitcases and it was loaded.

"Whooooooo!" Nina screamed. She jumped in Rick's arms and kissed him all over. "Let's go, baby. Take me to Barbados, or should I go to Rodeo Drive first?" She tossed two handfuls of coins up into the air. All three kids jumped up and down and started yelling and swooping them up.

Rochelle had been blowing Shawn and Cream's phones up. "Y'all muthafuckas think y'all can play me like this? I got news for y'all!" Neither one of them ever got back to her.

*   *   *

Rinaldo was on top of the world once again. It was Friday morning and he was having a meeting with his Platinum Sales Team with Frank sitting at the helm. He had lit a cigar and was boasting on how he was taking the wife and kids to Hawaii this weekend when Deanna announced over the intercom, "Rinaldo, guess who just pulled into the parking lot? Charlie."

"What?" He hit the intercom.

"Charlie is here."

Rinaldo had a baffled look on his face. *He didn't tell me he was coming.* "All right, this meeting is adjourned." He cleared everyone out and went to the front.

Charlie had barged into the front door.

"Hey, Char, man. I didn't know you were coming. What's up? Come into my office."

Charlie followed him down the hall. He slammed Rinaldo's door. Rinaldo sat down. "What brings you to my side of town?" Rinaldo joked.

The look that he saw on Charlie's face let him know that this was serious. Rinaldo leaned back, bracing himself. "What's up, man? Why didn't you tell me you were coming? Is it that bad?"

"Where have you been, man?"

"Out running errands."

"Not that bullshit! When is the last time you been to Florida? To our spot?" His voice boomed.

"Not since the last time. You know when I was down

there. I never go there without you knowing about it. You know that. Why? What the fuck is wrong?"

"All of our stash is gone, Rinaldo. That's what the fuck is wrong. I don't have time for these games," Charlie gritted. "I'm too old for this bullshit. Now I'm gonna ask one more time, when—"

Rinaldo was now up and on his feet, his face red. He had startled Charlie. "Man, you know I don't fucking joke about my money. What do you mean our stash is gone? Charlie, you talking about over fifty million dollars." Rinaldo reached over into his desk and pulled out and sucked on his asthma inhaler. He hadn't used it in months.

"Cut the theatrics. I went to pick up something to put down on this plot of land and the shit was empty. Cleaned the fuck out. I hoped you had an explanation, and like I said I'm too old to be playing games. So cut the jokes." Charlie was looking intensely at Rinaldo, looking for any signs, a clue, something that let him know that his little protégé was pulling the wool over his eyes. *The asthma pump is definitely a nice touch*, he said to himself.

"Only you and I have the keys and combination to that spot and I haven't been there since the last time. So what the fuck are you trying to pull, Charlie? I may be young, but I am not into playing games either."

They were now glaring at each other.

BOOM! BOOM!

"What the fuck?" Rinaldo jumped out of his chair and charged out of his office.

"On the floor, hands behind your head, you maggot!" the agent yelled. "We got both of you muthafuckas this time!" It was the same agent who led the last raid and investigation. He handcuffed Rinaldo and the other agent handcuffed Charlie as the rest of the agents swarmed the offices, guns drawn. Déjà vu.

Everything rained down on Rinaldo at once. Rochelle and his son weighed heavily on his mind. She wouldn't come and see him and whenever he called home she was very distant and short with him. She kept asking him how did he expect her to live. He sent Mack by the house to check on her and she would only question him about his finances.

Now he couldn't believe what he was hearing as he paced the client-attorney room. Matt, Mack and Dave, all three attorneys had a look on their face that said, "I told you so."

He was denied a bond and had been sitting in the Federal Detention Center for three weeks now.

"All right, lay it on me." Rinaldo wearily ran his fingers through his hair.

"Where should I start?" Mack smirked. "You would be free if you hadn't went back and opened up shop. But we could delay the trial for at least a year."

"I don't pay you to tell me what I already know," Rinaldo barked at him.

"Okay, well the girl Nina is gone. Her house is up for

sale. The tall guy Milt, he's still around. He did call our office to check on you. Your brother made bail."

"Damn, I didn't know that." Rinaldo sighed. "I was hoping he would have been in touch by now."

"If you want us to track him down, we will," Mack assured him.

"No. No. That won't be necessary. He will eventually surface."

"I'm not so sure about that. He's talking about taking a deal."

"What?" All of the attorneys nodded.

"And I think you should know that Pete died just last week."

"I thought he was just hit by the truck. He died?" Rinaldo yelled.

"I'm afraid so. He was in critical condition from day one. Sorry, Rinaldo," Mack stated apologetically.

"Sorry," Dave said. Matt just looked at him and shrugged his shoulders.

"Geesh. This is fuckin' unbelievable. Where is Shawn?"

"We don't know yet," Mack told him.

Finally, Rinaldo stood up and began pacing the floor.

"What do you want us to do, Rinaldo?" Mack asked in the tone of a concerned parent.

Grabbing the seat and sitting back down, he said, "It's nothing you can do, man, but get me out of here. What's the strategy?"

Dave opened his briefcase, pulled out a folder. He slid Rinaldo a stack of papers.

"Here is the discovery motion. There was a bug placed under your desk. So not only do the feds have all of your phone conversations, but they've got sales meetings and the office chatter as well."

"Okay. What else do they have? What else am I looking at? I'm not worried about that."

"Mack." Dave nodded to Mack. He wanted him to have the honors.

"Rinaldo, there is a second superseding indictment, new charges of tax evasion and, in layman's terms, I guess they threw in for good measure charges of running a prostitution ring."

"Mack, they got me fucked up! I am not going down by myself. Get me somebody to talk to. This was Charlie and Shawn's operation. They were in charge. I just worked there. I need to talk about a deal."

"A deal?" Mack asked incredulously. "Who are you gonna flip on? Everybody on your sales team has already taken one except for Milt, and there's no word on Shawn or the girl. To add insult to injury, Charlie may even flip."

He tossed another file in front of him.

"What's this?" Rinaldo didn't touch it.

"They are charging you with the murder of Darwin Branson. Armand is the witness the government has to testify against you."

"Man, that's bullshit and I know that's beatable. It's his word against mine."

"One more thing."

"One more thing? Y'all muthafuckas keep piling shit on piece by piece. Just give it all to me. Y'all muthafuckas are on the clock."

Mack pushed a small recorder in front of him.

"What is this?"

"Obviously your boy Armand didn't trust you, because he taped every meeting and phone call you guys had."

Rinaldo burst into laughter. "So everyone is flipping, talking, missing in action, and y'all muthafuckas sittin' here like the Keystone cops."

All of the lawyers looked at one another. Matt was the first to speak.

"Since you have all of the answers and we work for you, what is the strategy?"

Rinaldo looked around at all of them. He lit a cigar and sat back. He puffed, blew out smoke rings and was deep in thought. He did this for about ten minutes.

"You know what?" They all scrambled for their note-pads waiting to hear what he had up his sleeves and ready to take notes. "I played the hand that I was dealt and I wouldn't change a muthafuckin' thing!"

READING GROUP GUIDE

1. What do you think of Reese telling Nina that he had a family?

2. Did Nina appear desperate for love?

3. Should she have taken her children to Georgia with her from the very beginning?

4. Did you ever get the impression that Nina didn't want her children?

5. Should Nina have tried harder to find her baby, Jatana?

6. What were your thoughts of Cream?

7. What was your opinion about the firm WMM (We Make Millionaires)?

8. What did you think about Rinaldo? Did he have to run his operation with an iron fist? Or was it totally unnecessary?

9. Should Rochelle have shown more loyalty to Rinaldo?

10. Were you surprised at Rick showing up in the story? Did he fall for Nina a little too quickly?

11. If you were Nina, how would you have handled the situation with Deacon Rutherford, her mother and daughter?

12. What should have been Rinaldo's fate?